For six weeks, I'd carried this book inside its protective case, never knowing what I had in my hands. The printed manuscript from the hand of Joan of Arc.

I couldn't let the Adrianos burn it.

Glancing around the locked vault, I searched for a way out. The ceiling showed the upper reaches of a fireproof room. No escape. But the floor… I followed the lines of the floor to a crack in the shape of a square. A trap door. A way out?

Lying flat on the floor with the case beside me, I was finally able to lift one side and slide the square cover away from the hole. The sudden smell of human sweat stung my nostrils. I forced myself not to cough. I couldn't afford to make any noise that might bring Simon back.

The trap door led to some sort of room below, but the opening gaped down a long tube without steps. I glanced around the vault for a ladder or rope and settled on the fire hose near the vault door. Pulling it over to the hole, I used it to lower myself down the tube.

My feet had bar a man's hands on

Dear Reader,

When Vicki Hinze, Evelyn Vaughn and I first conceived THE MADONNA KEY series, we wanted to examine different aspects of motherhood in each book, including the story of a mother who had left her child behind. Because I have a wonderful relationship with my own teenage daughters, I could not fathom ever leaving them, so I wanted to explore Aubrey's past and find out what turned her into the "bad girl" thief so many people perceived her to be, as well as what she might sacrifice to protect her daughter.

I never expected this book to become a reclaiming story. I wrote *Dark Revelations* shortly after my divorce, during a time when I was starting over, figuring out who I really was and what I wanted out of the rest of my life. I realized through Aubrey that life doesn't always turn out exactly the way you plan it, no matter how many plans you make or how good you are at planning, and at the same time, that the best things that happen in life are often the things you didn't plan for or that didn't happen exactly the way you planned. No, they are even better!

I hope you enjoy Aubrey's story as she takes back her life, and that she inspires you to reclaim all the good things in your life that you left behind.

Bendith Y Mamu (Blessings of the Mother),

Lorna Tedder

Lorna Tedder

DARK REVELATIONS

Silhouette®

BOMBSHELL™

Published by Silhouette Books
America's Publisher of Contemporary Romance

THE MADONNA KEY series was co-created by Yvonne Jocks, Vicki Hinze and Lorna Tedder.

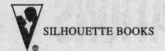

SILHOUETTE BOOKS

ISBN-13: 978-0-373-51420-5
ISBN-10: 0-373-51420-4

DARK REVELATIONS

This edition published by arrangement with Harlequin Books S.A.

www.SilhouetteBombshell.com

Printed in U.S.A.

Books by Lorna Tedder

Silhouette Bombshell

Dark Revelations #106

Silhouette Intimate Moments

A Man Called Regret #582 (written as Lauren Shelley)

LORNA TEDDER

By day, Lorna Tedder hangs out with rocket scientists and negotiates technology contracts. By night, she kicks ass with her fictional heroines. In her spare time, she conducts experiments in unified field theory and teaches workshops on setting up interdimensional portals for communication. The author of more than a dozen books, she holds a doctorate in metaphysics and a third-degree elevation as a Wiccan high priestess. Her popular blog, SuperGirl@40, can be found at her Web site, www.LornaTedder.com.

To all who have attended my famous
Sunday Night Gatherings: I am forever grateful
to have had you in my life and in my home. Without
you, I might never have learned firsthand about sacred
geometry, radiological electromagnetic energy fields,
the Nolalaln High Order, geological healing frequencies,
geopathic stress, dowsing or ley lines. There is so much
around us that is unseen and so much yet to see!

Prologue

Once, in the early fifteenth century, there lived a maid of Orleans who saved her king and led his people to victory on the battlefield but offended the priests and died at the stake. From the blood of her mother rose another like her, whose name was obliterated from all lips but who secretly wrote of their mission and hid away a dangerous legacy, in hopes that one of her descendants would one day save the world....

Chapter 1

Late summer
San Francisco, California

Hanging upside down is for bats and Spider-Man. Not for an Oxford-educated literature professor like me. Then again, I was no longer a professor. I was nothing but a thief. One in a lot of trouble.

It wasn't the first time I had been in that position. Wouldn't be the last, either. But then, life doesn't always turn out according to plans. For me, it never has, but I make them anyway.

Tonight's assignment was to be my last job for the Adriano family, a decision that normally only an Adriano can make. They don't exactly offer a hefty retirement plan, though it's rumored they always pay for the funeral—whether or not there's enough left of the employee for a coffin. I'd heard everyone from high-tech security specialists down to kitchen servants murmur the same epitaph: *Once an employee, always an employee.*

I intended to break that rule. Soon.

I flexed my bare feet hard, twisting them around the rope and held my breath. Only the crooks above my heels—where Achilles took his poison—held fast to the line strung between the rooftops. My tendons tensed and burned. Twenty-three stories of gravity called to me, but I refused to look down. The smell of garbage and exhaust rose from the street below, stinging my eyes and nostrils. The wind between the hotel buildings swatted at me, whining in my ears so loudly that I could barely hear the sound of the angry traffic below.

I didn't worry that anyone would notice me hanging by a thread in the night sky, stripped down to a cat burglar's black leotard, belt and bare feet. Too many things had gone wrong already on this job—enough that I had to wonder if I'd been set up. The Adrianos simply did not make mistakes when they gave instructions. If anything did go wrong, they were always careful not to be responsible. That's what employees were for.

With a deep but steady breath, I rotated one ankle, looping the rope around my foot. It wouldn't keep me from plunging to my death, but it was a step in the right direction.

The muscles in my calves ached and burned. The

human body, no matter how well maintained, simply isn't meant to hold this form for twenty minutes. Especially when one knee is weaker than the other from being bashed to hell and back.

Still, a setup didn't make sense. Why would the Adrianos want me to fail? I was their best acquisitions consultant—a lovely euphemism for a thief—and tonight's prize was considered a very important artifact, even though I wasn't deemed important enough to know what was in the package I was to confiscate.

Yes, okay, so my last mission had been botched, thanks to an Interpol agent named Analise Reisner. But as far as the Adrianos knew, it wasn't my fault I hadn't retrieved the Madonna statue and instead had nearly lost my life when I'd followed Analise in search of the statue and had wound up helping her get away from some truly scary Adriano henchmen. The Duke himself had agreed I wasn't to blame and had paid me a handsome fee for my efforts despite his severe disappointment. None of the henchmen had lived to tell tales.

Why then had he had his underling—a soft-spoken henchman who'd identified himself by phone as Eric Cabordes—give me follow-up instructions for this job? My training days were long over. Details on the job usually came from the Duke himself or, on rare occasion, from his youngest son, Joshua.

Even after all my loyal years of service—like I had a choice!—I sensed I was on shaky ground. I liked to think that the Duke treated me differently from other employees, that he had developed a fondness for me. I was hoping to parlay that fondness into some special treatment I'd heard didn't exist—release from his employ. Truth was, maybe his soft spot for me was in my imagination. Maybe I just wanted somebody to appreciate me for me, somebody who didn't demand I earn his love. So far, I'd lost the only two people who fit that description.

With a deep breath, I tightened and relaxed my calf muscles. My good leg was starting to cramp up. Not good.

I couldn't afford to make a mistake and return to Italy empty-handed a second time. Not and face the wrath of the Adrianos! Sure, to most of the world they were dashing philanthropists with a direct link to the Vatican, the White House and every remaining royal family in Europe. To those who knew better, either first-hand or from studying history, failing them meant misery, not hazard pay for injuring your leg.

I gritted my teeth against the pain in my knee, against the doubts that plagued me. It's times like these—when a heist goes badly—that I think of the little girl I left behind, of the man who was her father and of what might have been.

But my memories were a danger to fine concentration. For this moment, it was all about instinct. About survival. About how to hang on to a rope no wider than my little finger and propel myself upside down until I reached the hotel's penthouse window. Fortunately it wasn't the hardest job I had ever had.

I sucked in a deep breath and grabbed for the rope with both hands. I pulled myself up again, fighting the wind for balance, and held the rope gingerly under my crossed knees. Not the best or fastest way to move from one building to another, but I hadn't had much choice.

The information on the security of the hotel next door—the one with the higher vantage point that would allow me to propel down to the neighboring hotel's penthouse—had been faulty. Error number one, and it had cost me two hours to get past the metal detectors and security guards with the barest of my gear. Knowing the stealthiest ways in and the quickest ways out of a job site was vital, and I was no longer sure if I could trust anything Eric Cabordes had told me.

And yet I dared not balk at this job now. That would get me killed. Or—my worst nightmare—they might hurt my daughter to punish me. If they found out about her. And I wasn't so sure they didn't already know.

Stuck in midair, I inched toward the window, stopping to rest after a few feet. My calf muscles twitched from the earlier strain.

My knees trembled. I was exhausted but running on sheer adrenaline. My bare palms had started to sweat.

The rope jerked and I dropped several feet in a split second. One of the strands had caught on a metal edge along the railing above sharp enough to chew halfway through the rope as my weight pulled on it.

I glanced at the penthouse window, twelve feet and a good one-story drop below me. I wasn't going to make it! But I had to. The Adrianos had a long history of getting what they wanted, particularly when I was the one getting it for them.

I shook my head and held on tight. I thought of my lover's green eyes, which I would never see again, the same eyes my little girl had inherited. I never should have accepted this job. Never. I should have retired last week, changed my name yet again and spent the rest of my life living my dream—lecturing in some remote university and living the safe, boring, legitimate life of an academic. But there was always the lure of one more job, especially one that paid a half million dollars plus expenses. The Adrianos thought I did it for the money, but I had other reasons. And, too, there was the refusal to admit that my body had aged a year in the last twelve months and that I desperately needed time off to let my knee heal properly.

I breathed in the aloneness of nothing but night air around me. If I fell or if I failed, I didn't want anyone watching. But that's always been my preference. Succeed discreetly, fail anonymously. I'd simply be a shattered corpse found on the street below and later identified through my fingerprints. The local cops would pity me that I had no obvious family or friends to miss me. Later, the Interpol agent who'd been on my ass for the past few months would show up to claim my body, and if anyone mourned me, she was as close as it would come. Catrina Dauvergne and my other acquaintances in Europe would never even know what had happened to me.

I felt the rope jerk in my grasp and flung my head back to see what had happened at the secure end. I watched in horror as the rope frayed toward nothingness.

Both feet hugging the rope, I pushed off, propelling myself forward as hard and as fast as I could toward the penthouse window. The rope swirled into a spray of fiber and snapped, and I fell hard against the wall below the penthouse window, banging my shoulder against the dirty brick. Still I held on, and the rope was caught securely above me.

I cursed under my breath, then remembered I had a three-hour window to acquire the package and I was two hours behind schedule. I didn't have the luxury of licking my wounds. Best if I didn't waste time.

I hauled myself up the rope to the window. My hands stung with blisters, some of them bloody. I ignored the pain and focused on the window.

Fortunately at this height the windows didn't have bars or external security of any type. Unfortunately they couldn't be raised enough even for a five-foot-two-inch woman like me to squeeze through. If I'd had my tools with me, I would have been following my plan and inside already. But then, so much of life is about improvising and simply doing the best you can with what you have. Especially if what you have is faulty intel.

I'd chosen this particular window based on the blueprints that had been faxed to me. Why then didn't the blueprints match the building I clung to? Error number two. If I ever met this Eric Cabordes, I was going to give him a piece of my mind...or the back of my hand across his face. No, maybe I'd simply report his lack of thoroughness to the Duke and let *him* explain how dangerous little mistakes can be in the middle of a job.

Given what I knew of the blueprints and what I now knew personally of the building, access through the window was probably a bad idea. I'd expected to make a quiet entrance into an unused bedroom, courtesy of my glass-cutting tools, but the unforeseen metal detector had rendered that plan useless. I could crash through, counting on the element of surprise to aid me, but by the time I emerged from a guest suite, the crash would have been heard and every alarm in the building would have been activated. I would be trapped.

Do I really have a choice? Get caught, get killed or let the Adrianos make me wish I were dead.

Wind whistling in my ears, I grasped the rope and shoved backward with my shoeless feet, then swung against the window, my shoulder meeting it hard. I braced for the splintering of glass, for the burst through the window into whatever waited on the other side, for the surge of adrenaline I felt every time I broke and entered a building. Instead the window merely crunched under the force of my body. Then slowly a few shards of glass fell inside.

I smiled to myself. American architecture is stronger than that of Europe's centuries-old castles and inns, ones I normally smashed right through to get to whatever artifact needed extracting. I'd have to remember that next time—if there *was* a next time.

Still grasping the rope with my knees and one hand, I used my fingertips to tap out an area large enough for me to step through. I didn't worry about my fingerprints on the glass.

Why should I? They know who I am—my current identity at least—and I've never been caught. Yet.

Then again, I'd never received my instructions from anyone except a blood relative of the Adriano family.

The suite was a showplace indeed. Plush velvet curtains, hardwood floors, chandeliers burning brightly. According to Eric's research, the safe had been concealed behind a tapestry in the main room, somewhere beyond the closed door of the suite I'd slipped into. All I had to do was open the safe, grab the package and take the fire escape downstairs to where my taxi waited on a side street.

I paused, bare feet acknowledging the coolness of the floor as I listened for sounds of life. The penthouse was supposed to be unoccupied tonight, but given my luck in the past few hours, I expected to find a surprise party waiting for me, complete with balloons and whistles. I crept forward, unlatching the door and opening it only enough to peer through. The main room appeared to be as empty as it was opulent, with a large tapestry demanding my attention.

Opening the door a little more, I eased through, my ears trained for sounds of disaster. The only noises were the wind from the broken window behind me and the desperate sounds of a man grunting and a woman faking an orgasm in the master suite. Yes, someone was home tonight. Error number three.

I cringed. The occupants were too busy to notice an intruder, but those weren't sounds I wanted to hear right now, whether or not they were real. I hadn't had a romantic liaison in over two months. That was strictly my choice, of course. I still had a couple of lovers in France who would have welcomed me with open arms, but I'd become disenchanted with them. It was just physical, for them and for me. Try as I might, my heart wasn't in it.

My reflection, lean and petite, stared back up at me from the spotlessly shined oak floor. I still had what it took, whether it was to get a man into bed or to acquire his most precious possessions. Tonight would certainly be the latter, particularly since the man of the house was already otherwise engaged and I couldn't stop thinking about the only man I'd ever loved.

I scanned the room, noting the elevator across from the fireplace and the huge spray of lilies on a marble table, all fit for a palace. The fire escape was behind the window on the far side of the room. Good. So far, so good, even with occupants.

Padding across the room to the tapestry, I admired it from top to bottom. Sixteenth-century. Flemish. At least ten feet across and hanging from a jointed rod that could be swung away from the wall. The garden scene had faded over the years, and the lovers who had modeled for the tapestry were long since dead, their immortality left to the patterns of thread and dye as surely as famous lovers in literature lived forever on the page.

Against my better judgment, I reached for the tapestry and brushed my fingertips over the pattern of flowers and lovers on holiday. It's artifacts like these that call to me, that seduce me like a siren luring sailors to the rocks. There's something about old treasures that have outlasted generations of hearts that loved them and hands that fought for them. Something about their luck to withstand the ravages of elements and time where their human contemporaries could not. Something about the way they link modern society with all of its technological marvels to simpler medieval times and concerns as surely as a time-travel machine, if one existed.

It's treasures like these that I steal for hire. But an artifact even more precious than this one stole me away from my only daughter—a relic from the hand of Joan of Arc herself, and a promise that my lover was still out there somewhere, waiting for me to find him and love him again. My little girl had grown up without me. Of all the things in my life that I've done wrong for whatever good reason, giving up my daughter was my greatest regret. Even if I'd done it to save her life.

The moans from the master suite continued as I swung the tapestry away from the wall to reveal the walk-in safe, a fancy computerized one that was supposedly impenetrable. The tapestry tempted me, but I was familiar enough with the era to know that it was a legitimate sale and so not of interest to me. What was in the vault behind it was a piece of artwork that had been stolen from the Adrianos in the seventeenth century and moved throughout Europe and Asia to keep it hidden from its rightful owners. It had found its way back into old Max Adriano's hands when he'd been a very young man, only to be lost in Nazi raids. Whatever it was, Max's son—the Duke—considered it one of their most valuable acquisitions.

What is it? I wondered. *The source of their power? Their pedigree?*

I stifled a chuckle. Duke Simon Adriano, the distinguished sixtysomething man who'd hired me for no less than thirty-five jobs, would have admonished me for my sense of humor. His youngest son, Joshua, would probably have laughed at my insolence. But the remaining son, Caleb, would have wanted me publicly stripped and flogged and gladly would have done the job himself.

Caleb. I shuddered. One more reason not to get caught or screw up my mission. Simon kept his son in check. "And when it comes to Caleb and his father," I whispered, smoothing the threads of the tapestry to make room for my safecracking work, "I definitely want the elder Adriano protecting me."

I knew to steer clear of Caleb, my most dangerous mistake. Sometimes when I closed my eyes, even now, I could still feel his thumbs on my throat, could still feel the gray fog of unconsciousness seep into my vision. I hated him for that, almost as much as he hated me for refusing to let him touch me ever again. He'd sworn to kill me if he ever had another chance. That was but one more reason to finish this heist and put an end to my connection to the Adriano family.

If Simon will let me go.

The moans from the master suite subsided, then started again. I ignored the actress's shrieks and fidgeted with my belt until I extracted a safecracker's key no bigger than a penlight on a key chain. I held the cylinder close to the panel on the wall next to the safe. The red digital letters, SECURE, scattered into dots and reformed in a bright green OPEN.

The vault door clicked. I slid it open and expelled a sigh of admiration. Paintings—originals—lined one corner of the vault. Some were strictly black market and might have been worth my effort to—shall we say—*liberate.* But I had no time for such pleasures.

The package I'd been told to retrieve seemed to sizzle on its own shelf. Exactly as Eric had described, the soft-sided briefcase with the long shoulder strap covered a hard plastic case of…something…wrapped in a protective liner. For once, Eric had been correct about something. I understood at last why he had insisted I deliver the package to Simon "off the grid," even though it would take me weeks to return to the Adriano compound in Italy. No airport in the United States would dare let me board a jet without forcing me to open the package or, at the very least, to shove it through an X-ray machine. The Duke, when he'd first told me about this job, had been adamant about my not letting the package out of my hands and especially not allowing it into the hands of anyone in authority, such as a customs agent or that woman from Interpol who seemed to be two steps behind me no matter where I went.

Slowly I backed out of the vault, the briefcase tucked under my arm, its strap over my shoulder, and closed the door to the safe. I swung the tapestry back into place and turned just in time to catch the wide-eyed shock of a blond woman walking out of the master suite and dressed only in a satin sheet.

"B-b-burglar!" she screeched at the same pitch as her fake orgasm. Her overly pouty lips trembled, but she was too terrified to say more.

I didn't know whether I should be proud or hurt that she found me so frightening. For pity's sake, I wasn't even carrying a knife or a revolver. I was fully twenty pounds lighter than she, twice as disheveled and equally barefoot.

"Bill!" she screamed loud enough to pierce my eardrums.

I didn't hang around to get a good look at the guy who was probably just turning over for a good snore. I bounded for the window on the far side of the room, for the fire escape I could slide partway down, for my taxi waiting discreetly below. I'd be gone by the time she called the front desk to complain about an intruder. I flicked the window latch with my thumb.

It wouldn't open.

"Error number four," I whispered. The window didn't lead to the fire escape. It led nowhere. The blueprints were wrong again. I slammed my palm against the cold glass and it cracked under the force. "Damn you, Eric."

I dipped behind the marble table with the lilies on top and slid toward the elevator, pounding the button with my thumb. I glimpsed the blonde as she threw herself at the fire alarm on the wall. I couldn't let her do that. I couldn't let her pull that alarm. If she did, the elevator control panel would lock up, and the elevator car would glide to uselessness on the ground floor. Even if I could find the stairwell quickly, I'd never make it down the stairs on a bum knee without being caught.

There was no need to kill her. Not if I had any choice. I'd killed before, twice, but then only in self-defense against men who earned their living in the death trade. This woman wasn't a plant, wasn't a bodyguard, wasn't an assassin. She was an innocent. A bumbling innocent who didn't deserve to die for being in the wrong place at the wrong time, and I wouldn't sacrifice her for myself.

Twirling around, I shoved her backward—hard. She hit the marble floor and slid the length of the room, letting out a little "Oof!" as she bumped into the wall.

I scrambled toward the elevator, still looking over my shoulder. The blonde sat there, dazed, then shook it off and clambered to her feet. The elevator doors opened, and I fell inside, breathless but with the briefcase in tow. The last thing I saw before the doors closed was the blonde making a wild grab for the fire alarm. Sirens erupted throughout the building.

Damn.

The elevator locked up and dropped quickly, speeding toward the hotel lobby fast enough that my ears popped. I knew what would be waiting for me below.

Freedom or capture.

Chapter 2

A fire alarm might have been a perfect cover for me to leave with a crowd if I had been dressed like a normal guest and hadn't just heisted what Simon had alluded to as the "artifact of the second millennium," but I couldn't risk the likelihood that the blonde's companion would be intelligent enough to call hotel security and have them waiting at the elevator doors in the lobby.

Thankfully, I had a long ride down. Bare feet against the brass handrails in the elevator, I climbed one mirrored wall, punched at the plastic grating in the fake ceiling until I found the access door, thumbed the screws loose and then pulled myself and the briefcase onto the top of the elevator car just before the doors opened and the grate fell back into place.

Two security guards poked their heads through the door and checked the blind spot near the control panel, shook their heads, and backed out without looking up. Chest heaving, I tried to keep my breath quiet and under control. I watched through the plastic grating as they stood in front of the elevator for a few seconds, then bolted off in a different direction. I started to lower myself into the elevator.

"Stay by the elevators," I heard one of the security guards order between sirens. "She's here somewhere. What goes up must come down."

Meaning me. From my vantage point, I couldn't see anyone through the open elevator door, but I could hear the chaos of hotel security barking orders and hotel guests oddly demanding information instead of fleeing the building, but I couldn't tell why. I tucked the briefcase closer to my heart. Everyone in the hotel would be looking for a barefoot woman in a black leotard and a briefcase. How would I ever get out of the building? And when the three hours on my taxi's meter ran dry, so did my chances of escape.

Except…

Elevators have always been one of my specialties. They've been around for many decades and yet people still fear them, especially getting trapped inside or dropped or bisected by the doors. Even rescuers hate them because it's so difficult to extricate people when they're trapped inside or between floors. Most people don't know how to get out. There are at least fifty different manufacturers, and every elevator model is different, which is why good intel is so important before a job like this.

The elevator car was stationary and likely to stay that way as long as the alarms were blaring off and on in the building. The elevators were controlled by a central computer system, so a fire alarm would send every elevator car in the building to the ground floor. From inside the building, the only way back up would be through the stairwell—or the elevator shafts.

I peered up the darkened silo and tried to remember the blueprints. Maybe something about them was right. The lighting was dim, mainly from the fluorescent bulbs below and a few slits of light above. The longer I blinked into the shaft above me, the more accustomed my eyes became, and I could discern a thin metal ladder on one wall leading upward to the next floors and eventually to the roof. An escape from the roof wasn't feasible, not without my ropes. And as much as I would have liked to, I couldn't blame even Eric Cabordes for the elevator.

I'd have to improvise to get to my taxi. Standing carefully, I kicked at the emergency toolbox amid the equipment on top of the elevator car. It held a short ladder for rescues, too short to be of any use to me. Instead I grabbed a screwdriver, clenched it between my teeth, slung the briefcase over my shoulder by its strap and then started the climb up the shaft.

I'd done my share of rock climbing, and this would have been easy had my knee not screamed with every push upward I made. That and the fact that I had to be careful of everything I touched so I didn't electrocute myself.

I reached the second story and leaned in front of the doors, hanging on to the ladder by my feet as I worked to pry the doors open with the screwdriver. The blare of the alarm blasted through into the quieter elevator shaft. I slid the doors open just enough to see that the hall was clear and then tumbled out onto the carpet.

Too bad my daughter couldn't have seen me do that. I would have been the hit of show-and-tell. Then again, those show-and-tell days had ended years ago, and I'd missed seeing what had come after them.

At least I'd found what I was looking for on the second floor—the gym. The one place I could be dressed like a gymnast on a mission and no one would take me for a thief.

I squinted through the floor-length windows. The treadmills and recumbent bikes had been abandoned. *Good.*

The alarms still shrieked at intervals. I ignored them and bounded through the glass doors with the gym's hours etched in white.

My plan was to hide in plain sight because they would be looking for someone in a defensive posture. I've always had the kind of looks that people notice. Not the best feature for a thief. The security guards, and by now the police, would be looking for black leotards, bare feet and a briefcase. Surely the blonde would have gotten that much of a description right. Those three things, if nothing else, would have to be hidden.

I tore through the locker room, finding it empty, as well. Someone had left a navy-blue gym bag on the changing bench, smelly shoes included. The bag looked generic enough not to be spotted by its owner. The briefcase was a perfect fit, but I could tell by looking that the shoes were too small for me.

Using the screwdriver, I jimmied open one locker and then another, finally pulling out a pair of expensive athletic shoes. About one size too big, but if laced up tightly, they'd do fine. I salvaged a bright blue sarong from the pool area and turned it into a skirt that hid the legs of my leotard and made the top look like a swimsuit. I dampened my hair and threw a white gym towel over my shoulder.

"Hey! What do you think you're doing?"

I spun at the voice, screwdriver hidden in my palm. A well-muscled security guard eyed me frantically from the gym door.

"Can't you hear the fire alarm? Come on! Go, go, go!"

Before I could say anything, he grabbed my elbow and escorted me into the hall. His gait was a little too fast for both my oversize shoes and my knee injury, so I pulled away from him, nodding as he pointed to the stairwell.

I limped down the stairs both flustered and relieved. Every footstep ached. For the kind of bashing my knee had suffered, the worst thing in the world for it was walking down stairs. But the good news was the security guard hadn't recognized me.

Free, I thought. *I'm going to make it. This time.*

I had barely enough time to get to the first floor and out the door before my taxi was scheduled to leave, with or without me. He'd been paid cash in advance, with a nice bonus promised for waiting the full three hours if

I returned. I'd always found it best to use cash as an incentive, a little something I'd learned from the Adrianos.

The alarm stopped, but it still rang in my head. The scene in the lobby was a little less of a zoo than it had been when I'd almost descended into it earlier. Hotel guests milled around, some grumbling about being kept downstairs and others looking bored. Some wore pajamas or bathrobes, and one man with shaving cream on half his face had obviously hastily tugged on a trench coat over his flip-flops and God knew what else. The lobby was so thick with people that I had to stop a few times to wait for someone to inch around me.

As for me, I did my best to fit in, something that's never been an easy chore for me. I made shy eye contact with a couple of guests as if I were an old friend, shrugged and waved and kept walking through the crowd until I had passed the danger of being caught. The main exit was straight ahead. None of the security guards or police seemed to notice anything out of the ordinary about me. I was just a normal guest whose swim had been interrupted by the fire alarm.

"Ma'am?" An auburn-haired security guard stepped in front of me. He was older and not as buff as the one who'd dragged me out of the gym. "You can't go that way."

I swear I batted my eyelashes at him. "Excuse me? I thought there was a fire. We're supposed to stay inside a burning building?"

"Yes, ma'am. I mean..." He blushed. "I mean, no, ma'am. You must have missed the announcement. It's just a false alarm. Some prankster pulled the alarm, but we have to check it out. You'll have to wait down here for a few more minutes."

Hmm. So the hotel management didn't want it known that they were looking for a thief? The guy I'd taken the briefcase from must have been pretty important to get this kind of service. I wondered if the hotel employee in front of me was important enough to know who had pulled the alarm and why. Judging by the presence of police officers in the lobby, I guessed that even if he didn't know, the ones guarding the doors had an idea that they had a dangerous thief in their midst.

I looked past him at the front doors to the hotel. Another twenty feet and I'd be free.

"Ah," I said, "a false alarm. So that's why I didn't see any firefighters running through the building."

"Yes, ma'am. We'd rather no one left the building until we get it sorted out." A flimsy excuse, but it was working for the mangle of guests in the lobby.

I flashed him a smile. "But I need to leave the building."

He pointed to the concierge desk. "Just show the officer over there your room key or some kind of identification." He must have seen the look on my face. "If you left it in the pool area, you'll have to wait until that area is cleared and then you can go back upstairs for it."

Not what I had in mind. I could barrel through the doors and outrun the cops, lose myself in the sidewalk traffic, disappear between buildings and double back to the taxi. Yeah. I could do it.

No, I couldn't. Not with a bum knee.

Nodding my thanks to the guard, I tucked the artifact

closer to my heart and kept my head down as I rounded the corner toward a service exit I'd noted on the blueprints. Hotel guests wouldn't be aware of the exit. I just hoped something Eric Cabordes had told me was correct.

The briefcase seemed to hum with energy, but it was probably just my imagination. I myself was putting out a lot of heat and energy. I'd been told it was an artifact from the fifteenth century, but for all I knew, it was a bomb or a deadly biological agent. I'd have to get the briefcase back to Italy before I could find out what was in it. Simon had assured me that I was not to open it, not under any circumstances. Eric, on the other hand, had said no such thing.

Through the glass partitions of the restaurant, I could see the red letters of an exit sign above a side door. Down one hallway and over another and I'd be there. I'd be free.

The rush of adrenaline made me tingle all the way to my toes. I was so close! All the doubts of earlier in the evening started to fade. Over three hundred heists—thirty-five solo for Simon—and I was still the mistress of the game! Pain stabbed through my knee, but I couldn't let it stop me. Never mind the money and the nice, safe retirement I longed for, I didn't want to admit it, but I really did love the excitement of getting away with it one more time. I was addicted to the thrill of it and I had to admit, too, that even with all of Eric's erroneous information, tonight's job had made every cell in my body come alive, first with doubts and then with victory. Ever since I lost the life I'd had with my little girl, the adrenaline rush had been the only thing that made me feel alive.

I couldn't avoid the smug twist of my lips as I focused on the marble tile of the foyer near the bank of public elevators. My taxi would be waiting for me across the street. I was practically home free. According to the blueprints, all I had to do was reach the service exit around the next corner and—

Dead end.

I stared at the framed sign: Pardon Our Dust While We Renovate. My heart sank. Sure, the new fountain and lounge would look great in another week, but my last-resort escape route had just been shot to hell and back. I spun to check my options.

Damn, damn, damn. A move to the right and I'd run into the unyielding arms of hotel security. If I bolted to the left, I'd meet face-to-face with the San Francisco police at the public exits. In either case, the most likely person to come to my aid would be Analise Reisner, the Interpol agent who'd been right behind me as recently as two days ago. Not exactly the rescue I wanted, even if she did owe me one.

I cursed under my breath. I was sick of the roller coaster this job had been. A minute ago I'd loved it, and now? Failure at every turn, then finding a way out, then failing again. It was almost as if someone wanted me to get caught red-handed with the artifact. Which made me wonder even more about the contents of the package.

My lover used to say that when one door closes another one opens, but I'm not sure he'd meant it literally.

I had to make a plan. I'm just that way. I can't do anything on impulse. I had to think it through and know where I was going. Planning, analysis, studying the situation—it's my scarecrow when I feel out of control. And yet, in the back of my mind something reminded me of how my plans for a heist were almost always perfectly executed whereas the plans for my life had gone awry at every opportunity.

I stalked back to the lobby to look over the situation. The exits on the first floor were blocked. The roof was out of the question. I couldn't take the stairs because they were blocked off now. *Trapped.* I was trapped. That's the worst feeling in the world to me, having to stay somewhere I don't want to be and being powerless, being controlled. Just like having to work for the Adrianos. *Damn.* I needed a place to hide until things cooled down.

One of the police officers at the front door skimmed the room and then did a double take. I watched in heart-sinking slow motion as he tapped another officer on the shoulder and inclined his head in my direction. I glanced down. My sarong skirt had caught on the corner of the table, snaring it and revealing one leg of black leotard.

The second man nodded and disappeared into the crowd. I caught a fleeting glimpse of him halfway around the lobby. When I looked back at the first man, he'd left his post, too, and had started nonchalantly making his way around the lobby from behind me.

Setup! If I was caught with the artifact, I'd rot in jail until Interpol showed up to haul me back. And that would be if I was fortunate. Along the way, a stray bullet was likely to find me. That had happened more than once with former Adriano employees who'd been captured and expected to face a jury in the States. Employees with far paler reputations in the criminal world than mine. The Adrianos couldn't allow any of their secrets to come out in exchange for a lighter sentence. As if anyone would believe the Adrianos were anything other than wonderful philanthropists without an ill-intentioned bone in their bodies!

Weaving through the crowd, I closed in on the elevator. I patted the gym bag, checking for the exact location of the screwdriver I'd need shortly either for defense or for an escape. A tall man sauntered through the swarm of hotel guests, and I matched his steps, keeping him in my line of vision so that for a few seconds neither cop could see me. I dipped into the open elevator, the same one I'd come down earlier, and scrambled up the wall and through the hatch.

Strong hands caught my feet as I strained upward, but I kicked and the too-big shoes came off in their hands. Barefoot, I dragged my feet to safety. I jammed the emergency toolbox crosswise over the escape hatch. I could hear them yelling below, calling for backup.

My eyes were still wide in the dark, unaccustomed yet to the absence of light. I fished the screwdriver out of the bag and bit into its handle. I'd need it soon enough. One way or another.

I reached for the ladder and began pulling myself up, hand over hand, relying mainly on my uninjured knee to push myself along. Adrenaline got me to the second floor. Willpower alone helped me reached the third. My breath came out in wheezes around the screwdriver handle. My eyes adjusted, but the tears of pain blurred my vision. I climbed with my eyes closed, by feel. Fourth floor.

My escape was a matter of who would get into a corridor first. Me, in a dark elevator shaft with a knee that burned and begged at every grunt? Or several cops who needed to run the length of the lobby, up at least three flights of stairs and then meet me as I tried to pry the doors open? Were I uninjured, the odds would have been in my favor.

Then I heard a click below and a slight electrical buzz. No. *No!*

I climbed faster, harder. The last thing I wanted was to be trapped in that shaft with a moving elevator!

The elevator car moved up one floor at a time, almost like a warning, reminding me they wanted me alive and not dead. Either that or they were afraid the artifact would be damaged. By the time I couldn't take another step, it was two floors below me and moving again.

At the seventh floor, I jammed the screwdriver into the crevice between the doors enough to ease my fingers over the edges and then forced open the doors. The screwdriver slipped, pinging off the sides of the shaft and then skittering across the elevator car below me, bouncing and then falling out of earshot somewhere far below. I tumbled into the corridor, gym bag pulled close, and squeezed my eyes shut as the doors swished together behind me.

"She can't have gotten too far," I heard faintly.

Cops were in the elevator! The door would open in another couple of minutes and they'd see me lying exhausted on the floor, and I wouldn't even have the strength to put up a fight.

I shook myself and struggled to my feet. I pushed hard down the hall, limping as I turned the corner. I hugged the wall, carefully avoiding the video monitors mounted at ceiling level and angled toward the outer edges of the corridors. The elevator dinged behind me, barely out of sight. I stopped cold.

So did the girl in front of me. A teenager, frozen at the door of one of the suites, key in hand. She stared at me through a mass of dirty tangles. We both knew that she wasn't supposed to be upstairs. The doorknob jiggled in her grasp and she shoved inside.

I sprang at her, catching her from behind. We rolled into the room together, me landing on top of her. I clamped my hand down hard over her mouth and with one foot eased the door shut behind us.

"Don't make a sound," I warned. Her eyes studied me, shifting a fretful gaze toward one side of my face and then the other. She looked as though she might cry. I felt bad. She wasn't much younger than my Lilah. "Shhh," I whispered, "and you'll be okay."

Outside, the cops pounded up and down the halls, then back to the elevator. The doors swooshed shut and somewhere a faint bell dinged as the elevator stopped on the eighth floor.

Change of plans. Again. I'd have to stay here for a while. Long enough for the hornet's nest downstairs to calm down. I had no choice, and by now my taxi was long gone. I slowly pulled my palm away from the girl's mouth but continued to sit on top of her, pinning her belly-down on the floor.

"I'm sorry, I'm sorry!" She covered her face with one hand. "I didn't mean to break in!"

I lightened my grip. "This isn't your room?"

"N-no. Isn't it yours?"

"No." So the look on her face had meant she not only wasn't supposed to be upstairs during the fire alarm but she wasn't supposed to be here at all. "Then if it's not yours, whose room it?" I asked.

"I don't know. Some guy. I heard him say he wouldn't be back until after midnight. Maybe not until morning if he got lucky."

"Then what are you doing here?"

"I—I stole the key from the maid." Before I could ask why, she backhanded a trickle of blood from her lower lip and added, "I have to eat."

Something twisted in my heart. Helping the girl sit up, I cautioned her with a finger to my lips. "You're a runaway?"

"You work for the hotel? You one of their cops?"

I shook my head. "No. Just somebody in a little bit of trouble. Like you. How'd you get in the hotel after dark?"

"Didn't. They only check IDs at night. Walked in

here in broad daylight. Stole a key from the maid and I've been living here ever since." She hiked her chin just a little to show me she was proud of her resourcefulness.

"What do you mean *living here?* For how long?"

"Two weeks ago yesterday. People who order room service don't eat everything on their plates, you know?" Insolence crept into her voice. "And all I have to do is watch people come and go and I figure out when I can slip in and sleep for a few hours. Sometimes I find a room that's empty all night. I put the Do Not Disturb sign out and nobody bothers me."

"You can't keep doing this forever. You're going to get caught." The expression on her face told me she'd come close already.

"Don't have to do it forever. Just for three more days. When I'm eighteen, no one can make me go back to my bastard of a stepfather." She set her jaw. "He won't ever touch me."

I grimaced. She looked like an underage hooker in her belly shirt, jeans that barely covered her butt cleavage and spiked heels that would make a grown woman cry. I recognized the look in her eyes. I'd seen it often enough in my travels. Runaway. Alone. Still proud but one step away from selling her affections to whatever scum would pay cold, hard cash just to keep from going home to a situation that really wasn't much better. She still had the slightest glimmer of innocence. Something about her touched the mother deep inside me, the part of me that I kept buried, and I wanted her to keep that innocence.

She was pretty underneath her greasy tangles. She had a nose ring and green eyes. Not as bright as Lilah's green, but in another time and place she could have been my daughter. But my daughter was in a safer place than this girl. At least I hoped she was.

"What about your mother?"

"She'd never believe me. Not over her new husband. She's the one who told me to get out. She didn't want me."

I sighed aloud and didn't try to hide it. I thought of Lilah when she'd hugged me goodbye at the age of ten and begged me not to go away on the academic expedition to Europe that, in the end, had been a terrible mistake. I'd planned carefully. I'd assured her everything would be all right and Mommy would be back in a few short weeks. Even the beloved auntie and cousins I'd left her with hadn't been able to cheer her. Maybe she'd known then that I would never return to her. But I myself hadn't known.

This girl, this runaway, was tall but too thin, and probably not from choice. She was right about having to eat. The mother in me wanted to feed her, wanted to *mother* her. And get her into some decent clothes.

"You've been wearing those for two weeks?" I asked, nodding at her too-tight jeans.

"No, just today. I borrow clothes when I can find them."

"You mean you steal them." I felt like a hypocrite. For once, I was glad not to be having this conversation with Lilah. "You shouldn't steal," I said lamely.

The girl jutted her chin out at me, then smirked at my leotard and bare feet, at the gym bag full of loot. "Who are you to say?"

I didn't say. I didn't say anything at all. What *could* I say? Except that I didn't want her or anyone else to live the kind of life that had made me a fugitive from the law as well as from my own past.

And then I did the unthinkable. I opened the tiny birdcage bars around my heart and let this girl step just barely over the threshold.

Three hours later, I'd become fast friends with a runaway named Nicole. She was certain the registered occupant of the room wouldn't be back until after midnight, and I didn't intend to cut it too close. Things had returned to normal downstairs—or at least it seemed so. I didn't doubt that the exits were being watched. Eager to please, Nicole had slipped down the hall to the ice machine and filled a pillowcase with ice, which I'd applied to my knee to bring down some of the swelling. My knee still ached, but it was feeling…tolerable.

Then the girl had slipped out again and returned with fresh clothes for both of us, courtesy of some prim and proper family that was probably still trapped downstairs and waiting for clearance to return to their room. Nicole's new wardrobe consisted of boy jeans and a band T-shirt, but her curves were still obvious underneath.

I smiled and turned back to the mirror and the job of making myself over. Nicole had obviously considered it amusing that my new clothes should be so conservative. She'd picked out an ankle-length dress for me, small floral print with a lace-trimmed Peter Pan collar. She aimed to have me mistaken for an English teacher, she said, and I didn't tell her that I really was an English teacher. Or had been. Regardless, when we left the room together, I wanted to make sure we didn't attract attention, especially since a few cops might still be hanging around in the corridors.

I lifted the glass of pomegranate juice—the secret of my youth—from the dressing table in front of me where the room-service waiter had left it and then I drained the last drops. We'd waited until life outside the room had returned to normal, and I'd paid in cash from the stash inside my belt. But as I finished the pom juice, the girl's reflection in the mirror stopped me cold.

She sat at the desk, chattering about how she'd evaded the video monitors in the halls, and finishing the last bites of the steaks I'd ordered from room service. She seemed to savor each mouthful. From her constant prattle, I knew how long she'd been on her own and what had driven her to this life on the run, but tomorrow she would have a fresh start. I'd see to it. A chance to rewrite her life. I had connections and I'd drop her off along the way with instructions to take care of her as though she were my own daughter, as though she were Lilah and I was doing for Lilah something I'd never been allowed to do. I wouldn't send Nicole back to whatever hell had brought her here. Seventeen, almost eighteen, was too young to lose her innocence, and there had been some innocence still in her eyes when I had offered her a decent meal, a hot shower and a chance to leave the city with me.

I'd been seventeen once, too, and lost after my mother's death as surely as this girl felt lost after her mother's rejection. Three events in my life had altered any plans I'd ever made for a bright future: losing my mother, losing my lover and—ten years later—losing my little girl. At eighteen, alone and scared, my fate had been to die at the hands of an assassin. I'd escaped that fate, but all else had been sacrificed. Something about this girl reminded me of myself then. If I could help this runaway, if I could keep her from getting herself killed on the streets, then maybe she could get her life back on course for the bright future I'd never had.

"Are you done, sweetie?" I asked Nicole's image in the mirror. I tried to imagine how Lilah would have looked at seventeen, shortly before her guardian had died. A private investigator sent me photographs regularly, but it wasn't the same. Children can change so much from the time they're ten until a few years later, especially a girl when she loses her baby chub and gains a few curves.

Nicole nodded vigorously as I turned to her. "Yes, ma'am. It was delicious." She'd suddenly started treating me like the mother she said she'd never had, complete with all the little courtesies a stricter mom might expect.

"Don't *ma'am* me." I slipped on the shoes she'd acquired for me. "Come on. We're leaving." I ushered Nicole toward the door as I gathered the gym bag under one arm.

"Are we going out through the lobby?" Nicole asked while I swept the hotel room with one last glance.

I shook my head. "Tonight I'm going to show you how to shinny down a fire escape."

She giggled. I grinned back at her, then sobered. It was something I would never do with Lilah. My daughter would never know this side of me. To her, I would always be the loving intellectual who'd told her bedtime stories from medieval manuscripts and recited Chaucer right along with her bedtime prayers. I wanted to keep it that way. I wanted to keep her alive, and that meant I'd never read her another story. I couldn't risk it.

"Wait," Nicole said. "I have something for you." She held up a key with a Mercedes emblem on it. "It belongs to the hotel. They use it to pick up VIPs. I know where it's parked right now."

As I took it from her, I started to ask where she'd picked up the key but laughed instead. Somehow I always ended up driving a Mercedes, and that meant the cops weren't quite so quick to think I was a thief. I never drove one for long. Safer that way. I'd leave this one with the Sisters in Los Angeles and find something less flashy for tomorrow afternoon.

By the next evening I would have crossed the border into Mexico with the newest Adriano artifact. The "artifact of the second millennium" would be on its way home. In spite of Eric Cabordes's bad information.

Unless the Interpol agent found me first.

The girl and I left the room quickly, quietly, and headed for the fire escape stairwells. Instead of keeping a low profile, Nicole slipped ahead of me, excited and full of life in the way that only a girl on the verge of womanhood can be.

I remembered those days. I might have forgotten them if the second tragedy of my young life had not burned those feelings of both foolish bravery and fear into my heart. I'd been barely eighteen and madly in love with Lieutenant Matthew Burns, the young American soldier who'd risked his life to rescue me. Looking now at the girl, at Nicole in all her naiveté, I couldn't help but wonder what had happened to Matthew after he'd smuggled me out of Britain. I had not even known who we were running from, but I'd trusted him when he'd said we were in danger.

After the third tragedy in my life—losing Lilah—I'd flitted like a gypsy all over Europe, between heists, always a few steps behind where he'd supposedly been spotted. As long as I held out hope of finding him again, I never dared let another man into my heart, though my bed had been another matter. I had to believe that Matthew was still somewhere out there. My daughter deserved to know her father.

As for Lilah, I knew exactly where she was, yet I could never see her again. I was dead to her. But better that than have her be dead to me.

"Which way?" Nicole asked at the bottom of the stairwell.

One fire door in front of us led back into the lobby area. We took the other door, which opened onto an open grate with rails. I kicked at the ladder, and it extended below us as I tested my weight on the top rung. Nicole climbed down behind me, paying attention as I caught the metal pole with my sleeve and twirled my way to the ground. She mimicked my movements and joined me seconds later on the ground.

"What now?"

I smiled at my protégée. "Now you do your thing, kid. Take us to the car."

I didn't complain as we climbed two culverts and dropped to the concrete floor three times to keep from being spotted by security guards in the underground garage. Nicole motioned to the gray Mercedes in a line of luxury automobiles and mouthed, *That's the one.* She held out her hand for the key.

"Uh, no. I'm driving." I swear she looked disappointed, but I'd been to far more driving schools than she had. I thumbed the door release on the Mercedes's electronic key, and the vehicle's taillights flickered. We both tiptoed, hunkered over to keep from being spotted, to the Mercedes, where I discreetly opened the driver's door and half shoved the girl into the passenger seat before slipping inside and clicking the door shut.

"Cool," Nicole whispered. "Do you do that all the time?"

I steadied my breathing and rubbed my knee. "Yeah, all the time." Somehow the novelty of it had worn off.

"What now?"

I nodded at the mirror and the image of a young man in his twenties crossing the garage behind us. "We wait for that valet and follow him out the security gate."

"I mean…what about me?"

"You're going with me. I'll take you someplace safe. There's a church in L.A. where I have a contact."

"A contact in a church?"

"I have contacts all over the world." I tried not to let my life sound so glamorous. It wasn't. Most of my contacts had come through criminal activity, and very few could be trusted beyond whatever they were paid to do.

"Who's your contact?"

"Just someone who helped me out a few times." I caught the wide-eyed expression on her face and decided to nix it while I had the chance. "Nothing glamorous at all. A nun who's hidden me from the cops on several occasions. One of the few contacts I truly trust."

Her upper lip curled. "You're leaving me with a *nun?*"

"Temporarily. In three days or a week or whenever you want, you can leave. I can arrange a new identity for you if you want. I have…connections who can do that." A contact named George who I didn't entirely trust for my own work, but he was in L.A. and his work was credible. I'd used him on a couple of Adriano jobs in Southern California. He made a damned good fake ID package and he could give Nicole whatever papers she needed.

The girl smiled the first genuine smile I'd seen on her face. She watched me expectantly. "So you're certain my stepfather won't be able to find me? He'd…he'd hurt me if he could find me."

I stopped cold. *Anyone hurts you while you're under my protection and I will kill them. Just as I would if you were Lilah.*

"There are no victims, sweetie, only choices." Me,

I'd made bad choices, but like most adults, I won't admit them to a teenager. "And tonight you're making a choice for a fresh start. If you want it."

She moved her head in a single slow nod. "More than anything. I just want to leave my past behind." She bowed her head.

I knew just how she felt. Except I didn't want to leave my past behind, I wanted it back.

"I've had to start over a few times myself, Nicole." When Matthew vanished. When I left Lilah for six weeks to find the Joan of Arc relic. When I met the Adrianos. But had I ever really started over? I seemed to be going in circles and I was dead tired of it. Nicole wasn't mine, not by any means, but talking to her sent an ache through my heart to step up my plans to leave the Adrianos and change my life completely. I'd have to leave my old life behind to live again and I was so damned unsure about whether I could do it. "Maybe tonight will be a fresh start for both of us," I told Nicole.

She nodded enthusiastically as I cranked the Mercedes and backed out of the parking spot, quickly falling in line behind the valet and the emerald-green Jaguar he drove. We waited patiently for the yellow-and-black-striped bar at the security gate to rise for the Jag, and then I pushed forward until I was almost touching his bumper. I glanced up at the bar, half expecting it to come down at any second and hold us in place.

"Hey!" A security guard at the gate frowned at me. Then he realized that the Mercedes wasn't mine and that I was trying to tailgate my way out of the secured garage. "Hey!" He ran toward me, drawing his gun as a threat but more bark than bite.

A petty criminal would have stopped rather than risk a bullet whizzing past. Not me. I floored the accelerator, pushing hard against the Jag's bumper, shoving the automobile directly into the side street in front of us. Other vehicles honked as he landed in their path. I shot between them, fishtailing into the street and stomping the accelerator as I straightened out the automobile's trajectory.

"Wow," Nicole breathed. "Can you teach me to do that? I'll be your daughter any day!" Her words sliced through me.

"No!"

"But—"

"No."

I glanced in the mirror and concentrated on growing the distance between the hotel and us. "Nicole?" I tried not to let her hear the tremor in my voice. No one could ever take Lilah's place. Even if I managed to leave my life of crime, I could never have Lilah back. Ever. To have what I wanted most would mean putting my daughter in danger, and I wouldn't do that. To see her happy, I'd gladly sacrifice my fondest wish to have her back in my life, and if she were branded as my daughter, she'd never be free to have the life she was meant to live.

"Nicole, do me a big favor, okay?"

"Anything."

"Don't try to be like me. Ever."

"Why not?" She sat up tall in her seat and tugged at her buckled seat belt. "You afraid you might get caught?"

"No." In the mirror, the last gleam of the hotel marquee faded in the distance, and I let the night hide my face as we headed south. My throat filled up with unshed tears for the daughter I'd lost, and I could say no more.

Chapter 3

Autumn
Outside the Adriano palazzo, Italy

I had no idea why the compound where the Adriano family hides itself away always seemed to crackle with energy. I had felt the same surge of restlessness and power in a few other places—at Stonehenge and again on the misty Glastonbury Tor in Britain; near the legendary Temple of Delphi; at an archaeological site in Peru; and later at an underwater Greek temple that no one will ever know about. Maybe it's because the Adriano home base is built on the tower ruins of an old castle close to such a famous volcano, old Mount

Vesuvius, and the fact that modern technology has little effect on acts of God and Mother Nature. Storms, hurricanes, volcanoes, earthquakes—men are powerless in such conflicts, resorting to far-flung prayers in moments of crisis.

Then again, I thought as I waited at the main gate to the compound shortly after sunset, maybe it's the fact that the Adrianos are always on alert, the air thrumming with dozens of unseen henchmen straining to distinguish any movement in the acres of darkness.

Careful not to let my cleavage fall too far out of my velvet dress—which was normal attire for me—I leaned out the window of my rented Mercedes, thrusting my identification at the pimply faced guard who didn't look a day over sixteen. He barked at me in Italian to leave my automobile outside the gate and enter on foot. An older guard with a scar across his lips and large nose stood behind him, one hand on a low-slung holster. Neither seemed to have a sense of humor. They motioned for me to get out of the automobile, so I obeyed, taking the briefcase with me.

Hmm. Strange. I'd been to the compound thirty-eight times—thirty-five on official business—and I'd always been allowed to drive to the main building. Of course, I always had to exit my automobile while the guards scooted an X-ray machine on a slender trailer beneath the body of the vehicle, jabbed underneath with mirrors to look for bombs and then brought out the bomb-detecting dogs to sniff inside the automobile, under the hood, around the wheel wells and in the trunk. What had happened to ratchet up security several notches since my last visit a few months before?

"What's in package?" the older guard asked me in stilted English, his head bobbing at the briefcase. His tone was as harsh as his apprentice's, and they both seemed impervious to my usual feminine charms. Contrary to the allure of other Italian men, these thugs didn't warrant a second look.

"What's in package?" he barked again, knitting his thick eyebrows into one.

"I don't know." Why were they giving me such a hard time? I'd always been treated as an honored guest in Simon's home. Or at least a very valuable employee. Had something changed?

"Explosives? Guns?" the guard asked.

I shrugged. These guys weren't very creative. If I had plans to assassinate anyone in the Adriano family, it would have been Caleb and it would have been with something a lot slower than a suitcase bomb or a bullet. Hell, a little biological or radiological something would have been more in line with what the bastard deserved for what he'd done to me. That or a grenade up his ass.

Then it occurred to me that I really *didn't* know what was in the briefcase I'd been sleeping with for the past six weeks.

The guard drew his gun. "Give me package."

I shook my head. My grip tightened on the briefcase and its precious contents. "No one touches this package but Duke Adriano."

"Fine. We shoot you. Then we give him package." The older guard laughed at his own joke. Without warning, he grinned. "Meanwhile, we feel corpse for weapons. Maybe have to look everywhere."

His leer made my skin crawl. Why did men always make me do this?

Before the younger guard could move, I kicked the gun out of the older man's hand and left the heel print of my boot on his forehead. I caught the gun midair and swung it in the direction of the adolescent guard, who backed up against the wall with his palms facing me. Neutralizing him, I turned the gun on the older one on the ground.

"Please tell Duke Adriano that Dr. Moon is here to see him."

Damn it. I'd twisted my knee again. I seriously needed some downtime to recuperate. Months' worth of downtime.

The younger guard pressed the intercom button and mumbled something in Italian. Simon's face appeared on the black-and-white screen. The video camera at the corner of the gate swiveled in my direction. Simon's blank stare shifted to recognition.

"Dr. Moon! How delightful to see you," he said in perfect English with a smooth-flowing Italian accent sprinkled with the slightest hint of British brogue from his long stays in London. I was well traveled enough to have noticed it where others may not have. He narrowed his eyes at me through the camera. "What's that in your arms? Besides the firearm, of course. Have you been taunting my guards again?" He laughed. "Do you have something for me?"

"The question is, do you have something for *me?*" Like half a million American dollars, plus expenses. And hopefully a promise to release me from his employ. I'd trade the cash any day for an early retirement. The Adrianos thought my motivation was money, and I fed their assumption wherever possible. They knew that the money allowed me to keep up my international contacts and my expertise and still be on call whenever they demanded my services. I wasn't some poor schmuck they forced into servitude with threats and no extra pay, and that made my status far more prestigious than that of most employees.

"Ah, yes. *Cara mia.* My dear, sweet mercenary, Dr. Moon. Have one of the boys drive you up to the house."

I glanced at the eat-shit expressions on the guards' faces and considered my throbbing knee. "Thanks, Simon, but I think I'll walk."

I didn't mind the walk, but it had always bothered me how they'd overplanted trees and gardens along the driveway to the main house, mostly to hide the grounds from satellite coverage. In the dark, the walk seemed more like a nicely paved trail in the jungle, with small footpath lamps placed at intervals, so that I could see the toes of my boots in their glow.

The palazzo was far more impressive in daylight, especially with the four towers from the original castle standing like sentinels over the property. A series of earthquakes over the past year had damaged the towers, and on every visit this year scaffolding had tainted the picturesque view of the old stone architecture and its intricate crosswalks between the towers. Almost as soon as they completed the refurbishment, another tremor would rock the whole region.

Odd, I thought. So many earthquakes here in such a short time.

Not that Naples was immune to earthquakes. Besides the famous earthquake and volcanic destruction of nearby Pompeii in the first century, the area had been hit in the late 1600s, killing ninety-three thousand people, and as recently as 1980, injuring over sixty thousand. These small shakers within the past year were not a good sign of things to come, but the locals seemed more concerned with recent sudden rainstorms.

The walk along the driveway took almost twenty minutes. I didn't let my knee injury slow me down, but I needed every second of the way to cool down and mentally prepare myself. I slid the borrowed revolver into my bra between my breasts and ignored the feeling that I was being watched by silent mouth-breathing security guards hiding in the shrubbery and behind the olive trees along the driveway. I was far more worried about the unseen video cameras photographing every step I took.

Caleb would be watching.

Biting my lip against the pain in my knee, I bounded up the stone steps to the main house and reached for the knocker on the door. I just wanted to get this over with, collect my fee, get Simon's agreement to let me resign or retire and quietly disappear to some quiet little university town in Florida where the Adrianos would never find me. If that was possible. With any luck, tonight's visit to the compound would be my last. That was my plan, anyway.

Cold steel brushed across my cheek. I held my breath and didn't move. I kept my eyes straight ahead. The gun barrel caught the fall of hair above my eyes—the trendy style I'd chosen to hide the crinkles at the corners that some idiot had nicknamed *crow's-feet*—and lifted my hair away from my face. I didn't move as the metal traced my hairline to my forehead and examined my face with an intimacy that made me tremble. I felt naked. Worse—*vulnerable.* I had my props, my clothes and hair and makeup, to hide my flaws, and yet when your enemy inspects the lines of your face and knows how often you've smiled into the sun or frowned at your pain, there is nowhere to hide.

"Your weapon." His voice was low, quiet, but sounded vaguely familiar. "Don't move." He reached into the open neckline of my brown velvet dress and withdrew the revolver, barely touching my skin between my breasts as he did, but it was still enough to make my breath catch. "Sorry," he whispered in a Parisian accent that sounded like home to me. "We don't allow guns in the house."

I turned only my head to face him. I wasn't sure if it was safe to move. He lowered both guns and exhaled audibly.

We stood there for a minute longer than necessary,

sizing up each other. He was tall, very un-Italian, with brown hair that curled a little long on the collar of the sleek black leather jacket he wore. He had classic features and, for a man in his early thirties, nary a sign of a smile line or a frown crease. A good poker player, probably. His face held no expression at all, but I lost myself in his pale blue eyes.

It's a man's eyes that I'm always most attracted to, and in a split second I'd planned out the rest of our lives in my head. How we'd slip away from here and spend our days on the run, changing our identities and seeing the world together. Never able to slow down or become bores but always intense and exciting and thankful for one more day of life together. This man had what it took to keep the fire in my belly—and elsewhere—and I knew it in an instant. I could feel alive again with this man, at least for a little while.

I blinked away the illusion and promised myself I'd fantasize about him later. He was one of the Adriano henchmen and therefore off-limits to me in reality, but I knew without a doubt that I'd lust after him in my dreams. At least until I could find Matthew again.

The door opened inward, and I looked down at a little boy who stood between the door and the threshold using all his strength to keep the heavy door from pushing him out onto the steps with me. He nervously dug the toes of his sneakered feet into the stone floor and peered up at me with the biggest pair of puppy-dog eyes I'd ever seen on a child. Then he reached for the hem of the henchman's jacket and tugged three times.

"Eh-wic?"

Eric? Eric Cabordes? The man whose shoddy information had nearly gotten me captured in San Francisco?

"Go back inside." Eric's voice stayed low and gentle even while the heat of anger rose in my temples. He hid both guns behind his back. I could still see them, but the boy couldn't.

Of course. Guns weren't allowed inside the house because of the child. Was that it? Or was it that I wasn't supposed to have my own weapon while in the house? Guns had certainly been allowed in the house when a child wasn't present. I'd seen Adriano Security on the job a number of times, though I'd never seen this man. Either he was new or he spent most of his time off-site. A courier, perhaps. Yet why would they trust someone new to help me on a crucial heist?

"Eh-wic?" The boy tugged again. "Would you play hide-in-seek wid me?" He stared up adoringly at the man, and I assumed the boy was his son.

"Not now, Benny."

Benny. Ah. Little Benedict Adriano. He spoke English, so I assumed his multilingual training had already begun for the day when he would be the international businessman of consequence that his grandfather was. I hadn't seen Benny since his crawling days. The boy was the son of the youngest Adriano brother, Joshua, and his sniveling wife.

Pauline was a waiflike creature with a big temper and even bigger ambitions, and I'd personally borne the brunt of both. I'd made the mistake once of commenting on the lavender-colored alexandrite in her necklace and actually reaching toward it, even though I hadn't planned to touch it. She'd accused me of wanting to steal it. Simon had admonished her gently, but I'd been livid at having my integrity questioned. Maybe that's a strange thing for a thief to feel, but I have my own sense of honor, even if I can't wear it in an obvious way.

And Pauline rankled my sense of honor just by breathing. One of my connections had sworn to me that Pauline had once been Simon's favorite mistress and that the two of them had worked together to install her as the wife of the youngest Adriano brother, who was somewhat gentler on the eyes and spirit than Caleb. Once Pauline had borne a male heir to the family dynasty, she'd been able to relax, and I'd not seen her again on my brief visits to the compound. Usually she was away at a spa, I was told. Which was fine by me. She'd performed the greatest service a woman could perform for the Adriano family—a legitimate heir—and as long as her son lived, she was safe.

But the kid…Benny… My heart broke for him. Had Joshua and Caleb once been the same? Or their brother Aaron, who'd died before I'd had the opportunity to meet him? Had Simon himself been an innocent boy?

Benny was all of four or five years old, with a freshness about him that made me want to scoop him up and hug him tightly to me as I had with Lilah at that age. Yet his destiny had been determined at birth, surer than any combination of stars and planets. He'd spend the next five years of his young life with private tutors, and the five after that learning the skills he'd need to be as cold and heartless as his grandfather. In another twenty years he'd know the cultivated pleasures of cruelty and manipulation as he prepared to take over the Adriano family. But at the moment he was just an innocent little boy who longed for a playmate.

And if Eric wasn't the boy's father, who was he? And why did he seem to care so much for the little tyke? He had to be someone they trusted to have been involved in my heist. Maybe someone they shouldn't have trusted, given his penchant for errors. But even if the man was an idiot where I was concerned, my heart still softened as I watched his response to the boy.

"Benny, go back inside. Ask your mother to play with you."

The child rolled his eyes. "She said to ask you."

I caught the slightest hint of an exasperated sigh from Eric, but otherwise he kept his opinions to himself. I had the impression that he disliked Pauline as much as I did.

"I'll play with you after the pretty lady leaves." He stood in silence, studying me while Benny studied him.

I clutched the briefcase to my chest. "I'm not leaving."

One eyebrow rose just enough to be noticed. "You shouldn't be here at all. If you want to live, you'll turn around and go. *Now.*"

"Can't. Sorry. I have a delivery to make." And a paycheck and a pink slip to pick up.

"Give it to me. I'll see that Simon gets his artifact. Leave before your pretty corpse is hanging on a wall like one of your stolen trophies."

Was that a threat? Or a warning? I ignored the chill in my bones but not the disdain in his voice. Unbelievable. He worked for the Adrianos, too, and yet he had the nerve to pass judgment on the way I earned my living? Who did he think he was? Did he think being a security guard was any more altruistic than stealing back lost treasures that had belonged to the Adrianos' ancestors?

"Simon will want to see me," I assured him through gritted teeth. "I want him to know I didn't fail." This time.

I still had to make up for losing that statue earlier in the year, and if this package was truly the "artifact of the second millennium," then maybe Simon would feel he owed me my release. I'd already rehearsed my resignation speech in my head, about how often I'd come through for him and how he was right to be fond of me. I was nervous but determined. Sure, I could take the money I had stashed in several South American banks and hope to disappear, but without Simon's blessing, I'd never really be free of the Adrianos' grip as long as I was alive.

"Listen to me," Eric warned in a whisper. "Your pride will be your failing. You're fooling yourself about how much Simon likes you. You are not the teacher's pet."

Teacher's pet? What was that supposed to mean? A reference to my former life as an English literature professor? The Adrianos knew nothing of those days.

Eric leaned into my ear so that only I could hear. "You're special to him but not in the way you think."

Before he could say another word, I pushed past both man and boy, through the door and into the lion's den. Eric and Benny followed me, and out of the corner of my eye I saw Eric hand off my borrowed gun to a security guard called Algernon in a hallway and then discreetly holster his own weapon.

No matter how many times I had entered the compound's main house, it always amazed me that people could live in so much luxury. The house reeked not only of money but of centuries-old wealth. But there was no warmth in this place. The air was as sterile as any I had breathed in the world's most closely guarded museum vaults.

My boots clicked on the marble floor as I stalked across the foyer and into the reception area where I had previously met with Simon on thirty-five occasions, all of them successful. Always before, I'd felt calm and in charge. I'd never had butterflies in my stomach, but I did now. Then again, the only Adriano I'd ever said no to was Caleb, and that had ended badly. Very badly.

"Hello, *Ms.* Moon."

I stopped in my tracks and clenched the briefcase. Panic rose in my chest. I took a deep, measured breath to calm myself. Just the sound of Caleb's voice was enough to unnerve me, especially when he made the effort to discount my talents by ignoring my usual title of Dr. Moon, the one old Max Adriano had ordered given me on my last incarnation as an art thief. Caleb thought my name was Ginny and I'd let him think it. By the tone of his voice, I knew something was up.

Slowly I turned to face my ex-lover. He was as handsome as ever. Dark blond hair discreetly dyed to make him stand out in a family of dark-haired Europeans. Tall. Piercing Adriano eyes. Expensive casual clothes. Devastating smile. The physique of a muscular teddy bear.

Yeah. A teddy bear with fangs and claws.

I forced a smile but kept my distance. The twenty feet between us wasn't nearly enough to make me feel safe. The fact that Eric, Benny and a host of servants and security guards stood watching on the periphery didn't help, either.

"Can I get you anything to drink? Wine? Hemlock?"

Caleb snapped his fingers, and a svelte servant in a black dress and white apron appeared at his side with a tray of crystal glasses and dark red juice. "Oh, that's right. You have a preference for *pomegranate* juice."

The servant offered the tray to me, but I shook my head. How did Caleb know I enjoyed pom juice? Unless he'd been watching me. Checking me out. Spying on me to learn more than just what I considered the secret to my youthful looks or that, like the goddess Persephone, I made regular trips into hell. I frowned at the crystal pitcher of juice and the empty glasses on the tray. Caleb had gone to extra effort to let me know he was aware of this particular secret. In any relationship, you must follow the effort to know whether the other party is interested, and Caleb was interested…in something.

Another liaison in his bedroom? No way in hell was that going to happen. I'd told him that a year ago. I'd told him again on the two occasions I'd seen him since, and he hadn't taken the rejection lightly.

"I had the juice prepared *especially* for you." He

winked at me over a smirk that told me he knew something he shouldn't.

Drink whatever poison Caleb offered? "Not damned likely," I murmured too softly for him to hear. My fists tightened. I wouldn't put it past him to try to force me to drink something more dangerous than antioxidants. Tonight he was more treacherous than usual because he was alone—he didn't have a new conquest on his arm to keep him in line.

I'd warned his newest love interest, a woman named Scarlet Rubashka, what he was capable of. I doubted he'd bedded her yet, but he was definitely courting her, and she wasn't letting the relationship move too fast. *Smart woman.* I'd liked Scarlet. Something about her reminded me of Lilah, even though Scarlet was a grown woman in her thirties and Lilah—according to the last photos I'd seen—still had a slight sheen of adolescence.

If Caleb hadn't already hated me enough, he'd vowed to kill me after my little conversation with his new infatuation. Scarlet had reminded me that I was a criminal and hadn't believed me, then she'd told Caleb all about my warning. *Stupid, stupid, stupid.* Caleb had promised to see me dead for telling her about his bedroom antics. He didn't need yet another excuse to want me dead, but I'd given him one.

I should never have gotten involved with the older Adriano brother. I'd known better. And yet, true to form, my years of rejecting Caleb's advances had brought his pursuit to fever pitch, just as Scarlet's slower pace was doing now. He always wanted what he couldn't have, and my denying him just made him that much more determined to have me.

Glancing around the room, I suddenly felt self-conscious. What the people in that room must have been told about me! Eric Cabordes included. Even the servants eyed me as if I were some kind of slut. I knew without a doubt that if I needed help from them now, not one would risk his life to save me. None of them knew the whole story.

Caleb had worn me down, gotten through my defenses, and I'd relented after six months of his constant attempts to court me. Over several dinners at the palazzo, including one private rendezvous on the old tower ruins before the first quake of the past year skewed the stones, he'd shown me a tender side of him that seemed incongruous with the man I knew now. Probably the same lies he'd told Scarlet on every attempt to get her into his bed. He'd been wildly passionate and intense, and I'd let go of my worries and found myself acquiescing.

Once. Just once.

Caleb was an experienced lover, almost fanatically competitive about bringing me to climax, as if it were a power over me that he simply had to wield. Then, when I'd been lost in the throes of passion, he'd closed the fingers of his large hands around my throat and pressed his thumbs into my carotids, cutting off the flow of blood to my brain until I'd felt dizzy. I'd fought the intensity of the physical pleasure, fought to live instead, fought him, scratched at him with my long fingernails, cut his chest and face.

The people in this room...the ones looking at me with such disdain...they don't know the truth.

He seized my wrists then, held them down with one hand while he'd borne down his full weight onto my chest until I couldn't breathe and cupped his other palm over my gasping mouth and nose. His candlelit bedroom had given way to gray sparkles of nothingness. Later I would remember thinking, *I'm going to die and the last thing I'm going to see is the look of delight on this bastard's face.* I'd felt my body give way to light and a sensation of floating among angels.

Then I'd felt the sting of his palm on my face, again and again, slapping me to bring me back to life. I'd gasped and choked and crawled to the bathroom to throw up.

"Ms. Moon?" Caleb asked more forcefully as I stared at the glass of pom juice.

I shook myself and then glanced back at him. As more than one man can attest, I'm by no means a prude when it comes to sex and I wouldn't mind surrendering control to the right lover. But Caleb Adriano had stepped over the line. I'd ended our affair then and there, which had stirred up an anger I'd never seen in any man. He'd threatened my life several times since that night, and I had no doubt he knew exactly how he wanted to see me executed and whose hands would be around my neck.

"Aren't you going to drink your juice?" Caleb grinned at me and gestured to the tray as the servant poured a glass from the pitcher.

"Why?" I found my voice last. "So you can drug me? Poison me—"

"Juice!" Benny screeched from across the room and dashed for the tray. He grabbed the glass in his two small fists and pulled it toward his lips.

Chapter 4

Eric was by his side in four quick strides. "Here, Benny. Let me."

He shot a doting look at the boy, and Benny willingly gave up the glass. Eric glanced at Caleb, but Caleb only blinked, bemused. Everyone else in the room seemed frozen in time.

My God, what if it is poison? Would Caleb do that to his own nephew? To the heir to the Adriano dynasty?

Eric brought the glass to his lips and sniffed, then drank deeply. He closed his eyes and waited. Silence fell across the room. Then at last Eric opened his eyes, poured a second glass half-full and handed it to the little boy. Benny grinned and took it, but after a single sip made a face and handed it back.

"Fucking babysitter," Caleb mumbled.

"You watch yourself."

I was stunned. A henchman for the Adrianos had just threatened his boss. Unheard of! I could almost admire that in a man, even one who'd screwed up my heist. Eric Cabordes would certainly be dead by dawn.

"Watch myself?" Caleb closed the distance between them and leaned into Eric's face, but Eric didn't move. "What are you going to do about it, Cabordes? Tattle to my baby brother?"

"My only concern is protecting Joshua's son. I couldn't care less about your games with women." Eric didn't bother to look in my direction. He set the glass down hard on the tray, sloshing juice onto the servant's white apron. "Come, Benny. I'll play hide-and-seek with you." He grasped Benny's hand and led the boy out of the room.

Watching him go, I felt a little less safe in a room full of people…and Caleb. So Eric Cabordes was Benny's bodyguard. Other than our dislike for Pauline, we had one more thing in common: we both hated Caleb Adriano.

"Caleb, will you stop taunting the hired help?" Simon swaggered into the room, waving his hand as if to dismiss his elder son. "Dr. Moon, *cara mia.* Ginny. So nice to see you again." He eyed the briefcase, then crossed the room to me and gave me a civilized peck on both cheeks, lingering too long to inhale my scent.

"Thank you, Duke. I've missed you, too."

Strange as it may seem, I actually liked Simon Adriano with his clipped words, stylish air and promise of intensity. I don't know. Maybe it's something like Stockholm syndrome, that effect where the hostage takes on the necessary traits of the kidnapper to earn his affection and approval. I'd been working for the family for so long, heard so many disquieting rumors, seen so much unsettling evidence of their true power, yet Simon had never mistreated me.

I breathed in the sudden realization. Since when did lack of ill treatment equal fondness and appreciation? After my talk with Nicole in that borrowed hotel room in San Francisco, I'd become aware that I'd started to identify with Simon psychologically, which I found disturbing—and further evidence that I needed to get the hell away.

Until then, I'd found Simon a lot more likable. He was sixtyish or more and charming, and I'd thought more than once that it was too bad I had a preference for younger men because I thought Simon would have been a hell of a lot more my type than his brute of a son. Not that Simon was a sensitive and gentle soul. I knew exactly who he was and what he was, but he'd always been honest with me, which was something I could appreciate in a world of dishonest power brokers.

Typically Simon told me exactly what item he was looking for or what item he'd located from their lost cache of treasures, and either he or Joshua gave me instructions on the job. I would retrieve an artifact for Simon, and he'd pay me and pay me well even when he could have forced me to work for nothing out of fear of reprisal from such a powerful family. Unlike most

Adriano employees, I was allowed to roam the world and keep my outside contacts, ostensibly because it made me a better-educated and better-connected thief. Simon was fond of me. Why else would I have been given such special treatment? Aside from my business dealings with other art lovers of the world, I'd amassed a small fortune from my dealings with Simon Adriano—if you can call seven million American dollars in untraceable accounts small.

"Dr. Moon, my dear, do I detect a limp?" His concern seemed fatherly, as usual, and quite normal for our mutual admiration society.

I felt myself blush. My knee still throbbed, but I was more concerned that I had let a weakness show. Simon didn't tolerate weakness. I hadn't been able to hide the fact that I favored one knee, and that was an invitation to my enemies to regard it as a target. If I took another blow to the knee, I'd find myself on the floor and unable to rise to whatever occasion I might find myself in.

"Just a tiny limp, Duke. I'm sure an ice compress and some rest will suffice."

"Enough of this!" Caleb thundered from where he stood, arms crossed, Italian profanities spewing from his mouth. "Take the package from her and be done with her. Better yet, give her to me and I'll personally pack her legs in ice."

Simon glared at his son. "Be silent, Caleb. She's under my protection. You know that. When I'm done with her, then you can have her. Until then, you won't…touch her…again." He pointed to the exit, and Caleb grudgingly walked through it without looking back.

I stared at the Duke, at this harsh man who had drawn my admiration in a world where there was so little to admire. So he knew. *My God.* He knew what Caleb had done to me. *And he'd let Caleb have me when he was done with me?*

"Oh, wipe that worried look off your face, Ginny. You're safe from Caleb for now. I have no intention of being done with you for many, many years to come. By then, he'll have forgotten all about your lovers' spat."

Simon poured two glasses of pomegranate juice and handed one to me. He took a sip of the other and made the same face his grandson had made. "Wouldn't you prefer wine to this? We have our own vineyard here as well as the famous one in Languedoc-Roussillon, the Chateau L'Astral. Our wine is respected as some of the finest in the world. It's the ley lines, you know. Our grapes are rooted in the very life force of the planet."

I sipped the juice and didn't speak. To me, it tasted like wine without the alcohol. As for ley lines, I wasn't sure what the Duke had meant, though I'd heard about them from New Agers and Bohemian types like Scarlet. I was still stung by the fact that he'd known about Caleb's misbehavior and had done nothing to protect me. As long as I'd worked for him, I felt he owed me something more than a good paycheck. I'd felt he actually cared what happened to me. And if he didn't, what about his tentative agreement months ago to let me retire from hanging by threads?

"You were gone a long time." Simon replaced the glass on the tray and sank his hands into his pockets. His gaze fell on the briefcase under my arm. "I was worried that you might have decided to keep the artifact for yourself." Then he raised his gaze to my face. "Did I have cause to doubt you?"

"Obviously not. I'm here."

"But it took you a long time. Longer than usual. What were you up to, Ginny?"

"You're the one who wanted me to travel off the grid," I reminded him. "I didn't expect it to take me six weeks."

He lifted an eyebrow. "I never said that. You were expected back within the week, and you were to contact me if you were late."

That's not the message Eric had delivered. He'd been emphatic that I take the long way back, take as much time as I needed, do whatever it took to keep the artifact out of the hands of any authorities, particularly Interpol. He'd never said anything about being back within the week, but he'd been specific not to contact the Adrianos until I arrived at the gate.

I started to say something, but at the last second I clamped my jaws together. I could get Eric into trouble with Simon, and that might be bad for Benny in the long run. Or I could make myself look good and earn points toward leaving the Adrianos freely. I turned it around several ways in my head, but I could think of more honorable reasons to say nothing than to rat Eric out.

"I'm sorry. I thought your primary focus was safety

for the artifact, not speed. I must have misunderstood what you ordered."

He shrugged. "Actually, I was otherwise disposed. Joshua handled your supplemental instructions."

And Joshua's personal bodyguard for his son had made the follow-up call. Maybe that's where the mistakes had come from. Did Josh not take his father's wishes seriously? Did he have his hands full with Pauline enough so that he had to rely on his most important employee? Maybe that's where the mistakes had come from. Maybe Eric hadn't realized how important this job was. I cleared my throat. "The job specifications weren't precisely as described."

"Did you have any trouble?"

I finished my juice and set the glass on the tray, then waited for the servant to leave. "Some," I whispered.

Simon flicked his wrist and the remaining servants and security guards filed out of the room and shut the doors. "Speak."

"I stayed out of the U.S. airports, as I thought you—um, Joshua—wanted. No chance of the package being X-rayed or opened. Spent most of my time in automobiles, trains and puddle-jumper airplanes. I had to bribe an official at the Mexican border and again in Guatemala, but you did say you'd cover my expenses in addition to my fee. Or...Joshua did."

Simon shrugged again. "Indeed."

"I spent an extra two weeks in the mountains of Colombia, hiding from the police. That's where I reinjured my knee. But I managed to elude them."

"Anything else?"

I silently debated with myself and decided not to mention the three close calls with the Interpol agent. She'd been gutsy, determined, athletic as hell. Simon had found Analise Reisner a little too fascinating on their one meeting that I knew of, and she was one package I didn't intend to bring to his doorstep.

"I managed to get a flight out of Rio with only a few minor bribes to help me along. Once I breached Europe, it took me three days by train and automobile to get here. Off the grid," I added.

I purposely didn't mention the runaway I'd liberated or that Sister Mary Margaret had left a message on my answering service that Nicole had waited until the day after her eighteenth birthday to leave. They'd arranged a job interview for her in another city with another contact of mine, who was told to treat her as my daughter and do what he could to help her set up a new life for herself. I prayed she was in as safe a place as Lilah was.

Simon smiled. "And I suppose you're anxious to be paid and on your way."

"Something like that, yes. Plus there was another matter I wanted to discuss regarding my retirement."

He didn't seem to hear me. "I have a proposition for you, Dr. Moon."

The butterflies in my stomach were back with a vengeance. I didn't want propositions, especially not from Adriano men. I wanted my money and I wanted my freedom and I wanted to leave. I wanted to reclaim the life I'd left behind as much as possible. Just as soon as I could. But saying no to an Adriano is a delicate thing.

"What kind of proposition?"

Simon paced around me in a circle, weighing each word. "I have another assignment for you."

"So soon?"

"Several weeks ago, actually. But you weren't available. It's a tapestry. Another one."

I thought of the tapestry in the penthouse in San Francisco. Best if I didn't return there for a while. "It's not Flemish, is it?"

He frowned. "No. It was stolen from my family many centuries ago. Just like the package you brought me tonight. I'm sure I can count on you to get the tapestry back for my family."

I hesitated. I'd retrieved a Black Madonna tapestry for him earlier in the year. The acrobatics and rope work had been downright daring. I wasn't up to it. Not yet. And how was I going to tell Simon I quit? Instead I said, "How soon?"

"This week. We know where it is."

"Duke Adriano…Simon…"

He stopped pacing to study me. "You're not going to turn down my offer, are you?"

"Uh, no, but…" I hung my head. I hated to admit a weakness, especially to someone so strong. Someone who might use it against me. "It's my knee, Duke. I botched it on that statue job for you. Remember? I spent two months in physical therapy in an obscure little beach town in Florida. Then I took this assignment for you and overworked my knee." I caught myself. I was nervous and talking way too much. "I'm sorry, Duke, but I seriously need a break to rest up and let it heal. I've been pushing too hard for too long, and maybe it's time I retired...."

He let his gaze drop to my knees, hidden beneath my velvet dress. I was tempted to lift my skirt and show him the swelling around my right knee and how tight it made my boot but thought better of exposing any bare skin to another Adriano male.

"I need that tapestry," he said finally. "Scholars say there's a family crest woven into the margins. It could be very valuable."

"The scholars are wrong," I told him. "I've seen that tapestry." I didn't tell him that I'd read of certain dyes that became invisible until the design was introduced to lemon juice. This was a job I didn't want.

"I'll decide if they're wrong." His voice tightened. I'd never argued with him before.

"And I'll get it for you—or find someone who can—but first I need to rest my knee. It's not like I need surgery, Duke. Just some rest and ice and elevation. Maybe some more physical therapy. But mainly rest. I can't be hanging by my knees in midair. Give me a couple of months to recuperate and I'll be as good as new." The less Simon talked, the more I seemed to babble.

"I need that tapestry," he repeated. "Within the week."

"Duke, I can't."

"You can and you will!" Simon went stiff all over, his eyes as full of fury as Caleb's.

My heart skipped. I'd never seen him *this* angry. Not at me, anyway. Had I done something wrong other than disagree about discreet markings on an artifact? Or was he more stressed than usual? I was his favorite employee out of many, many thousands. He'd told me that. He'd told me once that there were times when he liked me more than his own children. He'd told me I was special.

Then his face softened. "I'll make it a challenge for you, Dr. Moon. I know how fond you are of money. I'll hold your fee for your most recent acquisition until I get the tapestry. Once it's delivered, I'll double your fee. Deal?"

A million American dollars, plus expenses. No. It wasn't about the money. It was about fear. For the first time in my life as a thief, I'd been injured in a way that hadn't healed in a week or two. The physical work was getting harder, less fun. My heart wasn't in this kind of work anymore. The history, the thrill of discovery, the joy of holding a relic in my hands that people long since dead had cherished or stolen…or died for. The rush had made me feel alive, connected. But I was weary of it. Ready for something different, something the Adrianos wouldn't find useful to them. I suddenly felt as helpless as I had as an eighteen-year-old girl not yet rescued by a brave young lieutenant.

"Duke…if I do this job for you, what about the next time? What if my knee doesn't heal?"

Simon lowered his voice so the guards outside the door couldn't hear. "If I send you on an assignment and you don't think you can handle it, I expect you to die trying."

"But, Duke—" His glare silenced me. He'd never spoken to me in that tone of voice until tonight.

"When you can no longer get the job done, you'll be of no use to me. Do you understand?"

I swallowed, then nodded once. Suddenly I didn't feel so special anymore.

"As for your injury, we all get older, my dear. But you don't have anything to worry about. Not if you've been truthful with me about…everything. You're only thirty-two and your knee's not bothering you that badly."

I took a deep breath. *Only thirty-two.* So I'd fibbed a little when I'd created my last identity. Now my lies were catching up with me. And my knee was killing me.

I didn't move. I couldn't. When had I lost my freedom? Even forced into a life as a criminal, I'd had some freedom with the Adrianos as long as I'd stayed inside their wishes. Or thought I had. How had the illusion of freedom slipped away so quietly? Somehow I'd gone from being a treasured employee to an indentured servant. And now…now Simon Adriano owned me. I could no longer come and go as I pleased. I could no longer take the jobs I wanted or arrange acquisition through one of my contacts. I'd ventured one too many steps on the dark side of life and I would never be free again. Either in illusion or reality.

"Did you hear me, Dr. Moon?" Simon paused. "Aubrey!" He smiled. "Or should I call you Lauren?"

I startled, not because Simon had just raised his voice at me but because he'd called me Aubrey. Oh, God, it was worse than I'd thought! Worse than I could ever have imagined!

Simon knew me as Ginny Moon. His own father was the one who'd given me the name, even though I'd never met Max Adriano. Before that, I had been a college professor by the name of Lauren Hartford, teaching English composition and medieval literature in a Pennsylvania university by day and telling stories of ancient folklore to my little girl at night.

But before that, I'd been someone else.

I'd arrived in the States pregnant and desperate, finding a home with my mother's cousin's second wife and creating an identity so I could hide from the people Matthew had warned me would kill me.

Simon shouldn't know that my real name was Aubergine de Lune. He wasn't supposed to know my mother had named me for her favorite color and given me the nickname. Aubrey. Yet Simon knew who I was, just as readily as Caleb knew my favorite drink. Simon's sudden disdain for me seemed to coincide with his newfound insight into my secrets.

In some cultures it's said that to know someone's secret name gives you power over them. I wore the Adrianos' power over me like an iron band around my neck.

But it was worse than that. If they knew that I'd once been both Aubrey de Lune and Lauren Hartford, then they might know about Lilah. And my daughter was no longer safe.

If she ever had been.

Chapter 5

"Dr. Moon?" Simon cleared his throat to catch my attention. "You're to follow me to the vault. I need you to authenticate the artifact."

I shook myself. I couldn't let Simon see how worried his new insight into my past made me, though he had to have known. Simon would never have divulged such valuable information without a reason, most likely to throw me off-kilter or make me understand my insignificance…or to give me a strong hint that none of my secrets were really secret where he was concerned.

"Authenticate?" I struggled to keep my voice steady. "I don't even know what it is. The artifact could be a medium I have no expertise in."

Simon laughed and pried the package from my

white-knuckled fingers. "Oh, I think you'll have expertise enough. I handpicked you for this job. No one—*no one*—was better suited." He laughed as if he knew a private joke and I was the punch line. "Only two people on this planet can authenticate this artifact, and the other one's not expected to live much longer." He gleefully watched my expression as this new information sank in. When his comment received the desired response, he explained, "My elderly father is hospitalized."

"Oh." I pressed my fingers to my lips. In all the years I'd known the Adrianos, I'd never actually met their patriarch, but I'd seen an oil painting at the palazzo. In his younger years, when the paint had been wet, he'd looked much like Simon, dapper and sophisticated but with darker hair. He'd always been away on business or at another of their estates when I'd been at the palazzo, plus he'd made Simon responsible for my assignments so there was really no reason that I would have seen him, although it was one of his own relatives, Ricardo Adriano, who had "recruited" me. Old Max Adriano, I'd been told, was far too important to be bothered with the acquisition of family artifacts and the day-to-day management of employees. That's what sons were for.

I'd heard something about the old man nearly being assassinated several years ago. No one in my circles had heard much about him since, and the Adrianos didn't discuss it. One of Max's secretaries who'd delivered papers to me in Paris had said something about him actually dying, but Therese hadn't responded to any of my subsequent attempts to communicate with her. If the old man really was dead, the Adrianos were certainly keeping it a secret, most likely to avoid trouble with business contacts. Then again, it's said that no Adriano ever dies of natural causes, so perhaps they were trying to avoid a publicity nightmare.

"I'm sorry about your father," I murmured.

"You should be more concerned with your own health." Simon shrugged. "Now follow me."

More curious than I wanted to be, I lamely trailed Simon down two flights of stairs. Each step down burned a circle around my kneecap. Walking on even ground wasn't so bad, but stairs—especially descending stairs—nearly took my breath away. My doctor had said it was the worst thing I could do for a knee injury. It certainly felt that way. I wondered if that's why Simon insisted on the stairs when the palazzo had been modernized with elevators. Still, I didn't let the pain show and fought against the need to limp.

To my surprise, the vault door wasn't guarded. I'd never been allowed this far into the compound, but then again, I'd never been asked to authenticate my own delivery. I expected Simon to have the finest of security systems, but the door to the vault was apparently only for fire protection. He considered the palazzo itself to be secure, especially with his internal camera system. I'd heard something once about the extent to which they trusted their security employees.

A camera in every corner. I smirked to myself. *And especially in Caleb's bedroom.*

The walls around me changed to an older stone as we

made our way into a tunnel carved into what must have once been the Adriano castle, which the modern compound had been built over and around. Simon cranked open the vault door and motioned for me to enter.

I had never seen a museum equipped as finely as the Adriano vault. The glass cases, the lighting, the brass placards beside each artifact. I don't impress easily, but I nearly whistled at the treasures inside. An odd collection of medieval keys. The Black Madonna statue similar to the one I'd botched my knee chasing. A da Vinci Mother and Child painting stolen from a castle near London. A tantric Hindu manuscript last seen in a Kathmandu museum. From Bucharest, a statue of a monk. An alabaster jar of medium size that could easily have been thousands of years old. Several stolen Afghan and Iraqi religious artifacts. A Picasso from a private collection. Two pieces lifted from an antiquities fair at The Hague. Various relics pilfered from castles, churches and museums.

Supposedly all of them had at some point belonged to the Adriano family, whether the family had commissioned them or purchased them. The family lineage was as old as the Catholic Church, so I'd told myself it was true. I guess I'd told myself a lot of things were true because it was easier to live with the fiction I'd created for myself. In my heart I knew I was a thief, that I'd sunk that low, but I didn't care to admit it to myself or anyone else on a regular basis. To do so would make it real, make it permanent. Lying to myself gave me a sense of control over my life. I'd learned that from a few hours with the runaway in San Francisco.

Some of the acquisitions I recognized as my own handiwork. Several I'd tracked down and confiscated discreetly based on Simon's "wish list," while most were specific assignments with specific instructions for how to acquire the piece. More often than not, at least one item on Interpol's periodic Poster of Most Wanted Art was one I had personally handled, though my all-time record was five of the six works of art on the poster. I wondered if my most recent acquisition would put me over the top or bury me.

"Come, *cara mia.*" Simon clucked at me. "Stop preening over your résumé and tell me what you know of my latest addition." He stopped at a clean worktable with a green halogen pendant lamp dangling from the ceiling. He set the briefcase on top and turned over his palm in a grand gesture toward the package, indicating that I was to open it.

Heart pounding, I unlatched the straps over the top of the case and slid out the plastic-encased package. At least I thought it was plastic. It looked more like thick plate glass but wasn't heavy. This was the first close look I'd had at my constant companion of the past six weeks. Whatever was inside had been sealed in a waterproof cloth or paper, but the encasement was like nothing I'd encountered in the art world. I had seen it, though.

Once, on a science exchange program at a military facility in Virginia, I'd talked to a scientist about robotics and watched a laser beam play across the surface of a liquid polymer until the liquid solidified under the laser's sting, leaving a quite solid and exquisitely rendered spider in place of liquid goo. Instead of shrink-wrapping a plastic sleeve over an artifact to protect it from the elements or even to keep it from falling apart, someone had gone to a great deal of trouble to use stereolithography to surround the item in a polymer or resin of some sort, the kind now used in medical replacement procedures and automobile assemblies and poised for mass production of machine parts once a few wrinkles could be ironed out. The encasement and the design of circles and triangles could not be duplicated without the correct computer drawing files and the proper equipment and supplies, so if I had been curious enough to open the wrapper, Simon would have known it.

"I knew I could trust you, Aubrey."

I met his gaze. I could tell by the twitch at his lips that he was teasing me. "I've never purposely disappointed you," I reminded him.

Simon ran his fingers over the design on the casing. "Purposely or not, no one ever disappoints me more than once."

I swallowed hard and refused to be put on the defensive. "So how do we get into the package? UV light? Heat? Run over it with a forklift?"

"No need to be dramatic, Aubrey. Or do you prefer Lauren?" He paused. "Finding the best things in life is only a matter of knowing where to look." Simon brushed his fingertips along a series of triangles and pressed down hard on the third triangle at the center of the package. The case gave way and popped open with the sound of a pull tab on a soda can.

Amazing. The case material had been formed in two partitions and snapped together yet appeared seamless until the correct pressure was applied to the heart. A bit like me, I supposed. I tamped down my excitement and proceeded to lift out the artifact and peel away the interior wrapping.

I was vaguely aware of Simon watching my face as I folded back the final layer of wrapping. My jaw dropped. He was right—I had the expertise.

Before I even saw the full-page woodcut of a mother with a sword in one hand, a jug at her feet and a baby in her free arm or before I mentally transcribed the first words from centuries past, I knew the book was rare. Books printed before 1501, before the advent of the printing press, are known as incunabula, and they're exceptionally rare. Of the known ones printed on vellum and sheep's gut, perhaps as many as thirty-five percent still exist, most in private collections or hidden in the bowels of dusty museums. This book was no exception.

It was the reason I'd made the worst mistake of my life—the reason I'd been lured into a trap and had lost my daughter. And if the relic proved to be genuine, then it was indeed "the artifact of the second millennium."

"This belongs to your family?" I asked.

"Of course."

Legally? Perhaps they'd purchased it from a dealer or maybe even a monk or priest centuries ago, but this artifact was more mine than theirs. My grandmother had spoken of it many times with me cuddled against her, but my mother had sworn it was a figment of an overactive imagination since no one in my maternal line remembered seeing the book. I stared at Simon and tried to give a measured response so he wouldn't know how much this artifact meant to me personally. Or maybe he already knew. Maybe that's what made me his preferred choice to authenticate it.

"It's...beautiful," I whispered in reverence.

If the book was legally an Adriano possession, I expected familial pride from Simon but found none. "It's bullshit, accusations, lies," he said instead. His lips curled as if he'd tasted acid. "But that's why I had to have it. The Church itself deemed this manuscript to be heresy. It was a charge written against my family in the 1400s in an attempt to destroy us, but thankfully Pope Martin the Fifth presented it to my family as a token of his appreciation for our services."

"Services?"

"Yes. My family did everything in its power to protect the Church. The Church was very grateful."

Extortion? I wondered. I was very familiar with medieval history—much of the knowledge coming from the literature I had studied and taught—and the fifteenth century had seen the Church torn apart by regional infighting and indecision over which of three popes was the true leader of the Church.

"The genuine artifact," Simon continued, "has been stolen from us and recovered more than once over the centuries. If this...accounting of lies were made public, it would send historians into an uproar. Do you understand?" He lowered his voice. "I have to know if it's authentic or if it's a modern hoax to discredit us."

Simon's family had been as powerful as the Catholic Church in the Middle Ages, just more quietly so, and more powerful than most governments of the era. Some said they'd controlled more than their share of kings and popes. No doubt the pope's little token of appreciation had been for some type of political assistance rather than building a new cathedral or clothing a few nuns. Had the Church declared the manuscript heresy or had the reigning Adriano of the times?

"And if it is authentic?"

Simon laughed. "Then we'll have a bonfire in two days when Joshua returns from business in Alexandria."

I almost choked. Burn a book? Especially an incunable of this age and significance? A book with a personal tie to my own ancestry?

As a professor of literature, I couldn't even fathom burning a self-published chapbook of bad poetry, let alone destroying an artifact that might "send historians into an uproar." But as someone with a vested interest in the manuscript, I knew I had to save this book. My hands itched to get started, and I intentionally let my excitement show. Simon needed to see that I could be a team player. Doing so might keep me alive another day.

"I'll need time to authenticate it, Simon. Several hours, at least. Maybe more. I don't really have everything I need here to do a complete job."

He shook his head. "I need to know only if it's real, not who wrote it or why."

I frowned down at the folio pages and immediately started to drone as if I were lecturing to a hall of graduate students. "It's faded in places, stained in others. Very delicate, of course. Some annotations in brown ink. Hmm, looks like family crests or names in the narrow margins. How curious. Bound in what appears to be contemporary blind-tooled pigskin over wooden boards with original brass clasps. A few wormholes in the pastedowns, but overall a handsome artifact. Two columns of text in a compact Gothic script used to economize on space. Hmm, Latin, which I can read relatively well."

I hesitated, wondering whether to continue, but Simon was already sure enough of what I was about to tell him. Lying was not an option.

"I'd put it somewhere in the fifteenth century, but I'll need time to translate it to be certain." Unfortunately I'd be alone in a closed room with no way out but the vault door. "I can't get my work done for you if I'm interrupted. Will I be safe to work here alone?"

Simon nodded. "Take all the time you need. I'll have guards at the door."

"That's not what I meant."

"I know very well what you meant." Simon walked away. "I'll inform Caleb that he is to leave you alone… tonight…while you work." He reached the door and looked over his shoulder at me. "I'll be back for an update in—" he checked his expensive watch "—two hours."

The vault door clicked shut behind him, but I barely

noticed. Even the air around me seemed old and leaden in my lungs. I already knew that the incunable was authentic. I knew because I'd sacrificed years and a life with my daughter and everything I held dear to find it. For six weeks I'd carried it in my arms. And now it was in my hands.

The printed manuscript from the hand of Joan of Arc. The heresy against the Adrianos.

My pulse pounded in my ears. I couldn't let the Adrianos burn it. This was more than an artifact; it was history. *My* history. And it was the only thing other than Matthew and Lilah that had meant anything to me in my whole life.

On a cold day in March the year my Lilah turned ten, I'd kissed my little angel goodbye and told her to be a good girl for her aunt and cousins in Pennsylvania while I was gone to Europe. I had been selected as one of only a handful of professors of medieval literature to attend a six-week workshop in Paris, studying old and forgotten manuscripts on an archaeological grant and chasing the rumor of a Joan of Arc manuscript. I'd written letters to Lilah every day, telling her how much I loved and missed her, and I'd sent her postcards of the French countryside. I spent weeks studying references to a memoir allegedly written by Joan of Arc and detailing a far greater mission than the ones given to her historical credit.

"This is it." I touched the pages with trembling fingers. The fragmented memories I'd tried to forget came flooding back.

I'd been told that my selection was a very prestigious honor funded by the Adriano philanthropic trust and that as many as a hundred scholars might be chosen to attend. It was odd that there had been only six women selected for the honor of attending the workshop, and all of us within a few years' age of each other and all of us profoundly interested in Joan of Arc lore. At the end of the fifth week, I'd become ill. On the last day of the sixth week, the day before I was to go home to Lilah, I thought I saw Matthew standing in the darkened door of a small French church. Maybe I just wanted to see him there or maybe it was the virus I'd picked up, but I followed the man I saw. Two hours later I'd become the most wanted thief in France and a woman on the run.

I rubbed my eyes. My breath came quick and shallow, and I could barely think. I'd never been able to figure out exactly what had happened or why. My life had changed in the blink of an eye, and I now held the clues in my hands.

"Later," I told myself. "I'll think about it later. Focus on the moment—and then get out of here." I squinted at the distant Latin words of the incunable and began to translate as I strained to read....

> I was born first, as the sun was setting on the Feast Day of Corpus Christi, and she was born second, when the last of the light had faded. We were two girl children born to a land that saw no worth in daughters. We were unwanted and doomed to be abandoned to starve or die of the cold, save for the

Grace of God. I was named Isabelle after our mother, and she, Jeanne. We lived for a reason that became clear with the years—to continue the tradition of our women, of warriors fighting in the name of the Holy Mother.

Perspiration prickled at my brow. Joan of Arc had siblings, yes. A sister even. But a twin? My mother's mother and her mother's mother before her had often said we were descended from Joan of Arc's womb. I'd had my doubts about the claim. Joan had died at eighteen, only months older than I'd been when Matthew had rescued me. She'd been far braver than I. She'd died childless, though not a virgin. Her jailers had seen to that with their horrific tortures long before they burned her at the stake.

But a twin? A twin who had shared the womb with Joan? A twin no one had ever heard of…until now? The times the young warrior had been wounded and still managed to rally her troops as if she'd never been hurt…? The girl had seemed invincible. Could it be that she'd had a partner in her revolution?

Hands shaking, I rewrapped the incunable and tucked it back inside the stereolithographic casing, then snapped the encasement shut. With a quick glance at the vault door, I slid the artifact back into the briefcase and fastened the straps. I had to get out of the Adriano compound and I had to do it with the book in tow and the hopes that I'd live to translate it when Simon wasn't around.

Glancing around to make sure there were no

cameras watching me, I clicked across the floor, searching for a second way out of the vault. The ceiling disguised the upper reaches of a fireproof room but no escape. But the floor…

I followed the lines of the floor to a barely noticeable crack in the shape of a square. A trapdoor. A way out. Maybe.

Lying flat on the floor with the briefcase beside me, I was finally able to lift one side and slide the square cover away from a hole big enough for a man the size of Caleb to crawl through. The sudden smell of sweat and excrement stung my nostrils, and I nearly gagged. I forced myself not to cough and instead breathed through my mouth. I couldn't afford to make any noises that might bring Simon back. Or worse. My ears rang. I felt ill.

The trapdoor led to some sort of room below, which had light and ventilation, but I couldn't see any more than that. The door gaped down a long tube without steps. Since the vault was on the bottom floor of the palazzo's main house, where the modern building met with the old castle, maybe the room below led to an escape along the seashore. It had to lead somewhere.

Normally I might have descended the tunnel using my back and my knees, but I knew intuitively that my bad knee would fail me tonight. I glanced around the vault for a ladder or rope and settled on the fire hose near the vault door. Although the vault seemed fireproof enough, I guessed that the Adrianos would take no chances with their personal art collection.

Leaving the briefcase on the floor beside the trapdoor, I lowered myself down the tube with hose to spare. My feet had barely cleared the tunnel when I felt a man's hands on my thighs and halfway up my dress!

Oh, God! Caleb?

I kicked hard, and the hands released my legs at the same time I heard an "Oof!" and a thud. I dropped to the floor, hammering my right knee hard as I did but fists outstretched and ready to fight.

All at once, I felt relieved and terrible. An old man lay on the floor, one feeble arm raised in self-defense. He blinked at me through straggly white hair as if looking at sunshine for the first time in weeks.

"You didn't have to kick me," he groused. "I was trying to help you down."

I peered up at the way I'd come. It was nothing more than an opening into a room that otherwise was without a door. An oubliette. A *trap.* Without the fire hose to climb out, I would have been just as trapped as the old man.

"Sorry," I mumbled, quickly taking stock of the room. No exit. No windows. Numerous artifacts on the floor, including several nineteenth-century tapestries. Prettily colored tiles of some sort. Several small air vents—which were greatly needed, considering the stench coming from the far corner of the room. I guessed that the old man had been in the oubliette for quite some time, and he'd been decently fed if not bathed.

"I knew one of you would come. But I'd hoped it wouldn't be you." The old man shakily rose to his feet and dusted himself off. It seemed an odd thing for him to do. His clothes were torn in places and hung loosely on him as if he'd lost several shirt sizes rather quickly. His eyes were wild, his beard unkempt and his hair drooped long on his shoulders. He looked for all the world like Gandalf the Wizard with an attitude.

I ignored his vote of confidence in me. "Who are you?"

"Just an old man who crossed the son of Max Adriano and lost."

"How long have you been down here?" He seemed in remarkably good health, especially for a man who was certainly well into his eighties, maybe more. But the air and walls around us seemed to pulsate with energy. My ears rang.

"You feel it, too, don't you? It's the ley lines. They can keep you healthy or they can kill you as quickly as any volcano or earthquake. Just as easy to feel as the earth's magnetic fields. As easy to feel as gravity. The whole Adriano homestead is built atop one of the most powerful geopathic stress fields on the planet."

"Why are you here?" I asked. I wasn't sure if he was crazy. The odds were in favor of it.

"They put me down here to punish me." He waved an arm at the colored pieces outlined on the floor. "For helping the daughters of their enemies. For helping *you*."

Had I heard him correctly? "I...I don't know you. I've never seen you before in my life."

"Oh, but I've seen you." His aged eyes seemed to come to life. "You have the manuscript, don't you?"

I nodded. How could he have known?

"We should destroy it."

What was with all the bibliophobes bent on destroying valuable old books? He sounded like Simon.

"I'm not destroying anything."

He sighed. "Might be for the best if you did. Simon will use it as a key to solve his problem, he will. Yes, burn it. Burn it before he reads it. You could save countless lives." He nodded emphatically. "You weren't supposed to be here, but I'm glad now that you came for us."

"Us who? I don't see anyone else here but you and me. And I didn't know until a few seconds ago that you were here."

He waved a hand in disgust. "Doesn't matter if you came for me or not. As long as you came for them."

"Them who?" Yes, definitely crazy as a loon.

"Them!" He flung his arm wildly toward the tiles on the floor.

Poor guy. All this time trapped inside the vault, half starving and completely mad. How could Simon and Caleb do this to an old man?

I strode back to the fire hose and tugged it to test its strength. "Look, I'll get you out of this hole, but that's about all I can do. I don't know if I can get you out of the room above, let alone out of the Adriano compound."

"Oh, I can get us out of the vault. And out of the compound. I can take us all the way out to the parking lot at the security gate if you want. You drove, didn't you? You always drive." Before I could ask how he knew, he plowed ahead. "There's a hidden exit or two that I know about." He sniffed indignantly at the trapdoor above us. "I could get out of this hellhole by myself, too, but I can't jump quite as high as I used to."

I almost smiled at him. He didn't seem to realize that somewhere along life's journey his body had betrayed him with the growing inability to do less than the day before. I suddenly felt a kinship with him that I didn't want to think about. One day, in at least another four decades, I'd be his age and just as unwilling to admit that I wasn't as strong as I once was. If I lived that long.

"You can get us out to the parking lot? Seriously?" I tried to study his eyes for signs of truth, but he wouldn't stand still. "Okay, if you'll put your arms around my neck and hold on, I think I can pull us both out of here."

"You can't leave without them."

I pretended not to hear. We had to hurry. "Or I could tie the hose around your waist and pull you up, but I think it would be easier to—"

"Aubrey!" he shouted in a stage whisper.

I let the fire hose drop from my grasp. "What did you call me?" What the hell was happening that, out of the blue, everyone knew my name after I'd kept it a secret for decades?

"Aubergine de Lune." The old man's voice dropped to a focused whisper. "Also known as Dr. Ginny Moon, aka Lauren Hartford, professor of medieval literature."

I stared at him. "You know who I am?"

"More than you do. You think you know who you are. You've spent a lifetime getting to know yourself, flaws and talents and all, and yet you've not even scratched the surface of who you are or what you're capable of. How can you? You spend your life in the past."

It's where the ones I love reside, I wanted to say.

He gritted his teeth as he leaned forward. "Aubrey, Lauren, Ginny…it doesn't matter how many incarnations you have if you refuse to reclaim the life that was stolen from you."

Stumbling backward, I leaned against the wall, still staring at him. "You know who I am," was all I could say. I still couldn't believe it.

"Yes, I know. And unfortunately for you, so does Simon. He doesn't know everything, but he knows enough that you'll never be free of him unless you take back your life. Maybe not the life you planned when you were a girl, but if you're not willing to live your own life, then you're already dead."

"I can't live my own life," I said, grating out the words. "I'm a prisoner. In a gilded Adriano cage, yes, but a prisoner."

"Prisoner? Child, only *you* are forcing you to wear that crown." The old man lifted his hands dramatically as if to ask God to strike him down. "Nobody's keeping you in chains but you."

"Look, you don't know what you're talking about. I don't have any choice but to work for the Adrianos. Now that he knows my name—" *Now that he knows my name, my daughter might be in danger.*

"Who cares about your name? He knows your *identity.*"

I started to tell him I didn't understand, but the old man took my hand and tugged me toward the tiles laid out on the floor. It was some sort of mosaic, life-size, with at least one person outlined, but most of the tiles were missing.

"What is it?" I asked.

"Depends on your point of view. It's history. It's treasure. But in the wrong hands, it's a weapon."

Chapter 6

I picked up one of the tiles and rubbed it between my thumb and forefinger. My ears rang, almost hurt. The texture was smooth but with a strange push-back, like two magnets pushing away from the same polarity. I'd seen tiles like this before. My friend Catrina had tiles like this. But that wasn't all. I'd *owned* tiles like this…a long time ago.

"They're some type of fired paste," I offered. "Maybe fourth century?"

"Very good. Gemstones of particular qualities. Seashells. Iron from meteorites. Atlantean dolphin stone—or *larimar*—like from the Dominican Republic. Lava rock, like from Vesuvius."

I nodded. "Elemental properties. Earth energies." Just

as historical texts told of ancient priests and priestesses who wore precious stones in their breastplates because of the power and representative qualities of the stones. Then I had a darker thought. "Maybe they're explosive?"

"Not exactly. They're radiological electromagnetic energy fields. The ley lines activate them, make them sing with purpose. Some people can hear them or feel them as a tingling in their extremities. Some see auras over the tiles. Some people see visions around them or hear sounds that resemble voices. It's the way the energy stimulates the human brain, and each person is different. Most people sense nothing at all. I've been putting the mosaic together to see how much of the complete picture the boys have."

"And how much do they have?"

"All but the best protected of the legacy collections of tiles. Your identity is tied to your legacy. See that corner? The wisps of hair and stars? The empty space below? The Adrianos knew the identity of the woman who inherited those tiles from her mother's mother. Her name was Nanette. A beautiful girl from Poland who trusted the wrong man." His eyes grew misty. "She died protecting those tiles." His puckered mouth twisted to one side. "Simon's father, Max Adriano. He killed her. With his own hands. But he never recovered those tiles."

I said nothing. Obviously this Nanette had meant something to him. I guessed I wasn't the only one with a penchant for living in the past. I wanted to hear about the tiles, but time was ticking away. We needed to get moving before Simon came back and left me down a hole permanently with a raving lunatic who felt as vindictive toward Max Adriano as I did toward Caleb.

"And that corner there, with the elbow and bit of cloak. That legacy was easier to take, from what I'm told. She was a farmer's daughter, widowed with five daughters of her own. Killed in 1802. Brigid. From Ireland's County Clare. They killed her daughters, too, except for one who escaped and was never found, but none of them ever knew their birthright. Her descendants are still out there somewhere, but they have no idea of the legacy they lost. The same with this one over here that was taken in 1719—"

"Look," I said, hurrying him along, "Simon will be back to check on me. If we're leaving, we need to get out of here before he shows up. Now come on, old man. Let's go."

"Myrddin. You can call me Myrddin." The Celtic name for Merlin of Arthurian legend. Obviously not his real name and a surprising pseudonym for an Italian, but a fitting alter ego.

I touched his elbow. "All right, Myrddin. Let's go."

"You lost your legacy, too, didn't you, Aubrey? Tell me about your tiles."

I stared at him. *How* did he know? "There's nothing to tell."

My mother had inherited the strange tiles from her mother with the understanding that they must always be passed on and protected by a daughter. A story went with the legacy, one that I would have been told on my eighteenth birthday when my family felt I was old enough to grasp the gravity of our history, something more than just my grandmother's fairy tales. When my own mother died unexpectedly and I was only seventeen and a student at Oxford, the tiles had been hidden away in my flat beneath the false bottom of a locked trunk, along with my mother's jewelry and my father's journals. I didn't think much about them in those days. I was still reeling from Ma Ma's death. Later, after Matthew rescued me from a near assassination, I never went back to my flat. My life had depended on it, he'd said. Trust me, he'd said. A friend had retrieved the trunk for me several months later, but it had been smashed and the tiles taken. My father's journals and my mother's jewelry had not been touched.

"Aubrey, are these yours?"

The old man knelt on the stone floor and turned over seven tiles of varying shapes and sizes, then placed them one by one in their proper place in the mosaic. All I could do was nod as the tiles took shape as a baby's face and small, chubby body. A cherub-faced lap-child beamed back at me from the floor as it *almost* had years ago. I'd seen the tiles before, minus the small ones with blue stone eyes in a pinkish setting. Maybe that's why I'd never liked the tiles—the eyeless baby had given me chills. But now, seeing the child's body and face, seeing it whole, seeing those larimar-stone eyes drew me in. Larimar, reputed to be a stone used for healing, to the point of dredging up pain to be released.

A whimper escaped from my throat. Memories from all those years ago flooded back. The fresh sense of grief from my mother's death. The difficulty fitting in at the university. Strange and loud men following me, invading the seminar taught in London. The terror of a masked gunman promising to kill me if I moved. Matthew. Matthew rescuing me, Matthew loving me, Matthew disappearing forever. And years later, me telling my aunt in a discreet phone call to tell Lilah I was dead, that it was best that way. All those painful turning points flashed through me with the heat of lightning, both illuminating and burning.

I squeezed my eyes shut and opened them. I didn't have time for sentiment. Not now. If ever. "Yes!" I blurted out. "They're mine. The tiles are mine."

Myrddin nodded as if he'd won. "The tiles weren't the only baby you lost, were they?"

I held my breath. You can poke at a wound only so long before it bleeds again. Especially if it never healed.

The old man studied me carefully. "You weren't pregnant when you left the country, were you? You'd lost the baby. That's what Simon was told." He squinted. "Or did you?"

"H-how do you know these things?"

"Simon and I were on speaking terms then. I knew everything." He jabbed a finger at my stomach. "Was that what Matthew was protecting? His own little legacy with you?"

I shook my head and backed away—straight into the wall. He didn't know about Lilah. Not Max, not Simon and certainly not Caleb. I'd kept her hidden as Matthew had made me promise to do. Myrddin seemed to know everything about me except when it came to Lilah. And if Simon and the Adrianos knew as much about me as I feared, how soon before *they* learned about Lilah? I hadn't seen my baby in years, but perhaps that's what had kept her safe. She was the only real legacy I believed in.

"Myrddin, we need to go. We need—"

"You don't know, do you?"

"Apparently there's a lot I don't know. But there's no time." Simon would be back soon. He'd said two hours, but Simon had a habit of showing up unexpectedly and changing timelines to suit himself—and throw others off-kilter.

"You don't know about Matthew. The boy-soldier who saved your life and seduced you."

"He didn't seduce me," I fired back without thinking. I had been the one to seduce him. He'd been all about honor and integrity, but I'd slipped into his bed and rubbed my body against his until he'd relented. I'd been barely eighteen, and he'd been a little older and sweet, and I'd been so lost and so hurt and so scared.

"You still don't know what happened to him."

My jaw worked but nothing came out. Finally I said, "He never showed at our rendezvous point. He vanished from the face of the earth. He…" I hung my head. I wanted to believe that Matthew was still out there, but my Matthew certainly would have found his way back to me by now. "No, I don't know what happened to him."

Myrddin's mouth snatched to one side in an awkward smile. "Still love the boy, don't you? Isn't that odd how the ones you lose end up perfectly preserved by time?

If you'd had a full life with him, you may have discovered his flaws. And he certainly would have found yours. He might have been just another notch on your lipstick case if your passions had been allowed to play out—"

"*Stop it.*"

"Or you might have married and divorced bitterly a dozen years later when he left you for a younger woman. Maybe that would have been better for you, child. At least you might have resurrected yourself after that kind of tragedy."

"Stop!"

"Or maybe it would have been a lasting love. With its rifts and joys, yes, but lasting. In any case, you can never know what future might have been waiting for you so you choose instead to honor him by burying yourself with his memory. Is that why you've never settled down with another man? You've had plenty of opportunities."

I said nothing. I felt sick. I didn't want to hear the truth and yet I did, just as it's impossible to look away from a tragic accident when you drive past on the freeway and you want not to look but the flashing lights and sirens and sheer force of life and death around you pulls your attention to the thing you most hate to see. If Matthew was dead, I didn't want to know. And yet I had to know once and for all the thing that I felt deep and cold in my bones.

"They traced the tiles to your grandmother," Myrddin said, and I was relieved that he was changing the subject. "There was a family crest drawn in the margin of an old book that Max had lost as a young man. He used it to find women like you. Aubrey?" He leaned closer. "That book was the artifact Simon sent you to get. So that he could find the women his father missed. And you brought it back to him, didn't you?"

After a few seconds, I remembered to close my mouth. The family crests in the margins. The notes. They were a treasure map to his victims' genealogy. I'd just delivered and authenticated a murder plan.

"But by the time he found your family, your grandmother had already died of a fever. Max and Simon had nothing to do with that."

"How reassuring," I growled, anger and grief rising in my cheeks. "Come on, old man. Let's get out of here."

Myrddin tossed aside a piece of embroidery and selected one of the thinner tapestries and rolled it out on the floor beside the tiles. Quickly he began stacking the tiles in the center of the tapestry.

"What are you doing?" I sniffed twice and wiped discreetly at my eyes. I didn't have time for emotion right now, not if I was going to survive the night.

"We're taking these with us."

"What if we break them?"

"It's more important that Simon doesn't have them, even if they're dust. As long as he has them, your life will be full of storms."

Rather than argue with his cryptic ramblings, I knelt beside him and helped transfer the tiles to the cloth. My fingers tingled when I touched them. I'd think about it later, when I could think clearly, about Ma Ma and Matthew and Lilah and Joan and me. I tied the four tapestry ends together and threw it over my shoulder, like the Fool in a tarot deck. I shinnied up the fire hose and left the tiles in the vault while I went back for Myrddin, who really wasn't much heavier than the tiles. With the tiles slung over one shoulder and the briefcase full of the words of Isabelle, sister of Joan of Arc, I turned back to Myrddin.

"You said you could get us out of here," I reminded him in a whisper. Guards still stood outside the vault door, and it was only a matter of time before Simon returned to see if I had authenticated the incunable. We had to escape before he returned or there might be no escape at all.

"Shhh," he warned, finger to his lips.

The guards outside were talking, but in Italian. It sounded as though they were being dismissed. Then I recognized Caleb's voice. *God, no!*

Myrddin pointed to a glass-and-brass case that held a Samurai helmet and armor. He ran his gnarled fingers under the edge of the ledge, found a button and pushed. The case swung open to reveal a passageway behind the wall. Myrddin tugged me inside and pulled the door closed behind us. We stood in the dark for a few seconds before Myrddin fumbled his way to something on the wall. The soft glow of a battery-powered lantern fell over us.

We stood in a small room no larger than a stall in a train-station latrine. I heard the vault door open and pressed my face to a small peephole in time to see Caleb stalk into the vault. I held my breath.

"Myrddin," I whispered, "what is this place?"

"Trap."

I jerked my head up to look at him in the dim light, but he smiled through dingy teeth.

"Not for us. For intruders. It's on a time release in case thieves—like you—try to escape with Max's jewels. The passageway opens in ten minutes if—"

"Ms. Moon?" Caleb called out. I watched through the peephole as he stalked around the vault looking under tables and behind counters. He didn't seem to notice the missing artifact I'd brought with me. "Ginny? Come out, come out, wherever you are!"

I peered up at Myrddin, but he shook his head and gestured for me to remain quiet. Caleb paused for a moment to look at the glass-and-brass case in front of our hiding place. He was close enough that I could see the outline of a child's dirty handprint on his shoulder. Benny, I assumed. Caleb squinted into the glass case and then a wide grin spread across his face.

"I see you!" he exclaimed.

Heart pounding, I stepped away from the peephole. Myrddin shook his head. Without exhaling, I leaned into the peephole again. No, he didn't see us. He thought he did, though. He'd seen the reflection of the oubliette's opening in the glass between us.

Caleb stomped over to the oubliette and addressed the opening as he flung the fire hose across the vault to prevent any future escapes. "I see you've found the old man. Excellent! I can't think of two people who deserve each other more. Now you can rot down there together." He kicked the trapdoor shut with one foot, then dragged a heavy Black Madonna statue over the door. "Enjoy your time together. You've got the rest of eternity." He stalked out of the vault with a grin.

"We have to get out of here," I told the old man beside me. "He'll tell Simon—"

"Tell Simon what? That he disobeyed his father?" Myrddin snorted. "The two of them get along almost as badly as Simon and *his* father and the father and son before them."

"Regardless," I said, glancing around our hiding place, "Simon will be back and it won't take long for him to realize I'm gone, you're gone and the 'artifact of the second millennium' is gone. Now how do we get out of here?"

"Another few minutes. Max had this precaution installed because of you."

I frowned. "Me? I never even knew him."

"But he knew you. He knew how talented you were. He was afraid you'd break into his home one day and take back all the things you'd brought to this vault, especially if you figured out the tunnel system around the castle ruins. He wanted to make sure you got only so far before he caught you." He laughed softly. "And now it's your only means of escape. How ironic."

But if the old man knew about the trap, then Simon…? "The Duke will be back. We can't wait here."

"You have two choices. Wait here with me or go back through that vault door and take your chances with Caleb and Simon."

I didn't like traps. I didn't like feeling closed in. I

didn't like limited choices. Maybe with the guards gone I stood a better chance of escape. I reached for the door Myrddin had closed behind us.

"Your mother would have found a third possibility, though I have no idea what."

I jerked my head up. "My mother? What's my mother got to do with this?"

"How do you think she died, Aubrey?"

"Broken neck." My voice cracked. "She was riding horses in the country. She wasn't a very good equestrian. Her horse threw her. She died before the doctors could reach her, but there was nothing they could have done anyway."

Myrddin eased his bony limbs down onto a low table not meant for sitting. "Yes, a broken neck. And yes, she was riding a horse shortly before it happened. But Aubrey—" he leaned forward with as much tenderness as he could muster "—she was fleeing Max and Simon's men on horseback and protecting those tiles of hers. And yours."

"*What?*" My mother? My mother had been a gloves-and-hat British-born lady who'd never raised her voice and would have been more concerned with tainting her manicure than with protecting tiles made of ground-up gemstones.

"Contrary to what you may have been led to believe, your mother was an excellent horsewoman. Sharpshooter, too. She was fast but not fast enough to outrun a dozen men after shooting another six of them."

I couldn't believe what I was hearing.

"They took a package off her body. Tiles." Myrddin laughed. "Tiles she'd made herself to fool Simon. It took him almost a year to find out they were fake and that you had the real ones in a false-bottomed trunk."

My head was reeling. My mother had been murdered? My mother had had a secret life—and I'd followed in her footsteps?

"I didn't know what they were. They were in a trunk with her other treasures and some weird recipes for plaster crafts. That's the only reason I kept the tiles." I'd been nauseated every time I'd looked at them. "Their only value to me was that they'd belonged to my mother. I didn't even know what they were."

"Simon found that out too late. He thought you knew your identity. That the tiles had been passed to you. That's why he sent a man to assassinate you."

Simon. Simon had been the one. It made sense now. I nodded furiously, suddenly seeing it again through eighteen-year-old eyes. "That guy meant to kill me. If Matthew hadn't shown up…"

"Matthew worked for Simon."

His words sank in. I shook my head. "No. No way. That man followed me and I ran into the medieval studies seminar and he took twenty of us hostage. He killed fifteen of my classmates, for pity's sake! Then this young lieutenant in the U.S. Air Force showed up. Special Operations, he said. There on vacation. He saved me."

How he'd gotten there or why he'd been armed, I never knew. I'd been eighteen and falling hard into love and I'd simply accepted his explanation in that naive way that very young women do when they'd led a sheltered life. Nothing but being with him had seemed important.

I could still feel his arm around me as he'd fired back at the gunman. I could still see the smoke as he'd led me to the rooftop of the building. Matthew had whipped off his belt and looped it over a cable at the roofline and twisted the belt around his wrist. Then he'd wrapped one arm around my waist, and we'd plunged over the side of the building, riding the cable to safety.

Instead of taking me to the police, Matthew took me away to the countryside. To somewhere in the thatch-roofed Cotswolds. He'd said the police could be bought and paid for and could do nothing to help us. We hid in the countryside for three months, and when we realized I was pregnant, he smuggled me into the Scottish highlands and told me to wait for his return. He never came back.

"He may have saved you, Aubrey, but his mission was to kill you."

"I don't believe you." I scanned the walls of our hiding place. I had to get out. I needed air.

"It's true. He went along as backup, in case the assassin failed. The man who was supposed to kill you got a little carried away. Panicked when you led him into a classroom full of students. Matthew was supposed to finish the job. Fortunately for you, he was also working for a higher power than the Adrianos. Simon had to abandon his plans when he realized you were gone, but his men did find your tiles eventually, exactly where Matthew said they'd find them."

"Matthew would never betray me." I was thinking seriously of leaving Myrddin in his hellhole for suggesting such a thing.

"He didn't betray you. Not intentionally." Myrddin rose from his makeshift seat. "Simon tortured the boy. Your lieutenant—he wasn't really a lieutenant—gave up the location of the tiles with his dying breath. Your Matthew never did give up your whereabouts, though. All he would say was that you'd left him after you miscarried his child."

I let my head loll against the wall. I shut my eyes and willed away any show of tears. So Matthew had died protecting me. *At the hands of Simon Adriano.* I had probably known in my heart for years that Matthew was dead, but I'd never let myself believe it. I had held on to the hope that someday I'd have back everything I'd lost—Matthew, Lilah, the Joan of Arc manuscript, peace of mind, something sweeter than the freedom to be unfettered by the bonds of normal relationships.

"Max found you almost ten years later. Lured you to Paris on a phony sabbatical. He knew you'd never stay on your own accord, so he set you up. Turned you into a criminal so you'd end up working for Simon."

I blinked at him. "Why? Why would he do that if he'd tried to kill me before? Why didn't he just kill me then?" Maybe it would have been better that way.

"He thought you knew who you were. He thought you'd lead him to others like you. So he let you live. And made you useful to him at the same time. But he didn't trust his own son not to make a mess of things. He never told Simon that the fearless Dr. Moon and poor little Aubrey were the same woman. And Max didn't know you'd never been told of your true legacy. That was his failing, and probably the one thing that kept you alive."

For so many years I'd wanted answers. Nothing more. And now I had them. The problem was, so did Simon Adriano. Now, somehow, Simon knew the truth. But how? Had Max Adriano, dying somewhere in a hospital, had a change of heart about his secrets and passed them on?

It was bad enough to be on his blacklist when he didn't know who I was, but now to learn that he'd tried to kill me when I'd been an innocent eighteen-year-old girl? That he'd killed my mother, that he'd killed my lover and that he knew my true *identity*, whatever that meant? If he knew about my life as Lauren Hartford, how much longer before he found out about Lilah and went after her? How could I warn her without putting her in more danger? I could only hope that she had a little bit of Joan of Arc's blood flowing through her veins, too.

Something clicked in the walls. A quiet whirring. The sliding of arched walls on two sides of us.

"When one door closes, another one opens," Myrddin whispered. "Sometimes your only choice is to wait for it."

We stood on a narrow plateau. The passageway led up more slender steps above us and looked the same below where it dipped deep into the earth.

Steps. Why did it have to be steps?

"How did you know about this passage?" I asked, following Myrddin carefully down the steps. My knee screamed with each downward motion. "What if Simon finds us here?"

"Simon doesn't know about it. I told you, I knew Simon's father, Max, quite well. When I was a boy, Max's father showed the passages to me. Of course, back then it was kerosene lanterns, not battery packs. Max modernized it over the years."

"So you used to run with the bad guys, but now you're a good guy?"

Myrddin paused on the steps to look back at me through the heavy wrinkles around his eyes. "I never said I was a good guy. I never said I was anything. The only thing you need to know, Aubrey, is that we're on the same side."

I followed him down at least fifty steps before having to rest. "What's up the stairs?"

"The passageway connects every treasure trove in case the Adrianos came under attack and needed to hide their most valuable treasures or escape with them. The vaults, certain bedrooms, Simon's office."

"And he doesn't know?" I asked for the third time.

"No. His father never trusted him. That's part of the Adriano legacy. It's because of what sons have done to their fathers for centuries. Later, when the son becomes the father, he fears history will repeat itself. It usually does." The old man was at least twenty steps ahead of me. "You should get that knee seen to, you know."

Damn. I was slowing *him* down? Time to head back

to that obscure little beach town with the eye candy of a knee doctor and relax and work the kinks out of my knee for good! Right after I figured out how to keep Lilah safe.

"Myrddin? Where does this passageway come out?"

"About thirty meters from the main gate. The tunnel levels off underground and comes up in a clump of bushes not far from the private beach."

"Meet me at my automobile," I said. "You go ahead and I'll follow as best I can."

"I'd hate to leave you behind. Would you like for me to carry the tiles?"

Arrogant tease. Arrogant *smelly* tease. "No, you go ahead. I'll carry the tiles."

"Suit yourself. But don't get caught."

I watched him walk ahead, turning on lanterns as he went. The weight of the briefcase and the tiles tore at me. I descended the steps sideways, which made the knee pain much more manageable but was incredibly slow. When the tunnel leveled out, I could walk normally and made better time. The last few steps swerved upward and I knew I was near the parking lot. I poked my head out of the bushes and then fully emerged from the tunnel.

A new pair of guards milled about at the main gate, but their attention was on the video monitors inside. I half ran, half limped to the automobile, spotting Myrddin bending down low in the front seat. Anxiously I fished in my dress pocket for the key and opened the trunk. I slipped in the tapestry of tiles, dumped in the briefcase, then closed it with the kind of solid click only an expensive German automobile makes. I turned to run to the driver's seat and heard a click.

"Leaving without saying goodbye?"

Holding my breath, I turned and stared into the blue eyes of Eric Cabordes. Then I lowered my gaze to the gun in his hand and nearly went cross-eyed. I exhaled and let my breathing become heavy as I looked from the gun to the man. I wet my lips.

"Maybe we could just say, 'Until we meet again.'"

His face showed no emotion at all. "Turn around," he said.

My pulse quickened. "Why? So you can shoot me in the back of the head? No, I'd rather watch." My jaw wound tighter until it hurt. "I'd rather see the look in your eyes when you pull the trigger. I don't want to miss anything."

"Turn around." He still didn't raise his voice.

"No. If you're going to kill me, you do it on my terms."

He rolled his eyes. "Turn around. Please. And put your hands up."

I took a deep breath and grudgingly obeyed.

"Goodbye." A whisper. That was all.

I closed my eyes and waited for bullet to splinter bone.

Nothing happened. Slowly I turned to look over my shoulder at Eric Cabordes, but he was gone.

Chapter 7

I left the headlights off until I hit the main road—a winding two-lane ripple of blackness—then gunned the engine of the rented Mercedes. Surprised as we lurched onto the pavement, Myrddin raised an eyebrow at me but said nothing. A sound like a mewling kitten rose from the passenger seat. I didn't know if it was the old man's stomach or his fear was showing through, but I was already on the verge of rolling down all four windows to air out the vinegar smell of his soiled clothes.

"Take a left up there," the old man instructed, pointing a gnarled finger to a strip of brown earth ahead and a flourishing field of drooping yellow sunflowers I'd seen earlier in the last rays of sunlight. The headlights bounced off the stone fences that lined the intersection. "That way leads out," Myrddin added.

I grunted. How many times had I been here, with and without Caleb? "I know these roads."

"And I know the ones you don't know." Myrddin seemed stronger now than he had in the oubliette or even in the tunnel, as if he'd caught his second wind or was running on willpower alone. I glanced across the seat at him and recognized the excited gleam in his eyes. Damn. Just like me most of the time. Relishing having a purpose.

I nodded to the road as we zipped along. "This one's faster."

"It is. But they'll catch up with you faster, too." Then a smile played across his thin lips. "Haven't you ever heard of taking the road less traveled?"

I nodded. Hell of a thing to ask a former English teacher if she's familiar with a Robert Frost poem or its sentiments. All my life I'd been on the road less traveled, and more than once I'd made my own path, usually not the one I'd intended.

"Then take the next road or Simon and his boys will find us and those artifacts before you reach the next city."

He had a point. I fishtailed the Mercedes onto the dirt road and bumped along over a wide grass path through the sunflower field. My knee throbbed as I crushed the accelerator to the floor. My ears rang, too, but not as loudly since I'd put the tiles in the trunk. It was more like the barely audible sound of a cheap burglar alarm in a jewelry store.

The kitten sound mewled again from Myrddin's seat,

but he didn't seem to hear it. Probably a little deaf, I told myself. Poor guy had lived for who knew how long in miserable conditions, half-starved. I'd find a place to get him a loaf of bread or a cup of soup as soon as I felt it was reasonably safe to venture out. For now, we needed to put some serious distance between the Adriano palazzo and us.

Simon had murdered my lover. All these years I'd been allowed to roam the world freely and been very well paid, and I'd thought it was because he favored me. Instead I'd learned that it was so I could lead Max Adriano to others of my kind. Max had had his subordinates, including Simon, give me a long leash instead of killing me, all because they'd been misinformed about how much I knew. And now Simon knew how much I knew. Or how little.

Simon had made it quite clear that I was expendable. If he ever got another chance, he'd kill me.

"You're distracted," Myrddin said after what seemed like an hour had passed with me lost in thought.

"It's been an eventful night. I have a lot to think about."

"Better if you focus on surviving and stop thinking so hard. You tend to analyze too much." He said it as if he knew me. Myrddin pointed to where the road vanished into blackness. "Turn up there." Then he continued, "Sometimes you have no time to study the alternatives, no time to make plans. All you can do is jump."

I slammed on the brakes and spun the steering wheel hard. When the automobile finished screeching to a halt, I looked out my window and down, a long way down, to where waters dashed over rocks in the moonlight. I let out a frustrated yelp. We'd come damned close to plunging over the guardrail and onto the rocks below.

"I told you, you're distracted. You'd better get a grip on your emotions. And your first priority, as long as you've got those tiles in your possession, is to stay alive. You're second priority is to make sure Simon never sees that book."

My chest heaved as I sat gripping the steering wheel. Foam danced over the jagged rocks below. The waves struck earth with a thunder louder than the ringing in my ears. I couldn't look away. I'd seen my own mortality tonight. Years of hanging from rooftops by a thread, and nothing had ever been as close to the bone as Simon's notification that I'd be working for him for the rest of my life, however long he chose for that to be. I wasn't sure that kind of life was worth living. No, I was sure that it wasn't. Not anymore.

As for my current priorities, my top one wasn't the tiles or the book. It was Lilah and making sure she never got pulled into my own miserable life.

Several local automobiles passed us, blowing their horns to insult my driving skills. They sped into the night as if their tires knew the road by rote and they weren't the least bit concerned with the inconsistent lack of a guardrail to keep them from tumbling down onto the rocks.

"Aubrey."

Myrddin's voice snapped me backward. "Wh-what?" I shook myself and crawled away from the edge, back onto the road. I waited for another automobile to pass before I maneuvered the Mercedes toward the south.

"Focus," he warned. "You're not any good dead."

I slammed one fist against the steering wheel and kicked at the accelerator. How was I supposed to focus? I didn't know what to think or how to feel! What the hell was all that about tonight? Simon's change in attitude toward me, my discovery that my mother had led a secret life, the revelation that my lover had been a hired killer.

"And Cabordes," I said aloud. "The gun. The disappearing act. What the hell—" I punctuated my profanities with another pound of my fist on the steering wheel "—is going on?"

It was almost as if all my unlucky stars had lined up in one night...or an early midlife crisis of catastrophic proportions had struck. One thing was for certain: my life would never be the same.

Myrddin rolled his eyes. "You either ask too many questions or you ask the wrong questions." Then he gestured ahead. "Slow down. This road isn't well marked. And watch where you're going or you'll blow out a tire on the decries ahead."

I swerved to miss the remnants of an automobile accident that had left glass and metal sparkling on the road. A flash of errant meal bumped under my front right tire and clanged under the Mercedes before disappearing in my rearview mirror. "I'm driving," I reminded him angrily as I took the next curve a little faster than I should have.

"Is that what you call that?"

"If you think you could do a better job—"

"Of course I can do it better. Look at you. You're letting your anger and your emotions get to you. That'll get you killed."

I ignored him and waited for the automobile riding my rear bumper to pass. Just being on this road was a life-or-death choice. The last thing I needed tonight was for someone to lecture me on my emotions, especially the ones I'd always been so good at hiding. *I'm a Pisces and I'll be emotional and dramatic when I damned well feel like it.* That's why it was so important to balance my emotions with so much analysis. Studying the situation, researching, planning—that was my scarecrow, the thing I held up to my fears to frighten them away. That's how I lived my life. And how I stayed alive. All the planning was absolutely necessary for my heists and had served me well. As for planning my own life, it seldom paid off, but that didn't stop me. Instead of all the planning, maybe what I really needed was to follow my heart. But I'd lost that opportunity when I'd wedded my life to the Adrianos.

"You're changing the subject," I told Myrddin. "We were talking about Cabordes. What's his deal?"

"*You* were talking about Cabordes. I was talking about driving. Watch this next curve." He ground his feet into imaginary brakes. "Slow down!"

I gritted my teeth. I needed to know what was going on. How could I make any plans if I didn't know anything? "We're fleeing for our lives, old man. I'm not slowing down. If I do, the locals will run me over." I shielded my eyes from the next pair of bright headlights coming up quickly behind and prayed the driver wasn't an Adriano. "I suggest you buckle up."

"Why? At my age, an automobile crash will kill me anyway. I'm more worried about those artifacts. That manuscript must either be buried where no Adriano will ever find it or it must be destroyed."

"There's no way I'm—"

"You don't need it. Not to find the others. I've seen the book. Long ago. I know the family names. I can find them myself."

He'd seen the manuscript? "What were you? Max's right-hand man?"

"You need those tiles unbroken, if possible. But even if that's not possible, you must to keep them away from Simon."

"Me?"

The road passed in an awkward silence between us.

"You," he said at last, his voice quiet, almost reverent. "You and all those of your kind. Those tiles are vital to your mission."

"I don't have a mission." What was he talking about? Then again, he was well into his eighties. Maybe his mental faculties had started to erode. "I have back the property that was mine. And a bit more. And that bit more will fetch enough spare change that I can use to change my life."

Including changing my face and my address to someone and something that Simon would never find. To a face my daughter would never recognize. To something Matthew would never… Ah, Matthew.

"I agree," Myrddin said, but I wasn't listening. "You need to change your life, but no amount of money in the world will do it for you. You have to change from within." He pounded his chest once to emphasize the words and then winced at his own strength.

Matthew, not Myrddin, was on my mind. I blinked back the tears that wanted to come, but I wouldn't let them. Not now, not ever. The time to cry for Matthew had long passed. He was dead. And according to Myrddin, he had been for more than half my life. And I'd grieved every minute, never ending my grief because I'd never really known for sure.

I sucked in a breath that came out just as ragged and I tried to breathe through the ache in my throat. I should have known all that time ago that he was lost to me, but I'm not a girl who gives up under normal circumstances. Matthew had died protecting me. He'd loved me. But that was all in the past. Right now, the best I could hope for was to stay alive and do whatever I could to protect my daughter from afar so maybe she could find the home and the life and the love that had eluded me.

My mind was a jumble. Myrddin was right about focusing on surviving. Everything else could be sorted out with daylight, provided I lived that long. There were so many things I wanted to ask, and yet Myrddin had insisted I asked too many questions. There was so much I wanted to know! About my mother. About her legacy. About the tiles. About the Joan of Arc manuscript. About Matthew.

Oh, God, about Matthew!

I'd learned everything I knew about him in a three-month span, but a whole lifetime ago. But what did I really know about him? I hadn't even known who we were hiding from! And how could anyone ever expect me to believe he'd been sent to kill me or that he'd worked for Simon?

Except that I, too, worked for Simon. *And I've done things that I'm not too proud of, either. Things it's best Ma Ma did not live to see.*

"My mother," I began, but when I glanced at the old man again, he'd fallen asleep in his seat. I sighed and concentrated on the dark road ahead punctuated by headlights and the edge of the guardrail that sometimes wasn't there at all. More than two decades had passed, and I still missed my mother as if I'd lost her yesterday. Almost as much as I missed my daughter.

I never let myself think much about my mother. We'd been close, the kind of close I later dreamed of having with my daughter. Losing Ma Ma was something that had still been raw in my blood when I'd met Matthew and he'd whisked me away. I'd felt so alone in the world, with no one to nurture me or protect me, and I'd been overwhelmed by the aloneness. I'd told myself that I'd get over losing her, but I never had, not even after all these years. I never really finished mourning for her either, before there was Matthew to grieve and Lilah to raise and a busy life to occupy my thoughts. Some nights, especially more recent nights when I was with a lover and still felt all alone, I longed to wrap my arms around Ma Ma's waist and have her pull me to her to be held, just held. More than anything, I missed the weight of her gentle arms around my shoulders.

A fine mist splattered across my windshield as the road seemed to become a bit bumpy. I let Myrddin sleep as I searched for the button for the windshield wipers. By the time I found it, the rain was already peppering down with the ferocity of pebble-size hail and the road was even bumpier than a few seconds before.

I squinted into the rearview mirror. Funny. It didn't seem to be raining at all behind us. Ahead, water fell out of the sky in sideways sheets, white in my headlights like some kind of translucent force field. I'd never seen anything like it. Almost as if we were entering the outer band of concentric circles and the inner circles were still clear.

Again I glanced at Myrddin. Poor guy. Still sleeping and just deaf enough not to notice the ferocity of the storm. Was he this hard of hearing all the time or was he still suffering from being locked inside a vault of energy that affects the senses? Either way, the old man was obviously exhausted, and frankly so was I. A few times I heard whimpering as he slept. Almost a soft crying.

The front right of the automobile shifted downward with every bump, and I moaned out loud. The debris I'd crushed a few kilometers back must have cut my tire just enough for the air to ooze out over the distance. We needed to keep moving, damn it. The storm flashed jagged bolts of lightning across the night sky, spotlighting the narrow road carved into the cliffside. If we stayed on this course, we might easily find the road washed out ahead or blocked by a small landslide that would leave us stranded and without enough room to turn the automobile around and go back the way we'd come. And going back meant facing an enemy who was, for the moment, stronger than I was. We had to get off this road, and the sooner, the better.

By the time I found a deserted road—a small dirt path already muddy—the rain pelted so hard I couldn't see beyond the three-pronged hood ornament on the Mercedes. I found a safe spot where I wouldn't bog down.

For the moment, I felt somewhat safe. We couldn't drive in the storm, but neither could anyone else. Even with the storm raging outside, I surprisingly managed to doze out of sheer exhaustion. Still, it was that fitful kind of sleep where you jerk yourself awake every few minutes. I dreamed of Matthew and of Ma Ma and of Lilah…and the whole Adriano clan after me, after my daughter, all bent on revenge. I didn't need a dream to tell me that they'd kill me if they ever saw me again.

Sometime after that, a panicked dream struck that I immediately forgot the plot of but remembered the fear. I opened my eyes wide, blinking at the clear weather and the palest pink hues of sky, signaling the coming sunrise. Myrddin slept peacefully while I slipped out into the morning and quickly changed the tire, muddying my shoes in the process. The sun was higher in the sky by the time I slipped back behind the steering wheel, and I was weary of cursing Mercedes tire jacks.

Myrddin stirred beside me, then startled awake. "Why are we stopped?"

I heard the panic in his voice but stayed calm. My adrenaline rush had crashed and I was tired. "Storm," I said, yawning. "You missed it."

"You stopped for a storm?" he asked, incredulous. He stared at me with his gray-stubble-framed mouth open. A greasy wisp of hair hung between his eyes. "Do you have *any* idea what you've done?"

"Saved our lives? Worst rain I've ever seen, second only to the traffic." I stretched and turned back to Myrddin. I was getting used to the smell of his dirty clothes; my eyes no longer watered. "You didn't want me to drive off a cliff, did you?"

"Might as well if Simon catches you. It may already be too late." He frowned at the stone fence beside us, the one made of lava rock that had kept us hidden from plain sight. "It's lucky for us that they can't track you in one of these storms. If they could, you'd be dead right now. Don't you realize that?"

I jammed the keys back in the ignition and twisted. The engine started right away. "I'll find a way out of here. That's my specialty—finding a way out."

"And you're a little too good at finding ways in. You weren't supposed to be here at all. We went to a lot of trouble to keep you from leaving San Francisco. You and that manuscript—"

"We?"

"Stop asking questions and drive. Concentrate! You need to get as far north as you can before it starts raining again."

Uh-oh. We were heading south.

I tilted my head to look out the windshield. Not a cloud in the sky. "I think the rain is over."

"I said before it starts raining *again.* The sky may be clear now, but that doesn't mean anything. Don't you think it was a little coincidental that a freak rainstorm forced you to stop for the night?"

"Oh, I don't think…" What was he saying? That the Adrianos had something to do with the sudden bad weather? They weren't gods, after all. Though Caleb would probably have disagreed with me on that.

"You've already been tricked. Simon's slowed you down. He probably has men scouring the planet right now, looking for you. Satellites, tracking devices. He'll be looking for those tiles and the manuscript. Aubrey—" the old man grasped my wrist and squeezed. "—whatever you do, you have to get to Paris. To a flat on the Left Bank."

My old stomping grounds? I'd been there three times in the past six months, mainly to impose on friends for a place to stay for a few days while on my way to a new assignment.

"There's a woman named Catrina Dauvergne. You have to—"

"Cat?" Speaking of friends I occasionally imposed on. "You know Catrina? She's a friend of mine."

Cat was really more acquaintance than friend, but she was as close as I got to anyone. At one point, after a particularly bad night for nightmares around the anniversary of my mother's death, I'd felt much closer to Cat and after a few glasses of wine I'd confided a few secrets, including my birth name and my identity as an English professor. Now I wondered if that might have been a mistake. Our friendship had cooled a bit over the past year, and I wasn't sure why. She'd asked a favor of me recently, a problem with an old letter written during the height of the French Revolution, and I'd been satisfied to answer her questions without asking any of my own. She'd given me a place to stay and a friendly smile on a few particularly bad occasions, and I owed her whatever favor she asked.

"It's not her friendship with you that matters. What matters is that she's one of your kind. Get the tiles to Catrina," he reiterated. "The manuscript, too. She'll help you hide them—and yourself."

"Do I need to be there today?" Old habits die hard. It was a question I frequently asked with assignments. A train didn't seem feasible, given the bulk of the tiles in the trunk. And an airport was out of the question. Leaving Italy by plane would be like waving red flags in front of the polizia and begging to be arrested. To keep a low profile and carry that kind of bulk, the best mode of transportation was by automobile. That would take a good day's drive if I stuck to the Autostrada del Sol. That would take longer, but the rural pathways would be safer for me if I needed to disappear, and I usually did.

"You don't necessarily have to be there today, but the sooner, the better." He pulled the door lever and it opened wide.

"You're not coming with me? Where are you going?"

He flailed one hand toward a small villa ahead, barely visible in the first rays of sunlight. "I have connections. It's best we separate so you don't slow me down."

I rolled my eyes at the old man. Always thinking he could do anything and refusing to consider the possibility that he couldn't. I liked him for that.

"I have a man on the inside, Aubrey. He has my full authority to do whatever he must and he knows more about you than you yourself know. He'll know how to delay Simon. I'll do what I can to give you some time, as well."

"To get to Cat's. And she'll know what to do."

He nodded. "Right. There are others like you." He shrugged. "Not thieves but...I need to find them. Quickly."

"What others? I don't understand."

"You're all descendants of some of the most powerful women in history. A few of you have tried to come together over the centuries. Before, you've failed. This time, you can't let that happen." He paused for a second, his gaze faraway in the dimness. "It's a shame that you and Matthew didn't have a child. It would have been a child of destiny. One under special protection from the higher powers."

I held my breath and said nothing.

Myrddin stepped out of the automobile, onto the muddy roadside, and then peered back through the open door at me. The words caught in his throat as if he had already decided we'd never see each other again. Then he added, "The child would have had a double bloodline. Matthew, too, was descended from your kind."

Chapter 8

Every few kilometers I caught a glimpse of a black Saab behind me, just at the edge of my vision. At first I'd thought it was a shadow, a cloud passing between the sun and Earth. I didn't recognize the automobile, but the driving patterns were familiar. The distance from the center of the road, the way the automobile hugged the curves. The reason I never carried a cell phone. The reason I changed automobiles frequently. The reason I cut my deals in currency and numbered bank accounts. Interpol agent Analise Reisner.

As much as I hated to admit it, she'd saved my life back in France. After I'd saved hers. Simon had sent me to follow her and find a Black Madonna statue she supposedly had, but in the end, we wound up working together to destroy Simon's electromagnetic device, which several strong Adriano henchmen had been *very* determined to fire off to cause a massive power outage in Europe. I'd left the scene battered and limping, my knee twisted in pain and promising an end to my physically active career in artifact acquisitions. We'd left that confrontation in a draw, but we'd both known that she had no choice but to come after me later.

I yawned, trying to unplug my ears and rid myself of the vague ringing. The radiological electromagnetic energy Myrddin had spoken of still played havoc with my senses. The last time my ears rang like this was during the fifth week of the six-week Joan of Arc seminar. Was there a connection?

If Reisner caught me red-handed with centuries-old tiles and a relic proving Joan of Arc had a twin, Interpol would declare it a mighty victory. It would be one thing for Reisner to arrest me based on an alleged history of art thefts, but I'd never be able to explain how a manuscript worth millions had legitimately fallen into my possession. I owed the athletic blonde a grudging respect for her abilities, but not enough to spend the rest of my life wearing a bland prison uniform.

In my rearview mirror I watched the Saab appear and then disappear on the horizon. Reisner was closing in too fast and she knew it. She didn't plan to confront me on the open road, where I could outdrive her. No, she'd wait until I was on foot, on my unsteady knee. That's where she had the advantage. That's where she'd act. And the fuel in my rented Mercedes was dangerously low.

Must ditch my auto, I reminded myself. *Sooner than planned.*

I glanced in the mirror again. Still there. Lurking. Waiting. She'd take her sweet time for the right moment. I couldn't keep my gaze off the Saab in the reflection. I was absolutely certain I would tangle with Reisner again. My best hope was to lose her in the next city.

The next city wasn't huge, but it was big enough to get lost in. I parked and slipped down a narrow street between stone buildings and waited in an alcove with a fresco of Mother Mary and Child painted on the wall, watching over me—I was glad someone was! Glass jars of red candles burned at its base. Some no bigger than tea lights burned on white trivets.

I lost myself quickly in the market-day crowd. Young lovers on the street corner kissing passionately. An elegant businessman with a cell phone to his ear. Nuns walking side by side. A dark-haired girl in a white apron listening to her iPod as she swept the sidewalk in front of her father's shop. Several elderly women haggling with a street vendor over a small white ceramic tile stamped with a red image of Mother Mary in prayer, a tile that seemed to be in popular demand as a coaster, trivet, candleholder and the like.

After a latrine visit, I gathered a loaf of bread, some cheese, fruit and several bottles of water and pomegranate juice in my arms, purchased them and headed back to the car. With Interpol agent Reisner hopefully several kilometers away by now, I fell into the driver's seat of the Mercedes and dumped my purchases into the seat beside me.

There it was again, coming from the far side of the automobile—that mewling sound I'd thought was the old man's stomach. Then soft crying.

I twisted to look in the backseat. A blanket? I hadn't noticed it before. Not in the dark. A deep, sleek navy-blue with a small crimson emblem embroidered at evenly spaced intervals. Two columns and a star behind them.

The Adriano family logo.

It was more than a blanket, though. More like a silken slipcover over a goose-down comforter. It exuded luxury. Owing to its dark color, the blanket hadn't been noticeable in the night. Myrddin must have brought it with him.

Then it moved. Someone was under it!

Without thinking, I reached for my keys to form a bear-claw weapon, but the Mercedes key was nothing more than an oblong chunk of black plastic over a computer chip. No metal.

Before I could scramble for any other makeshift weapons to defend myself, a pair of tiny hands gripped the upper edge of the blanket and pulled downward. The biggest puppy-dog eyes I've ever seen stared up at me.

Benny. The littlest Adriano. The heir to their philanthropic empire and more.

Oh, God. I pressed my fingers to my lips. What the hell was the child doing in *my* car? He'd been playing hide-and-seek with Eric. He couldn't possibly have gotten into my car by himself. It was too long a way for a child so small, especially at night. He wasn't even big enough to lug that blanket by himself!

He spoke softly in Italian, something about his mother. Benny sniffed a few times, then realized I was the "pretty lady" who'd spoken English with Eric. "I want my mother. I want my mother *now.*"

Realizing I'd frozen at the sight of him, I shook myself. I left the groceries in the passenger seat and quickly scrambled into the back with him, gathering his tiny body to mine.

"It's okay, sweetie. It's okay."

He nodded as I stroked his brown hair. He was so tiny, so innocent. I remembered those days with Lilah, the way she was always underfoot and clinging close to me for fear of strangers and monsters. Poor Benny was unaware that he lived among the monsters.

His body went stiff against mine. "Want my mother."

"It's okay, honey." I let him get a good look at my face. "I was just at your mommy and daddy's house last night. Remember? I was the nice lady with the juice you didn't like?"

I saw a flicker of recognition in his eyes. He nodded and relaxed against me. "Still want my mother," he whimpered, his voice catching.

"I know, sweetie. I know. It's okay. I'll get you back to your mommy."

What was I promising? Take him *back?* The Adrianos would shoot me on sight. But I had to. Tagging along with me was no place for a frightened little boy.

Or any little boy. Or any child at all. In my line of work, I had no business being around children at all.

I took a deep breath and bit into my bottom lip. *God, what now?* If Myrddin hadn't bailed on me, I could have sent him back with the child or at least gotten close enough to the palazzo to bribe someone into taking Benny back to Josh and Pauline.

"Look, Benny…sweetie…I'm going to see if I can find someone to take you back, okay?" Maybe I could find a courier. Pay them well. Well enough, anyway, to deliver the boy unharmed.

"No, you take me back. You take me to my mother."

"I—I can't!" How could I explain to him? Though he was destined to grow up to be as ruthless as Simon, he was a little boy, an innocent, with no concept of danger. Certainly the Adrianos knew already that I was gone, that Myrddin was gone and that their precious artifacts were gone. Once they realized Benny was no longer on the premises, they'd do the math and know he was most likely with me. If I returned to the palazzo, they'd shoot first and ask questions later.

Surely they'd know by now that Benny was gone. The Adrianos loved their cameras, as at least one sex scandal had proven. They weren't fond of paparazzi cameras and they preferred to stage their photo-ops for their philanthropic galas. They no longer liked cameras in the bedrooms, but I had the distinct impression Caleb had secretly videotaped his carnal pleasures with me, probably so he could watch over and over how he technically had taken my life and given it back to me.

The only place I hadn't seen cameras in the palazzo was in the vault itself and in the passageway that Myrddin had led me down. Simon had told me once that no one was allowed inside the vault and that not even his security team knew what was inside. I knew, of course, because so much of the contents was acquired by me personally, but he didn't trust his own security team. Their job was to watch the vault entrance, not to admire its contents. The fewer employees who knew exactly what was stashed in that vault, the better.

As for the passageway, it made sense that it, too, was without cameras. Especially if Myrddin was right that no one there knew about it.

Once they'd realized their heir was missing, the Adrianos surely would have checked the security cameras and would know Benny had made his way to my car somehow. They'd know he was with me. Never mind the priceless artifacts I'd taken from their vault—even if they were mine or partly mine—kidnapping their most precious treasure would be grounds for immediate execution.

The Adrianos guarded their pedigree with a ferocity that led back to a bloodline of kings. The family had little use for daughters. Maybe for a political alliance. Sons were preferred, imperative. Legitimate sons. Rumor had it their bastards were killed at birth—if they lived that long.

If an Adriano could bear at least three legitimate sons, even better. One became the heir to the Adriano empire. Another son was often planted with unscrupulous leaders in the Church or the government with the intent that he could gain some control that would benefit the family as a whole. All the other sons were spares in case of foul play or unforeseen circumstances.

Aaron, Simon's eldest, had died. Unnatural causes, of course. Adrianos rarely died of old age. Simon had then chosen as his heir the son who fathered the first grandson—in this case, Joshua. Caleb didn't have a solid place.

That's where Caleb, much to his dismay, fit into the family structure. A spare. Of course, he was angry. He had something to prove. He was too much of a playboy for a life with the church and too likely to cause another scandal for a career in politics. He didn't fit well anywhere within the Adrianos' fifty-year plan and had fallen out of favor with his father in the past year. Joshua was now the perfect son—reliable, responsible, appropriately behaved—and he'd produced a perfect heir with Pauline. Caleb's real worth was only if Benny died and he could produce another heir before his brother did.

"Want my mother," Benny blubbered into my velvet dress.

I stroked his hair. "It's okay, sweetie. I'll get you your mommy."

Though it was hard for me to imagine any child wanting Pauline as a mother. She'd always seemed so cold, so distant, so intent on her social life and her place in the Adriano household. Then again, I suppose some people might see me as cold and distant for not being with my daughter. Didn't mean I didn't love her.

Pauline, for all her faults, would certainly be devastated to find her baby boy gone, though possibly more so because he was an insurance policy that kept her position safe. I'd heard a black-eyed servant girl—she'd had a thing for Caleb—talking once about the possibility that Benny was not Joshua's son but Simon's. I never saw that servant again.

I hugged Benny to me. I couldn't just leave him in a strange city with strange people. Maybe I could sneak back, hide the car and take Benny up the hidden staircase to the vault and leave him there with his blanket. He'd be safe in the vault for a couple of hours. They'd find him after I had a chance to escape a second time and all would be well. Except this time they'd be watching for me. Probability of success was nil.

But what else could I do? I could feel the gears of my priorities grinding, chewing me up. I had to keep Lilah safe—as a mother, that was always my top priority. Second to that, I had artifacts that I'd been told couldn't be allowed back into Simon's hands. And third, there was my own future. Getting away from the Adrianos, starting over, reclaiming my life, having a second chance to live as an honest woman among honest people. And now a little boy was asking me to help him. I couldn't just toss him aside and run off to the nice, safe life I yearned for. How could I do that and ever look in the mirror again?

"Sweetie? Are you hungry?" I reached into the front seat and grabbed an orange. "Would you like some fruit?"

He nodded enthusiastically while I opened a bottle of water and offered it to him. He gulped the water, and after seeing the backwash in it that children tend to leave, I decided to let him keep the bottle. I peeled the orange and fed him half the slices, eating the other half myself, and then wiped his sticky face.

"I want you to be a big boy for me," I encouraged. "I'll find someone who can take you back to your mother."

"No!" He shook his head and poked out that petulant lower lip. I recognized a faint resemblance to his uncle Caleb. "Want *you* to. *You* take me to my mother. Not supposed to be wid strangers. My father says."

Typical Adriano male—insistent, not knowing how to take no for an answer.

Benny made a face and I knew what he wanted. I'd have to find a latrine for him. Any café would want me to stop and buy a cup of coffee at the very least. I'd done that once already and didn't want to call further attention to myself by going back, this time with a child I hadn't had with me before.

I sighed and looked around the alley, finally spotting a small chapel in the corner beyond the Mother Mary fresco. A priest who looked older than Myrddin stood at the door and nodded to me when I caught his gaze. I knew just enough Italian to ask for directions to latrines, gas stations and airports and I would have to fuel the car soon.

With as many assurances as I could make, I sent Benny to the priest to ask for help and smiled sheepishly back at the elderly man. He listened to Benny's Italian—which was much better than his English—then closed his eyes and nodded. The priest disappeared through the chapel doorway with the child.

I ducked back into the car for a bottle of pom juice and as I reemerged—half standing, half bent to keep from straining my knee—I came face-to-face with Eric Cabordes.

Chapter 9

For the third time in less than a day, he held a gun on me.

I dropped the bottle. Plastic, it bounced and skittered under the car. Neither of us looked down. Neither of us breathed.

He pointed the revolver at my heart but kept the weapon low, hidden between himself and the car door so no one else could see it. He stood closer to me than a lover. With all the people passing us on the street, all going about their daily lives, none of them knew how much trouble I was in at that moment.

Mentally I kicked myself. I should have planned ahead. I shouldn't have let myself focus so long on the child. Shouldn't have let my emotions get in the way. I was a sucker for children, and look where it had gotten me. Most recently, at the end of Eric Cabordes's barrel.

"Don't move," he instructed in a voice as low as a growl.

I couldn't see his eyes behind the dark sunglasses, but I imagined them as I remembered. Pale blue. Intense. Deadly. He'd let me go, just to catch up with me? Was that how he got his kicks? The chase? Couldn't blame him for that.

"Do you have the artifacts?" he asked, his voice barely above a whisper.

I said nothing. I didn't even glance in the direction of the trunk. So much for the child's bodyguard being interested in the boy. It was all about the mundane treasures, wasn't it?

He grabbed the neckline of my dress, hand halfway down my cleavage, and pulled me upright. The revolver pressed hard against my thigh. "Answer me."

"Yes," I said through gritted teeth.

I looked harder, tried to see through the sunglasses. The outline of his eyes. I saw my own face in the reflecting shades. Defiant, searching, ready to run.

In the few seconds he pressed against me, I took in as much information as I could. Something would be useful. It always was. He smelled like the leather jacket he wore. His chest heaved in deep, measured breaths. Ah. Eric Cabordes wasn't nearly as calm as he wanted me to believe. And *that* was useful.

"And the child? I saw him talking to the priest."

That was a pleasant surprise. So he'd already seen

that Benny was safe. He hadn't needed to ask about the child before the artifacts. Maybe my intuition was right—he was smitten with the boy.

The bodyguard held up his cell phone with his free hand but didn't dial. It was an odd gesture, a calculated one.

"In the latrine. He's—he's fine. I didn't kidnap him. He was a stowaway."

"Quiet!" His glasses fell forward on his nose, and I got a good look at his eyes and the strange fire that was incongruous with the tone of his voice. Amusement? "You expect anyone to believe you didn't kidnap Benny for a healthy ransom?" he spat out.

"It's the truth." He'd been there. He'd seen me put the artifacts in the trunk. Eric Cabordes knew I hadn't touched the boy.

"What would you know about the truth? The Duke took you in. He gave you a new life. A lucrative one. And this is how you repay him? Kidnapping his grandson? Stealing assets from his private collection? If you've harmed one hair on Benny's head..." He holstered the gun and then slapped the headrest behind me—hard. "If you've hurt that little boy, I'll take you out myself."

I stared at him. His movements were deliberate. So were his words. "I told you—" I started.

"Shut up, bitch!" He slapped the headrest again, and I almost fell backward into the driver's seat. "You don't look so fine now with a bloody nose, do you?"

But he hadn't touched me. I instinctively felt my nose and upper lip for blood and found none. I frowned up at Eric Cabordes, and he answered me with a wink.

"Stop struggling!" he snarled, making an elaborate gesture to me and to the phone in his hand. "You want me to hit you again?"

What the hell? What kind of game was he playing?

"No," I managed. "No. I'll do…I'll do what you want."

"Good." He thumbed open his cell phone and pressed a button. He didn't take his eyes off me.

"Duke," he said into the phone. "I have her. I have everything, including Benedict…. Yes, I'm on my way back now. I just have to throw the bitch in the trunk and we'll be at the palazzo in a few hours." He watched me watching him. "You want her alive or should I go ahead and…? No. I understand. She's Caleb's."

He snapped the phone closed and cocked his head, still speaking toward it. "Stop kicking! I said—" He hurled the cell phone at the alley wall. It slammed into the stone and shattered on the pavement. A girl on the street ran the other way without looking back.

I froze. Okay, I didn't know what his game was, but I wasn't sticking around for it. The man was crazy. The boy was safe. And I had no doubt the boy would be safe with the man even if I wasn't. He knew where Benny was and he could take Benny back. Me? I was getting the hell out of there and to Cat's as soon as possible. It would be nice to see a sane, somewhat friendly face.

"Benny's in the chapel," I offered quickly. Eric glanced over his shoulder, and in that moment I shoved him backward with one foot, jammed the key into the ignition and pulled the door closed behind me all at once.

He jerked the door back open. He grabbed my left

wrist and held it, leaning into my face. His sunglasses tumbled forward and fell into my lap. "*Don't* do that," he snarled. "I'm trying to help you." He reached over me and snatched my key, careful to keep his revolver out of my reach.

"Is that why you just went all homicidal on your cell phone?" I glanced at the bits of metal on the sidewalk. It wasn't even recognizable as a phone. I didn't know phones had that many parts. "You were trying to *help* me?"

He shrugged but didn't let go of my wrist. It hurt. I pulled away, but he held firm.

"That wasn't an ordinary cell phone. It was an Adriano phone."

"Aren't they all?" Had the situation not been so serious, I might have chuckled. The Adriano Communications subsidiary was well known throughout Europe and Asia and even in the larger cities in the States. Caleb had once bragged that the Adrianos held the largest market share of cell phones for major corporations, though the subsidiary's best marketing move by far had been a giveaway of ten thousand cell phones and free airtime to the teenage children of American military personnel.

Eric Cabordes didn't crack a smile. "Adriano cell phones are programmed to act as recording devices. They can be activated remotely, even when you think they're off. The Adrianos do it all the time." He released my wrist. "And I'm certain that my cell phone was activated as a recording device the moment I left the palazzo."

"Then that was all…an act?"

He raised an eyebrow. "Would you prefer I slap you for real? I will if I have to. To save your life."

"No, that's okay. I can do without the slapping. But the conversation you had with Simon? Telling him you were bringing me in? For—" I gritted my teeth "—Caleb's entertainment?"

"Didn't matter. I'm sure Simon and Caleb were listening to every word said, both before and after I ended the call." He paused. "That's why I needed to be convincing."

I tried to think of the last time I'd used a cell phone. Caleb had given me one as a gift several years ago and I'd purposely left it in a train station. Simon had offered me one for various assignments and I'd turned him down. I'd deliberately stayed away from cell phones because of Interpol. Certain audio software can detect a human voice pattern—which is as individual as a fingerprint—via airwaves and detect the speaker's location within a few feet. Global Positioning Systems—or GPS—combined with smart weapons made high-tech killing as impersonal as a video game but most definitely real. Governments secretly used this method for assassination plots all the time. I'd been very careful, using only landlines and a message service, so maybe I was safe from the übersurveillance of the Adrianos.

"They started reprogramming cell phones several years ago as part of their corporate espion—I mean *acquisitions*—program. I have no doubt they've heard every sound I've made since last night, when I volunteered to come after you. That alone may have raised suspicions."

"But you work for them." I could understand how they'd want to record a colonel's home life or an engineer's discussions of his latest designs. "You're just a bodyguard to the little boy."

"All the more reason to spy on me, don't you think? When his father's not present, I'm closer to the Adriano heir than anyone else, his mother included."

I shouldn't have been surprised. Simon didn't trust his own sons, not any more than Max had trusted Simon. Why would he ever trust an employee?

Quietly I eyed the relaxation in his muscles. The moment I'd been waiting for. For him to let go and believe I'd stay. I could still get away if—

"Don't even think it," he warned as if he'd read my mind. "I want you alive and free, but I *will* kill you if necessary. It would be better for me to be your executioner than Caleb." He lifted my chin. "I would make it quick. You deserve that."

I sucked in my breath and shook off a tremble. *I would make it quick.* By the look in his eyes, I knew he meant it. The strange thing was, there seemed to be a sense of nobility in that threat.

"How did you find me?" I rubbed the mark he'd left on my wrist. "Ever since I left the palazzo, I've been careful."

"You weren't careful when you were *at* the palazzo. Wait. I'll show you." He glanced back and held up a finger. "Do not run. I'm a good shot and I rarely miss."

As I climbed out of the car, I contemplated how fast I'd have to run to make it into the little chapel and whether I would actually find safety there. Then I remembered my injury. Sometimes I actually forgot it when the knee wasn't throbbing. I rubbed a slow clockwise circle around my swollen joint.

He strolled to the front of the car and fidgeted with the bumper. He bent on one knee, fished around under the bumper and then extracted a black box no bigger than his hand. Suction cups lined one side and a wire protruded from the other.

I blinked. "It's a tracker? Simon was tracking me?"

Eric laughed. "Simon always tracks you. Not for long, though. You switch cars and it's gone." He tilted his head. "Good move, by the way."

"Uh, yeah, thanks." It had had more to do with Interpol than the Adrianos.

He strolled to a car parked nearby. In less than two minutes he'd pulled back the plastic covering over the front bumper and inserted the tracking device. He pointed at the rental sticker on the car window and the maps of Italia on the dashboard.

"Tourists. They'll give the Duke a run for his money." When I frowned, he added, "Once I get us to a safe place, I'll let you go." He locked gazes with me as I leaned against the front fender of the Mercedes. "I swear by the Mother."

He'd risk his life to get me to a safe place, but if he couldn't, he'd kill me? *I would make it quick.*

"Eh-wic!"

I looked up in time to see Benny's face as he stood hand in hand with the old priest. His smile lifted his cheeks all the way up to his eyes. Benny tore loose from

the old man and ran frantically for Eric. His tiny shoes slapped the sidewalk with his all-boy bluster. I could have sworn he jumped from three feet away and landed in Eric's arms.

Eric grinned back uncharacteristically and swung the boy in a half circle. "Hello, my little hellion. Are you having a good day?"

Benny nodded. "Grrrrreat! I had oranges for breakfast."

"You did?" Eric snuggled against the child but watched me instead. "I smell them on your breath. Did Dr. Moon treat you well?"

"Yessss!" Benny smiled broadly to show a missing baby tooth that he was too young to have lost through natural causes. Obviously Eric hadn't been able to stop some of the tyke's shenanigans.

"That's good. Benny, I have something for you." He pulled an iPod out of his jacket pocket and snapped a pair of headphones over the boy's ears. "There. I'll turn it on for you and you can listen to a story while Dr. Moon and I drive. Okay?"

Benny nodded and crawled into the backseat of the Mercedes without any objections. Eric buckled him in, and the child sat quietly staring out the window and rocking back and forth as he listened to a story I couldn't hear.

"You sure that's not a recording device?" I asked, still leaning against the front fender.

"Yes. One, it's not an Adriano product. Two, I bought it this morning. And three—" he motioned for me to scoot into the passenger seat "—I verified it personally."

He propped his elbow on the roof of the car and

waited for me to move, but I didn't. Instead I said, "You take the boy back to his mother. I've got places to go and people to see that don't include you. No offense."

"None taken, but that's not the plan."

I still didn't move. "It's my plan."

"It changed. As a matter of fact, Dr. Moon, I'd say all your plans have changed in the past twenty-four hours. All your plans for the rest of your life."

Okay, so he was right about that. Everything in my future had turned on a dime last night and I was still as confused as hell. Nothing was certain any longer. Not my future. Not even my past. Everything I knew about everyone was suspect.

"Yes, everything has changed. But I'll still make my own plans. I always have."

"And where has that gotten you? In league with the devil? When was the last time your plans worked out?"

"Including the San Francisco job that your bad intel nearly botched for me?"

He squinted back at me. "You should thank me for that."

"Like hell I will!"

"I was trying to keep you away from Simon and Caleb. I was trying to keep that artifact out of his hands." Eric looked as though he was grinding his teeth with every syllable. "I was trying to save your life. I'm *still* trying to save your life. You don't make it easy."

"Yeah? Well, I'm sorry for making *your* life difficult." I shook my head and tried to stay calm. I didn't want to talk about my plans or where my life was going or where it wasn't. I was stuck. Stuck! But I refused to give over control of it to the Adrianos...even if they *did* control my life. "I make my own plans," I continued, "and they don't include you."

Then I remembered my manners. "Thank you, *Monsieur* Cabordes, for removing the tracking device, but my future doesn't include any passengers."

"Then consider me your copilot."

"No. I don't trust anybody to be my copilot. Especially anyone who works for the Adrianos."

"Who said anything about trusting me? You're not capable of trusting anyone."

I scowled back. True, I didn't trust anyone. It's a harsh way to survive, never letting anyone that close. But survive was what I did. And I didn't appreciate him pointing out my survival instincts as though they were deficiencies.

"What I mean is," he corrected, "you're not capable of trusting anyone *right now.* It's because you don't trust yourself yet. When you can trust yourself, it'll be easier to trust others."

I smirked and shifted against the front fender. Such sage advice from a bodyguard-slash-assassin. But it was a subject that was too close to the bone.

"You should take the boy back, Monsieur Cabordes. Alone."

"Can't." I saw the brief struggle in his eyes, then he decided to make a confession, maybe because he didn't think I'd live to tell it. "I can't take Benny home. Not yet. I need another day. His father's in

Egypt until tomorrow. I'll hand him over to Josh and no one else. Not even his mother. Besides, Benny is my responsibility, and if I don't bring him home, my corpse will be found floating in the Golfo di Napoli next week."

"Fine, but what has that got to do with me? Find a reason for a delay, besides a destroyed cell phone, and wander back at your own leisure. I don't care how you do it. But I have deadlines of my own."

"I know. But I need you to trust me on this." He seemed to regret his word choice immediately.

"No. Besides, you just gave me that speech ten seconds ago on how I don't trust anyone."

I did trust someone, didn't I? *Someone?* Maybe Catrina just a little bit? And I'd taken Myrddin at his word about the escape route out of the palazzo. Then again, I hadn't had a choice. Somehow I didn't feel that trusting someone when I didn't have a choice was really the same thing. The situation made the decision for me. There was no healing in my heart that rendered me willing to trust. Instead I was simply swept along.

"Even if I did choose to trust someone, why would I start with you?"

"Fine. If you can't trust me, I'm asking you to keep an open mind. You're not halfway around the world where I needed you to stay, far away and safe. You're here, right under the thumb of your worst enemies. You want to get out of Italy and get out alive, then you're going to have to work with me because I'm all you've got."

"I don't need you to fight my battles for me."

"Fine. Then maybe what you need is someone to watch your back."

I sucked in my breath. *Dead on target, Eric.* But that was more than I'd ever hoped for. Still, I had to travel this road alone. I didn't know any other way. "I told you, no. I make my own plans. I like to be in control."

"In control of what? Life? Falling in love? Losing the people we love? Death? None of us has as much control as we think. Life is what happens while you're making all those fancy plans of yours."

His words tumbled out, bitter and definitely unplanned. His voice was as smooth as ever, but his tone tore at the shields I'd erected around my heart. I couldn't remember the last time I'd talked to anyone in such a raw and intimate way. It was almost as if he really knew me. But how would a bodyguard for a child know anything about my life?

"It beats not having a plan," I said lamely.

"Just an illusion. To make you feel in control. Because you can't just let go and live. Can't you see where it's gotten you? You had a destiny and you've failed it. You haven't taken your power. You're the descendant of some of the most powerful women who ever lived, and look at you. Nothing but a common thief."

"A thief? Yes. Common? No."

"Okay, yeah, you're good." He folded his arms across his chest and leaned against the driver's door. "Maybe one of the best as far as art thieves are concerned. But for how long?"

"As long as I have to be. I don't have any choice but to be the best at what I do."

"Then change what you do."

"If I had any choice, I already would have."

Then, as if reading my mind again, he added, "You always have a choice. I'm asking you to make a choice to help me. To help me to help you and to help me to help that little boy. That's all I'm asking for now."

"And if I say no, you'll kill me."

Frowning at an imaginary spot on the street, he nodded. "I was going to say that I have no choice in the matter, but I do. If I can't save you, I'm to kill you—and rather than let the Adrianos catch you, I will choose to kill you myself."

"Oh, yes," I spat back. "And you'd do me the favor of 'making it quick.'"

He caught my gaze. "Because of who you are—what you are—it would be an honor to cheat the Adrianos of your death." He swallowed. "And because there are many more lives at stake here than yours and mine."

"Like whose?"

He nodded toward Benny, oblivious and innocent in the backseat. "That little boy, for one. Sometimes you can't do anything for your own future, so you have to do things for the children."

Eric and I stared at each other for a moment. I caught a brief glimpse of pain beneath the steely exterior and wondered if it was his or merely a reflection of my own that I was looking at.

He wrenched his head in the direction of a sleek yellow motorcycle parked down the street. "I can't take the boy home on that. Besides, I'm sure it's wired with a tracker. I just can't find it."

I rolled my eyes. "Okay. But I'm driving." Besides, he wasn't bad to look at. Maybe if I tried really hard, I mused, I could tolerate having a firm-bodied man riding shotgun.

He ducked into the passenger's seat while I buckled myself behind the steering wheel, checking once in the mirror to see that Benny was still entertained. I made a three-point turn in the narrow street and headed back the way I'd come.

"How long has Simon been tracking me?" I asked as we sped down a narrow street devoid of pedestrians and vendors.

"I don't know. Longer than I've been with them. A few years maybe. Every time you came to the compound and Simon's security staff searched your car for bombs? That was more than enough time to plant a tracking device."

Damn them. Always making a big deal about security, when I was the one being violated. Was I ever truly off the grid where the Adrianos were concerned? I had to believe I was, especially since they'd lost me for the six weeks it had taken to return with the Joan of Arc artifact. So it *was* possible to hide even when they knew my identity and most of my aliases.

Eric caught me eyeing the boy in the backseat. "You've a motherly streak in you," he observed. "That surprises me."

I felt my cheeks grow warm. Motherhood was something I didn't discuss. "He's a great kid," I managed to say. "You…you have children of your own?" I wanted to take the microscope off me.

Eric squared his jaw and said nothing for a few seconds. Then finally he answered, "Benny's my life. At least until he's a little older. Who knows? Maybe forever. Josh doesn't trust him with anyone else, especially when he's away on business."

"I didn't kidnap him. I swear. I don't steal children, not even from raving lunatics like Pauline."

Eric snorted. "Pauline doesn't deserve that kid."

I nodded my agreement. "I had no idea that he was even in the car until—"

"I know." Eric twisted sideways in the seat to look at me. "Stop straining yourself. I know how Benny got into the backseat of your car."

"You do? Because there's no way he lugged that blanket all the way from the main house to the parking area by himself. He's too little to even walk that far, let alone—"

"I put him there."

"You *what?*" I slowed the car to avoid hitting a businessman with a cell phone glued to his ear. An Adriano phone, no doubt.

"I know where the cameras are and where they aren't. It was easy to get him to your car, even before I saw Myrddin. Or you."

"But why?" I braked too hard at an intersection, and automatically my hand shot out protectively to brace my passenger. My palm landed squarely on his chest. I blushingly noted the muscles underneath and pulled back. Eric shifted uncomfortably in his seat, equally surprised by my reflexes…or by my touch.

"You were leaving last night and I couldn't," he explained. "I knew you'd leave the compound sooner or later. I didn't think Simon would have you executed last night. He still has use for you. Or did." Eric took a deep breath and exhaled slowly. "Benny was safer with you. At least for last night. You know what they say. Adrianos don't die of natural causes. They live into ripe old age…if somebody doesn't kill them first."

"What about Max Adriano? The Duke's father? Simon said the old man had been hospitalized and wasn't expected to live much longer."

Eric stifled a chuckle. "That's what Simon is telling everyone, isn't it? The truth of the matter is that yes, Max Adriano was recently hospitalized—after an assassination attempt."

I'd heard that. From Therese, one of Max's secretaries, as well as from several other sources of mine. "I've heard, too, that he was dead."

Eric nodded as I braked at another intersection and he braced himself discreetly. I fought the reflex and kept both hands on the wheel. I didn't remember being quite as protective of the old man.

"Is it true? That Max Adriano died?" I frowned into the rearview mirror. The gray BMW I'd barely noticed earlier had reappeared. Were we being followed?

"I understand he was technically dead for a few seconds before they revived him. As for Simon, you shouldn't believe everything he tells you." Eric shrugged. "Obviously."

"And the boy? You think someone would try to—" I glanced at Benny in the mirror, headphones over his ears as he stared out the automobile window, and I mouthed the words *assassinate him?*

Somberly Eric nodded. "It's already been attempted. I'm the only one who knows it. That's why I had to get him out of there. I can't tell Josh. Not yet. I have to do it face-to-face. And he won't be back from Alexandria until tomorrow."

"Why face-to-face?"

"Josh carries an Adriano phone. And though it's forbidden for security to activate a family member's cell phone, I can't take the risk and hope it doesn't really happen. I'd never make it back alive for a face-to-face conversation with my employer."

Activate Josh's phone. The words sank in. "Who would spy on Josh?"

Eric shot me a look and said nothing. *Ah.* He didn't have to. *Caleb.*

I glanced again in the rearview mirror and sighed. Good. The gray BMW was gone.

"For weeks now, Caleb has been enticing Benny to dangerous activities. Caleb knows he has to get past me to get to Benny, and I won't let him get past me."

From the tone of his voice, I didn't doubt it for a minute.

"You're saying Caleb's been trying to, um..." I cut myself off in case Benny could hear us beyond the insulation of the headphones.

"Yes. But Josh has been gone, and I can't exactly go to the Duke with that kind of information, can I? I can go to Josh and only Josh. He trusts me."

"And *can* he trust you?"

"Of course." He gritted his teeth. "I've paid for the privilege. In blood."

I desperately wanted to ask what he meant, but my intuition warned me not to. He was on thin ice, and I had the impression that if he cracked, I'd go down with him. I'd made my own sacrifices for the Adriano family. I guessed I wasn't the only one.

"You love the boy," I said. A statement of fact, not a question.

"Yes."

"Bodyguards shouldn't become attached to their clients. It's deadly for both of you."

"Agreed, but I didn't plan it. I thought my heart had been closed, but he got through, you know? I would lay down my life for that child. It's not just my job. It's my duty." He turned away and stared out the window for at least a whole block. "If any of the Adrianos are ever going to live up to their public image as philanthropists, I'll see to it that it's that little boy. I won't let them turn him into another Adriano clone."

I smiled to myself. Nice sentiments. But what could one man do? I wondered as I pressed the accelerator a little harder. I strained for a glimpse in the mirror of the gray BMW. For a moment I thought I'd spotted it, but then I lost it.

"Why me?" I asked. "Why my car? Why last night?"

He didn't speak for several minutes. I thought he'd not heard me. Just as I started to rephrase my question, he cleared his throat.

"Last night, after I took Benny out to play hide-and-seek, I brought him to his mother for the evening. Most of the time, she doesn't want to be bothered with him. Benny cramps her style. Last night was one of those nights. Caleb offered to play with the boy instead. That in itself was unusual. He's had nothing to do with Benny until this new girlfriend caught his attention." He raised an eyebrow. "Scarlet Rubashka."

"You don't like Scarlet." It was a statement, not a question.

"I don't like or dislike her. She gets on my nerves, though, always asking questions about where and when I was born."

I laughed. "Delving into your personality via your astrological chart, was she? Yes, I've seen Scarlet in action."

Eric curled his upper lip. "She said I was a Scorpio rising, whatever the hell that means. And that *that* explained everything. She never said what it explained, but I didn't care for it."

I shrugged. I liked Scarlet. She was vibrant and playful and intense with a hell of a sense of fashion. And too good for Caleb. There was something familiar about her that reminded me a little of Lilah, enough that I'd tried to take her under my wing, tried to warn her to be careful of Caleb. Instead she'd given me a cool shoulder. She seemed friendly to everyone but me. But then, I'd told her some rather unbelievable details about her suitor. My own sexual preferences aren't exactly vanilla, but Caleb's habits could be deadly. Obviously he was keeping his kinkier side hidden from Scarlet. That could mean only one thing: he really wanted to impress her.

"So Caleb's found a potential wife. Is that it?" He wanted to get rid of Benny and replace him with an heir of his own?

"Possibly. But his affection for her does seem genuine. It's Simon who doesn't like her. Not a conversation passes between father and son that doesn't include an argument over his focus on Scarlet Rubashka."

"Last night," I said, "I saw you leave with Benny to play a game. Later I saw Benny's handprint on Caleb's shirt."

"Caleb had me dismissed for the evening."

Hmm. Eric didn't seem easily dismissed. He was hard to set aside in my mind, even under the current circumstances.

"Can Caleb do that? Dismiss you?"

"He can't, no. But Pauline does have the authority to dismiss me for the evening so she can spend time with her son. Josh gave her that authority in his absence. But only because she's the boy's mother. While you were at the palazzo, all attention was on you and on the artifact you'd brought back. No one was watching Caleb. He took advantage of that. He played a game with his nephew, all right. I found the boy up on the scaffolding boards of the tower ruins. Not even within the walls of the tower. Just balanced up there with his blanket."

"On top of the tower? My God, that's dangerous! He could have fallen." Then it struck me, even before Eric could confirm it.

"More than dangerous. It's intentional. Benny's not allowed to play anywhere near there."

I remembered the four ruined towers of the old castle that formed the foundation of the palazzo. In places, the stone had crumbled, so the Adrianos were having it refurbished in an attempt to buck it up to last another century or two, but the recent earthquakes had played havoc with the repairs. The towers were always in the distance, high above the other buildings in the compound. Caleb had taken me up onto one of the towers for a private dinner one night, when he'd been courting me. The view was stunning, with the Bay of Naples visible in one direction and Mount Vesuvius in another.

A fall from there would be deadly.

I glanced again in the backseat at the boy, then checked the mirror again for gray BMWs and found none. "How could anyone do that to a child? Especially…his own uncle?"

"It would have been deemed an accident. They would have said the boy had been playing hide-and-seek and fallen. Even his own mother would have believed it. But not me. Benny's terrified of heights."

"Then how did Caleb get him up there if he's that scared?"

"He drugged him with cough syrup. With Pauline's permission, of course, to give him a single dose to help a nonexistent case of the sniffles." Eric's upper lip curled in disgust. "Pauline doesn't spend enough time with him to know if he's sick or not."

So that's why Benny had slept through last night's escape and the storm. I glanced in the rearview mirror again at Benny and then beyond to the street behind me.

"What's wrong?" Eric asked.

I kept my eyes on the road ahead, made a quick right turn, sped up and then another right. The road behind me was clear.

I shook my head. "Nothing. I thought for a minute there that we were being followed."

"We weren't. I was watching, too."

I smiled. Glad to know somebody had my back. That was a different feeling. I was used to doing it on my own.

"What are you smiling about?"

I shook my head. I didn't smile much anymore. Not genuinely. Most of the time I went through life with a poker face, even when my knee wasn't killing me.

"It's nothing," I said. "Nothing."

Again a movement in my rearview mirror caught my attention. A gray BMW. Three men. "Yours?"

Eric discreetly checked out the side mirror. "No. Yours?"

"Not unless Interpol just sent a whole entourage to pick me up. Which, I supposed, given my reputation, was entirely possible."

"You want me to drive?"

Jeez. What was with all these men? They thought they were the only ones who could drive? First Myrddin and now Eric. Give Benny half a chance and he'd want to take over next!

"I think I can handle it," I said drily.

I watched for the next street to the right and spun the steering wheel, barely clearing the corner of an old stone church that was probably three hundred years old. I fishtailed to the left, down an alley, and then threw the gears in Reverse, backing into a second alley. We waited a few seconds and the gray BMW passed. The men hadn't seen us.

"Made it!" I grinned and reached playfully to squeeze Eric's knee. "We made it."

Eric gingerly lifted my hand from his leg and squashed it back onto the steering wheel. "Please don't do that."

"If you're going to get persnickety about my driving—"

"No. Don't use sex as a weapon with me."

I stared. "Use sex as… What?" Had I heard him right? He was a great-looking guy. Sexy and determined, if not a little too reserved. My attraction to him was natural. "I didn't touch you because I had a hidden agenda!"

"No?" He raised a single eyebrow. "All I know is that you've left a trail of men all over Europe and the States, each one of them a victim of your, er, feminine wiles. To my knowledge, it's all flirtation to get what you want, whatever artifact you're after." He squared his jaw and peered out the window at the garbage in the deserted alley. "And, after all, you were Caleb's whore. A woman with so much potential, and you sank so low."

My jaw dropped. "Is…is that what you think I am?"

He turned back to me, his gaze burning condemnation into my flesh. "Weren't you?"

I shook my head and tried to speak, but nothing came out at first. "No! No. I..." Squeezing my eyes shut, I took a deep breath and found myself telling him the whole story, all about how Caleb had courted me and then nearly killed me for kicks. I don't know what compelled me. I'd never told anyone else but Scarlet, and only then because I'd thought I could save her the same humiliation and danger. But I told him everything. Every detail. I didn't open my eyes until I'd finished. I couldn't look at him.

"Aubrey."

I scowled at the steering wheel and then above it at the entrance to the alley. I couldn't face him.

"Aubrey." He turned my chin toward him with a single index finger. His face had softened, and for a second I almost thought he might kiss me. "I'm sorry."

He held his finger against my skin as we stared at each other. He meant it. Damn. He meant it. *Scorpio rising,* Scarlet had called him. I didn't know much about astrology, but I knew that an ascendant in Scorpio was special. All that emotion just under the surface, always hidden but utterly intense passion.

He blinked and looked toward the alley entrance. "Shit!" He went stiff.

I followed his gaze. The gray BMW blocked my view.

Chapter 10

I'm good at finding ways out, I told myself. I couldn't go forward. We were blocked. I had to find an alternative.

I gritted my teeth and threw the gearshift into Reverse. Hands hard on the wheel, I turned to look behind me and plowed backward through the alley and its garbage, then spun out into the street behind me, across traffic and into another alley. My earlier luck didn't hold out, and I scraped a wall as I backed out onto another street and spun into a courtyard full of flowers and small statues. We waited, Eric and I exchanging nervous glances. No gray BMW. In another silent minute, I maneuvered out the courtyard and back to the main road out of the city. No one followed. I looked in the mirror for the next few kilometers, but still no gray BMW.

"So what's the plan?" I asked, finally expelling a breath. "You and Benny tour the countryside for an extra day and then go home to Daddy?"

"Something like that. I'll spend the next day chasing you and finally report in from a pay phone to give Josh my status."

"And me? What happens to me? How will you justify your existence when I don't return with you? Benny may be too young to explain, but you'll be expected to." I looked at him hard. "I'm *not* going back with you, right? Now that you're here with Benny, there's no reason for me to go back."

"No, you're not going back with me. You're to meet your friend Catrina in Paris. If she's not there, then go directly to her farmhouse in Lys. Take the tiles and manuscript to her for safekeeping. Meanwhile, you're going to make a daring last-minute escape befitting one of Dr. Moon's famous getaways." His lips twisted in slight amusement. "Me? I will heroically save the child from your dastardly clutches and return him to his father. Consider it a win-win situation."

Wait a minute. "How did you know about Catrina?"

Before he could answer, a single raindrop splashed on the windshield in front of me. We were well out into the countryside, and on both sides of the road patches of sunflowers bowed their heads under a sudden light breeze. Then just as quickly they dipped low, their heads touching the ground and stems bouncing upright again and again as a heavier wind swept through the fields around us.

Clouds zipped in front of us, across the sky above the

road ahead. The single raindrop became two, then three, then a deluge.

I checked the rearview mirror. Benny yanked off his headphones and stared, horrified, out the passenger window. He began to whimper.

"It's okay, sweetie," I called back to him, fumbling as quickly as I could for the windshield wipers. I flipped them on high, but even then the wipers couldn't keep pace with the rain. "Put your headphones back on," I told him. "Close your eyes and listen to your story."

His reflection obeyed and he leaned back in his seat with his arms folded and his eyes squeezed shut.

The wipers slapped back and forth with little effect. I braked gently, then again, until I slowed to a crawl. Eric turned in his seat to check on Benny, whose eyes were still tightly closed.

"Answer me," I shouted over the pounding rain. "How did you know about Catrina?"

I could no longer see anything in front of me except for gray. I maneuvered toward the roadside, but Eric grabbed the steering wheel and swung us back onto the road.

"You can't stop," he said. "Do not stop. No matter what."

I wiped at the foggy windshield with my left hand and gripped the wheel with my right. "We have to stop. It's not safe to keep going."

"Do not stop!" Eric roared. "Keep going!"

"No." I swerved toward the roadside again, but he seized the steering wheel and angled the automobile back onto the road.

"If you can't drive in heavy rain, I will."

"I can drive just fine. This is ridiculous! I will not put that child in the backseat at risk when I can't even see the hood of my own automobile."

"If you do not continue to drive, you put us *all* at risk, including yourself. Including me. Including that boy." He leaned back in his seat. "Keep moving. See if you can get ahead of the storm."

"Get ahead of— There's no way! It's all around us."

"Exactly. It's all around *us*."

I veered sharply to avoid another car that had pulled onto the roadside in front of me, but I didn't see its blinking hazard lights in time. I heard the crunch of metal. My front bumper plowed the length of the automobile, denting in both doors and fenders.

"Do not stop!" Eric yelled as the other driver honked furiously back at me. "Keep driving!"

"But I just—"

"Keep driving!"

In the backseat, Benny started to cry. "Want my mother."

"Do not stop!" The veins in Eric's forehead bulged. I didn't like the look in his eyes. Not anger. Terror. The Adrianos' most important bodyguard was scared. When Benny whimpered again, Eric lowered his voice. "No matter what happens, you must keep driving. If we have a chance to get out from under this storm, we have to try. It may already be too late. They'll have to try for a visual of the car to follow you. They can't track you in the storm. Not until it stops."

So there was another tracker on the Mercedes? I motioned to the pounding water on my windshield. I could hardly see the metal rim of the hood at the base of the windshield wipers. Our entire universe had shrunk to no more than a finger's length outside the car. The road ahead was straight, but I wasn't sure I could navigate by the feel of the ground under the tires.

"How can anyone be expected to drive in this kind of storm?" I asked.

"That's what they're counting on."

"They who?"

"Simon. Caleb. If Simon catches us, I can salvage myself. I'm adept at cover stories. With Caleb, I don't know. I'd have to take the boy and run, hope to get to Josh before Caleb gets to Benny. But if they catch you?" He shook his head. "If they catch you, Aubrey de Lune, they *will* kill you."

I swallowed. Yes. That much I knew already.

"When it comes to torture, Simon is very efficient. Trust me, Aubrey. I've seen it." Eric caught my gaze for a split second but long enough. "Simon will use whatever emotional attachments you have—to any-one—to find out whatever it is you know."

"I don't know anything."

He took a deep breath. "Then that's unfortunate. Because rather than torture you directly, he'll make you watch while he dismembers the people you care about."

"I told you—I don't know anything. All the artifacts I've acquired for the Adrianos, I've given to them." I considered the contents of the trunk. "Until now. I never held anything back. I was always honest in my dealings." An honorable thief. My last sliver of integrity.

"He's not so much interested in your artifacts as your ancestors. The women you descended from. The women they told you about on your eighteenth birthday. The history of the tiles. In your family branch, that was the tradition."

"How would you know anything about my family?" Or that I was Aubrey de Lune? As for my family, I'd lost them long ago, but the wound was still fresh. "How would you know anything about *me?*"

"Because I've researched you thoroughly."

"Oh."

"In your family, on the eldest daughter's eighteenth birthday, the daughter is told the story of the tiles and given the oral history of your family tree. That's how your mother learned about the tiles. And her mother before her, and her mother's mother."

White-knuckled, I clutched the steering wheel. I leaned forward, flattening the accelerator as much as I dared. "I don't know any stories," I told him. Why couldn't he understand? Was that what Myrddin had meant? "I don't know what you're talking about. My mother died before I was eighteen. My grandmother died when I was a little girl. My father vanished when I was barely old enough to remember his face. I never heard any stories about the tiles. I saw them a couple of times, but that's all. The only stories I ever heard—ever—was how I was descended from Joan of Arc, but that was just a bedtime story my grandmother told me."

Eric stared at me, then started laughing. "All this time! All this time he kept you alive so you could lead him to the other women like you, the other descendants. And you knew nothing." He shook his head and wiped a tear from the corner of his eye. "Incredible! They lured you back to Europe, set you up, turned you into a criminal, made you useful to them, paid you a fortune with each completed assignment, and all with the hope that you would flit around Europe and eventually contact others of your kind. Didn't you ever wonder why so many of your acquaintances disappeared into thin air?"

Catrina. I pressed my fingers to my lips and then gripped the steering wheel again. She was the only acquaintance I had much to do with anymore, and because I didn't entirely trust her, I'd been extremely discreet with my connections to her. Other than an occasional professional contact, I'd simply never been able to keep a female acquaintance for long, so I'd pulled back, I'd withdrawn, isolated myself. I'd thought somehow it was my fault, that I was too cold, too distant. Why else would my newest women friends, year after year after year, not return my calls or ever show up for a planned lunch? Friendships seemed out of the question for me. As soon as a promising friendship started, it was over, and not once did I ever know why the other woman had dropped me. If what Eric was saying was true, becoming friends with me had probably cost them their lives.

"Catrina. How did you know about Catrina? The old man knew about her, too."

Eric sobered. "I work for him."

"Who?"

"Myrddin."

"I thought you worked for Josh."

"I do. But I'm Myrddin's inside man. I'm the one who took him food through the tunnels and kept him alive. Unfortunately I couldn't get him out of there without blowing my cover, so he insisted on staying. Everything he knows, I know. He's given me full authority to speak for him." Not even a smile. "So you don't know why all this is happening?"

"No. I mean, Myrddin was talking crazy stuff in the vault, but…I'm not sure about any of it." Too much had happened in the past twenty-four hours. Everything I'd thought was real had been shown to me for what it was: an illusion.

"Centuries ago, there was a group of women. They were enemies of the Adrianos. Quite possibly the only people the Adrianos ever feared. They were scattered to the corners of the earth and nearly wiped out. Max Adriano dedicated years of his life to tracking down their descendants and decimating their growing ranks. The manuscript in the trunk—that's what he used to find them."

"Myrddin told me. The family crests in the margins. A reverse genealogy," I murmured above the patter of rain.

He thought about my interpretation, then agreed. "A sort of reverse genealogy, yes. Instead of finding the ancestors, he found the descendants. He also found their tiles. Generations of his forefathers have been searching for them. But Max? He was methodical, ruthless. That's why Myrddin and I hoped to keep you away from the palazzo. And to keep you from getting that manuscript in the first place."

The rain lightened and a ray of sunshine struck the automobile. I pushed the accelerator with more confidence.

"The bad information you passed to me on the San Francisco job. You did that intentionally."

He nodded. His gaze raked across my face. Something sparked at me—a desperate tenderness, a wish, a desire that could not be requited. "Better that you be in jail and that manuscript in safe hands than you bring it back to Simon. Max lost it before the advent of photocopying, so there was only one copy. He took it with him to Poland to track down a family there, and while it was out of the Adriano vault, it was stolen and later fell into Nazi hands. All these years, it's been lost. It showed up on Simon's radar after the Berlin Wall fell, and he's been chasing it ever since. The private investor you took it from refused to deal with the Adrianos—bad business deal from years ago—and would never have sold it to them. It was incredibly valuable to Simon, mostly because it was the key to finding his enemies and making sure they never discovered their heritage."

And I had delivered it to Simon personally. The book was my history—and apparently my destiny. "And Myrddin told you all this?" The story seemed to match the scant bit of information I'd been given in the vault.

"Yes. Myrddin told me he's been fighting Max and his boys for several years now, since before the time I joined Adriano Security on the recommendation of my college roommate—Josh. Max and Myrddin were old friends, closer than brothers, the old man told me. Myrddin has dedicated the remainder of his life to tracking down those of your kind before the Adrianos can find you."

The rain in front of us suddenly vanished. The road was dry. I glanced in the side mirror and saw nothing but blackness behind me. Except the blackness was getting closer, closer. I urged the accelerator all the way to the floor.

"Whatever happens to you and me," he said, "we can't let that manuscript or those tiles fall back into Simon's and Caleb's hands."

I glanced in the mirror. Benny sat calmly staring out the window at the sunny fields, his headphones securely clamped over his ears while he lost himself in what must have been an incredible story to hold his attention through most of the storm. He couldn't see the storm behind us, only sunshine ahead.

I could only hope that Simon hadn't discovered my daughter, but I couldn't think of any easy way to ask Eric, not without tipping him off. Eric had been astonishingly candid with me, almost as if he had only a short time to get his point across and disappear forever from my life as so many other acquaintances and potential friends had.

There it was, then. All that hidden Scorpio intensity,

better seen with my intuition than my eyes. I wanted to see it close-up. I wanted to touch it. I wasn't positive that I could trust him, but I could work with him. For the moment, at least.

Eric shifted in his seat. His eyes glinted at me in the odd light of the sun ahead and the black clouds behind. "Faster," he urged.

I stomped the accelerator. He didn't need to tell me.

"They shouldn't have found us," I said. "The three men in the gray BMW. They shouldn't have been behind us. They found us after you removed the tracker."

"I know."

"How?"

"That, I do not know. Unless you had a second tracker on your car, and that's entirely possible."

A drop of rain hit the trunk of the car. Odd. The storm was catching up with us even though the wind outside was blowing against it.

"Drive faster."

"The polizia—"

"Don't worry about the police. You can outrun them. The weather? No."

I kicked the accelerator to the floor. The fields and the occasional automobile we met all blurred past. The speedometer needle rose until I could no longer see it.

"Myrddin said something about the Adrianos being able to control the weather. Is it true? Does Simon have some kind of new technology?"

"No, not new technology. It's ancient."

Rain splattered across the back of the Mercedes. The

storm was catching up with us. Again. We wouldn't be able to stay out of it much longer.

"I know you're not fond of making plans," I said to Eric in the seat beside me, "but I think it's time to make an exception."

Eric shot me a resigned look. "All right then. We'll find a place to stop. Defense will be a problem, though. We have only one weapon between the two of us. Unless you have something hidden under your seat."

I shook my head. The evening before, Eric had taken my sole weapon, the one I'd taken from the guard at the entrance. I knew better than to arrive at the palazzo with any kind of weapons hidden inside or under the automobile—Adriano security always confiscated them and made me look bad to Simon. I was expected to have some kind of weapon on my person, and in most cases I had to surrender that at the security gate, as well. So generally I didn't even bother.

"No other weapons," I said. "Nothing but our wits." A few raindrops splashed on the windshield. "If we could find a church—"

He laughed. "You think sacred ground would keep the Adrianos at bay? That's never happened before. They're not vampires or zombies. They're mortal men."

I sniffed. "Mortal men who never die of natural causes. I've heard the rumor."

"It's because of the ley lines under the palazzo. And under their other estates. The ley lines keep them healthy. Since I've been at the palazzo, I've been more…vital than ever in my life." He'd paused as if to say *virile* but thought better of it. Still, the pause was enough to make me bite my lip. "After a few days on the grounds, you start to feel invincible."

"The ley lines. The rivers of energy."

"Not just that. Power. Power to communicate. Power to heal. Power to kill. Energy isn't evil. It's pure. It's all in how it's used, and they've learned how to harness it. When it's tapped into, it's like opening a door. Some keys open doors and some keys keep them tightly locked."

"That's how they're able to send storms to block our path." I gritted my teeth. How could we fight that kind of power?

"Exactly. They've been experimenting with weather manipulation for at least a decade. The first big test was in the States. They were able to hold the jet stream in place for days. Endless rains. Broken dams. Flooded the Mississippi River and St. Louis. It was a big story then. In those days, there weren't that many weather anomalies. Now you've got tornadoes popping up out of blue skies and hurricanes that defy explanation."

"All because of ley lines? I thought they'd been around for years. I know I read about them when I was a kid." I heard about them once or twice, too. Mostly from Bohemian types who pretended to be psychic. "I'd never really considered them to be a scientific fact."

"Not just ley lines. More to it than that. It's the tiles, and who knows what else? Simon's become a little too interested in hunting down artifacts that emit unusual energies. Radiological electromagnetic energy fields."

I nodded. "Myrddin told me. They're some kind of energy waves that affect the brain, right? Makes people hear things or see things."

"Some people, yes. Not many. Not until recently. Most people who experience it won't even talk about it. They don't want anyone to think they're crazy."

"What about you?" I asked. "Do you feel it? See it? Hear it?"

He shook his head. "It doesn't seem to affect me directly. I do know, though, that there's more of this energy in the world than ever before. As the world becomes more populated and 'civilized,' the elements that give off this type of energy are brought together and the energy is magnified exponentially. For millennia they've been left alone, buried under continents or oceans, but now they're being combined in ways they haven't been put together before. Like your ancestors did in the tiles."

"They're benign when they're separate?"

"Everything emits an energy signature. Even inanimate objects. But put certain energies together…"

"And they change? Like in chemistry? Put hydrogen and oxygen—two gases—together and you have water?"

"Yes. The energies are different now. More people are feeling them. It's like the vibrations in the air have been ratcheted up a notch or two. The Adrianos have been studying the side effects of these energies for several years now. There's been a dramatic increase in anxiety attacks, depression, neurological disorders, especially in the States, where commerce and affordability make it possible for the average citizen to own objects that once sat thousands of miles apart. Chunks of New Age crystals. Jewelry with stones from all over the world. Some energies weren't meant to be mixed."

"The Adrianos mixed these new energies? These radiological electro—"

"No. The evolution of our race did. The Adrianos simply know how to use them."

A wave of rain washed over the automobile and was gone, almost as if it were the outer concentric circle of a hurricane.

"Eric, like I said before, I think we should find a church."

"And like I said before, it won't do any good. Simon and Caleb will not care that we're in a church. The Adrianos' ties to the Church are not holy. The Church is just another tool in their arsenal, and Simon may give his sons Biblical names to prove his devoutness to the pope, but it means nothing beyond politics."

"Actually, *Monsieur* Cabordes, I wasn't thinking of sacred ground. I was thinking of *higher* ground. We need the advantage of being able to see them coming."

"I have a contact on the coast. With some persuasion, he may be willing to shelter us for a few days until we can get our bearings."

"Great. How far?"

"About fifty kilometers."

"That's not going to work. We're almost out of petrol."

We stared at each other. I flexed my aching fists on the steering wheel. The BMW wasn't close by, as far as we knew, and the storm would hold it at bay. Cat was in Paris and too far away to be of any help at the moment. We had the tiles, the book, the boy, one gun and each other, but once again we were running out of options.

Eric studied the road ahead. "There. Up ahead, where you see that clump of trees. Turn there. There's a monastery up on the hill. Not a church, but it has the advantage of height."

I followed his advice, unable to keep my eyes off the sinking fuel gage. I was amazed we'd made it this far. The storm hit us from the side as I pushed down the tree-lined road toward the hill. The monastery had been built into the earth, and while it was centuries old, it wasn't vacant. Like many old holy buildings in the European countryside, it had been converted into a cross between a hostel and an inn.

"We're going to stay here?" I asked. The storm dumped water all around us so that we could see nothing of the monastery except the lamps on the posts outside.

Eric nodded once. "We'll be safe for a while. As long as it's storming, they can't track us. Even military weapons have trouble tracking targets in bad weather, so we'll use Simon's disadvantage to our advantage. As long as the storm rages, it buys us time, and time is what I need to get Benny safely to his father."

I turned the key and killed the engine. "And I need to find a way to slip away unnoticed while you're taking Benny back." That meant this would be my last night—

my only night—with Eric. I'd probably never see him again. And I *wanted* to see him again.

"You have to get away," Eric agreed. "We'll have a day, probably. Maybe two if we play it well."

"And if we don't?" My doubts started to set in. The Adrianos would most likely catch up. Despair washed over me. Not only might this be my last night with Eric but my last night, period. "Simon thinks I know more than I do."

"Aubrey, Simon will simply dismember everyone you care about, appendage by appendage, until you tell him about your ancestry or make something up. Then, after you've told him everything to his satisfaction, he will very quickly, very quietly, very efficiently put a bullet into the temple of everyone you care for, make you watch and then do the same to you. Simon is no killer. He's a cold-blooded assassin and he's just as efficient and courteous about it as he is when he's glad-handing at a gala fund-raising event."

I hadn't realized I was holding my breath again. I forced myself to exhale. "Simon promised to turn me over to Caleb when he was done with me."

"Caleb, on the other hand, is less concerned with efficiency than Simon. He will keep you alive for days. He will employ sexual tortures you can only imagine. He will deprive you of oxygen until your brain is damaged beyond repair. After that, he will keep you alive a few days more, long after your spirit has left you. Or he might drug you and fill your mind with irreversible madness, then turn you loose on the streets of Naples, slobbering and biting your tongue—"

"Stop! Just stop it!" I yanked my head in Benny's direction. "Don't let him hear you."

Eric shook his head. "He's listening to stories of a boy and his dragon. He can't hear me. Can you?"

"I read you loud and clear, if that's what you're asking."

"I won't let Caleb do that to you, Aubrey. I swear by the Holy Mother, I won't let it happen."

My throat tightened and I looked away. I knew what I had to do. Something I'd rarely done in the past decade.

"Will you… Eric, will you help me?"

He smiled, but there was no joy in it, only sadness. "Do you trust me?"

I liked this man. I really did. I liked his sense of integrity and his love of children. I like everything about him, including the way he looked. I wanted to know him better and I thought by the look in his eyes that he might feel the same.

But did I trust him? My head said no. My heart said no. But my gut instinct screamed yes. I told myself I had no choice, but I knew it was a lie designed to protect my heart.

"Yes."

Chapter 11

Inside the lobby of the monastery-inn, I carefully peeled back the curtain and peered out the window. It didn't matter. I couldn't see anything anyway. Even if it hadn't been night, the raging storm outside blotted out any light that was left.

"*Signora,*" the man behind the desk pleaded. "Come away from the window. You will be struck by lightning."

I smiled at him. He was a little younger than Eric but not nearly as handsome. His hair was close-cropped, except at the fringe, which hung low into his dark eyes. My presence aggravated the frown lines on his face. He fidgeted with a halogen lantern, setting it on the desk for quick retrieval if he needed it during the storm. He pocketed a small flashlight.

I shook my head at him. I was less worried about lightning than I was about a sniper's bullet. I permitted the heavy curtain to fall back into place. I had no idea if any of the Adriano henchmen were out there or how long we had before they found us, but for the moment, we were safe. We were alive. Thanks to a storm, no one could find us—yet.

"*Signora*, please," pleaded the night manager. "Go to your room. Enjoy your husband. Sleep. Storm so bad. You not go anywhere tonight."

I pursed my lips. Maybe he was right. Maybe I should go enjoy Eric. I might not get another chance to find out what made him catch his breath besides running for his life.

"*Signora...*"

Night manager probably wasn't the correct term for the man behind the desk, but neither was he a monk. Eric had been right—the inn was actually a monastery, at least five or six centuries old, refurbished in some places and in some places not. It wasn't uncommon to find them throughout Italy, but I'd never stayed in one before. This one had been converted into something more akin to a youth hostel than an inn, with a definite preference for backpacking university students.

There had been only a few automobiles near the cluster of stone buildings, and I was certain that most of the automobiles belonged to the family who owned the lodgings. The night manager's father, a more wrinkled version of the younger man, had met us at the entrance and welcomed us, ushering us inside, where the air had been warm and smelled of baked bread and homemade sauces.

I'd carried a snuggling Benny in my arms, with the child wrapped in his Adriano blanket and its ominous family logo of columns and a star. Eric had hauled in the contents of the trunk, the artifacts wrapped in a tapestry, and I'd found myself noticing his ass as he'd walked ahead of me and wishing for more time with him.

For hours afterward I'd watched the grayness outside, and no one had come. My mind had wandered across Eric more times than I could count. Maybe because there were so many other things I didn't want to puzzle through and he was a safe place for me to focus. Much safer than memories of a lover long dead or a daughter I'd left behind for what I'd thought was the right reason. The tempest inside me did not still and the storm outside the walls had not stopped. As long as the rain and winds wailed, no one would come. No one could make it through that. Me included.

After greeting us in flawless Italian and realizing I wasn't as adept as Eric, the old man had welcomed us in flawless English. His wife had prepared a sumptuous Italian meal for us of homemade pasta with fresh sauce. She couldn't speak a word of English but she'd been all smiles and in some ways she reminded me of Simon's current wife, even though this woman obviously didn't have the financial means to keep her face and wardrobe as sleek as any Adriano wife's.

She'd prepared an entirely different meal—risotto *di scampi* this time—for the evening meal for her guests as well as for her family. My Italian wasn't very good, but I knew enough to say *basta* for "enough" and *grazie* for "thank you."

The innkeeper's wife had made a special dessert of tiramisu for her grandson, who was a few months older than Benny. The two children had taken to each other immediately, and I could see Benny's Adriano charm showing through, even at his age, as he quickly persuaded the other boy to share his dessert and pet kittens. The two of them had eventually scampered off to play with the cats.

Later, I put Benny to bed in my room on a pallet of blankets on the floor. Eric took the small room on the other side of our slightly larger one. The two rooms shared a reasonably modern bath situated between them. It was ideal for the two of us adults to talk in Eric's space while Benny slept in my room with a kitten wrapped around his neck. We tucked the artifacts under my bed.

But Eric…

I'd watched him throughout both meals. He'd been nervous and careful at first, but he'd relaxed as the day had worn on and no one had come. A few times I'd caught him smiling or even looking as if he enjoyed the banter of family around him and good food. I doubted he ever relinquished the mask of stoicism that was required when he was on duty at the palazzo. His Scorpio-rising personality would have suited his bodyguard career quite well.

Occasionally across the table I'd caught his gaze and held it for a little longer than necessary. How long since

I'd touched a man? Especially one who had touched my heart, even the smallest bit? I wasn't looking for any port in a storm, but Eric suddenly seemed like a safe harbor in the tempest around me. God knew, I needed something solid to hang on to right now.

He mirrored me in some ways. Not only in the hidden depths of emotion just beneath his surface but in his survival acumen. Earlier in the day, not long after our arrival, Eric had gone back outside in the torrents of rain and hidden the automobile in a darkened archway that led to an interior courtyard.

Me? I'd waited until no one was looking, then I'd stolen a knife from the kitchen. It wasn't much, but if Simon and Caleb's men showed up, we'd need all the help we could get.

The old man who'd greeted us at the door had actually asked if we carried any weapons. Eric had lied about his gun, and the old man had reluctantly accepted Eric's insistence that we were unarmed and not dangerous. He had explained that the monastery had for centuries been a place of peace and was still sacred ground. Blood had never been shed on the premises—this place was a sanctuary. He'd pointed to the walls of the reception area, which were decorated with old weapons supposedly confiscated by the monks over centuries. Broadswords. Crossbows. An armload of sabers and foils. A couple of daggers that might have dated back to the Borgia era. With a few exceptions, the typical item on the walls might have sold for one hundred American dollars at any Internet auction house, but none were worth a second glance on the antiquities market. Still, they made for nice decorations and each had a story behind it, some of which the old man told us in excruciating detail.

Eric had retired to his room with clenched jaws. I knew what he was thinking—that he was turning over possible stories in his mind to tell Josh and Simon and that he was trying to figure out where to hide both the artifacts and us if the men in the gray BMW found us. Old monasteries like this had numerous places to hide things as well as children. As long as it kept storming outside, we still had time. Although the downpour kept us in place, it also kept everyone else out.

Tomorrow things would be different. Tomorrow I'd have to find a way to leave, to get to safety at Cat's, to check with my private investigator to make sure Lilah was still safe and clueless on her college campus in the States.

Ah, Lilah. I can't even get close enough to see you for myself without putting you in danger.

"*Signora? Signora,* please. Go enjoy your husband. Relax. Rest." He smiled feebly. "I go to bed now. I enjoy my wife. Relax. Rest."

I got the point, even before he reached for the room lights and held his finger at the switch as he waited for me to exit the room.

Alone, I walked the length of a dark corridor lit by dim bulbs where once torches probably showed the way. Outside, the winds howled, but inside the corridor, the stormy sounds were muffled. The only noise was the soft footfalls of my boots on stone floors.

I could tell by the ringing in my ears that I was getting closer to my room. I stopped outside the wooden door and adjusted the room key in my hand as I glanced up and down the corridor. No one was there. Just me and whatever ghosts of the past had died there without bloodshed.

Carefully I opened the door. I'd left the light on. Benny had insisted. Funny, our fearless little Adriano wouldn't sleep in the dark.

The ringing amplified as I stepped inside. Benny had crawled off his pallet on the floor and into my bed. The kitten still slept under his chin.

I locked the door behind me and shook my head as I did. The lock was flimsy, old, cheap. Meant for preventing peaceful people from accidentally wandering in unannounced on other peaceful *naked* people. Not meant for keeping assassins out. These locks wouldn't hold up to Adriano boots. Maybe there was some way we could sneak out, even in this storm, to someplace even safer. We could take one of the innkeeper's automobiles, one full of petrol.

We needed a plan. Or at least, I would have felt a lot better with one.

The tiles were safely hidden, untouched. Still, my ears rang. My energy seemed heightened, as if every pore of my skin had come to life. I felt my life force rising from between my legs, up through my chest and out the top of my head. What was happening to me?

I slid the knife out of my sleeve and stabbed it into the board over the door to the bathroom. Then I tottered through the narrow room on tiptoe so my boots wouldn't clomp on the floor.

"Eric?" I whispered, poking my head into his room.

I saw him just in time to duck. He drew back from the corner of the door. The bodyguard expelled a sigh that fluttered the hair over his eyes.

"Do not sneak up on me. I could have killed you."

"With what?" I smirked. He'd obviously left his gun by his bed. "I could have killed *you.*" I jerked my head in the direction of the knife wavering from the doorframe. "There. I brought you a present."

He frowned. "How romantic."

"Not exactly." My skin felt electric all over. As if I'd been hit with an energy field. Not just Eric's, either. I found it harder to breathe. "Anyway, no sign of…our employer…or any of his associates. But I doubt any of them could get through the rain."

Eric agreed. "If they're still manipulating the storm, something's wrong. There's no way they'd hold it in place for this long if they knew where we were. They've used the tactic before to slow down an adversary or hold him in place. If they were trying only to hold us in position, they would have been here hours ago, letting the storm die down as they got closer. I don't think they know where we are. Myrddin said it was very difficult for them to track us in bad weather, even when they're the ones creating the bad weather. So they'll keep the storm swirling over the whole area until they can locate us, but I've taken precautions so we won't be found."

"Oh?" I brushed at a raindrop on his sweater. He'd

been outside but not far. Anything beyond the door and he would have been soaked through.

"I paid the innkeeper's younger son to drive our car about ten kilometers from here and abandon it near a tourist spot where buses run regularly. If there's a second tracker on the car—and I'm sure now that there is—that's where they'll go. They'll think we've headed into the next city. That should throw them off long enough for us to acquire another means of transportation."

I cocked my head and continued to brush at imaginary raindrops on his chest. I liked the way the fabric lay against his collarbone. "So how are you planning to kill time until the rain stops?"

He lifted one shoulder in a shrug. "Sleep. Read. Any way I can."

"Any way?" I said softly. He couldn't miss my meaning. Under his sweater, Eric bulged in all the right places, and I already had the nervousness of our situation thrumming through my body. I would not be able to sleep tonight, no matter how demanding tomorrow might be.

"Benny's asleep in the next room," I hinted.

"He is."

Damn, but something had activated my kundalini. My life force sizzled through my body as if it started with my root chakra—or energy center—and rose through my core to my crown. Was that why my ears rang?

"The kid sleeps through anything," I told Eric. "He'll probably sleep until morning."

"Probably."

Most men would have had their clothes off by now. Eric seemed a little shy. All that Scorpio rising, I guessed. And I felt rather brazen. The likelihood of escaping the Adrianos, given all they knew about me, made me want to grab whatever passion life might offer before life itself ended. Their knowing how to manipulate Mother Nature did not bode well for me.

"I think, Eric, that I will...freshen up with a hot bath." The words came out low and guttural. He couldn't have missed my intentions, but he said nothing. If anything, he held his breath as if afraid to move. Instead he watched me turn and sashay into the bathroom, closing the door behind me but not all the way.

I stood in the middle of the tiny bathroom and stared at my reflection in the faded mirror. The florescent bulb over the mirror wavered, pronouncing the hollows under my eyes and making them look a bit deeper than usual. The bad lighting made my skin look sallow, lifeless, with a tint of blue, as if every drop of blood had been drained from me. It's not a bad look in some Goth clubs, but it's not the one I was going for tonight.

I peeled off my dress, first over my shoulders and then shoving it with my hands down over my hips, until it fell in a pool of brown velvet at my bare feet. Without looking down, I stepped out of the dress.

I thumbed the clasp of my black lace bra, and the forces of the earth claimed the scrap of cloth. And then I was naked.

I stepped into the claw-footed tub, drew the curtain around me and turned on the shower, which was cold instead of warm. I shivered in the flow and tried to let it wash away the weariness. Tired as I was, I was still wide-awake. There'd be no sleeping tonight. I wanted something.

I wanted…a moment of passion, of tenderness, of wild sex, of sweet kisses, of just being held and close to another human being, especially one who made my blood pump faster.

This man, Eric Cabordes, had traits I liked. Integrity, inventiveness, the fire in his eyes. And a tender spot for children. Always before, there'd been some hope of Matthew out there. Some hope that had held me back, that had kept me from giving myself wholly to a man—if I ever could. I'd given my heart long ago to Matthew with the hope that I'd have him back again someday.

Everything was different now. The nagging intuition had been confirmed for me. There'd be no more Matthew. He was gone. I'd had lovers since, but I'd never let myself care for any of them. Not really. A few had come close to worming their way into my heart, but then I'd simply left town, moved on, never looked back. I couldn't afford to. After all, Matthew might walk through that door any day, I'd told myself, or I might stumble upon him while away on an assignment. Somehow I'd find him again, I'd promised myself.

I'd lived for years as free as any woman could ever hope to live and still be in the Adriano's gilded cage. Traveling all over Europe and at times around the world. Living out of suitcases and airport lockers and crashing at the homes of acquaintances like Cat, who really didn't know me at all. Always on the move. Never settling down. Seeing everything in the world and being the gypsy I'd always dreamed of being and yet…always in limbo. Never willing to move on with my life and put down roots. The only thing that had held me to the planet was the memory of Lilah and the hope of finding Matthew again. My future, for years, had been entirely focused on my past.

Because of the past twenty-four hours, I was certain I could never go near Lilah. I'd just get her killed if I did. She thought I was dead, and maybe it wasn't so far-fetched for her to believe I was. Unless I was in the middle of a heist, I rarely felt alive anymore.

And as for Matthew, he was gone forever. And so at last I was free. Really free.

I let the chilled water splash against my face. Free. And I'd never felt so lonely in my life.

How much longer could I elude Simon and Caleb now that they knew my true identity? I sighed and shut off the water. I was as good as dead already. I wasn't free at all. But for tonight, if tonight was the last night of my world, then I needed something, wanted something, maybe passion, maybe hope. It was too late for anything more than that, anything more than just losing myself in the moment with Eric.

I dried my skin with a skimpy white towel and peeked through the door to Benny's room to make sure he was asleep and safe. I locked the door quietly between his room and the bathroom, then walked nervously to the door to Eric's room and opened it.

For a second I watched him on the bed, reclining, fully dressed, eyes closed, peaceful. The floor felt cold to my bare feet. Then he sensed me standing there and opened his eyes.

A very young woman might have played coy and let the towel drop with a well-placed "oops." Not me. I was grown-up enough to know exactly what I wanted and to let my partner know exactly what I wanted.

With one hand, I whipped off the towel and snapped it, then tossed it on the floor. I stood there and watched his reaction. He didn't move. Nothing but his eyes. He broke eye contact and let his gaze drift downward over my body. I didn't smile but rather cocked my head and waited. No doubt about it, the man definitely knew what I wanted—him.

"Do you, uh…"

I watched him swallow. I didn't move either, except to let my hands rake over my hips and drop loosely to my thighs. It was just enough movement to make him swallow again.

"Do you need some nightclothes? The innkeeper may have something for you."

"I don't need nightclothes," I whispered.

I ran one hand through my damp hair, then brought my palm down across my neck, over my breasts and stomach and back down to my hip. A calculated move, yes, but it warranted another swallow from a man who was otherwise calm, cool and collected unless he was screaming at me to drive faster. Let the twentysomethings be uncertain of their bodies and hide behind pillows and candlelight. Not me. I was old enough to know exactly what I liked and how I liked it—and that real men found my confidence sexy.

Though this one seemed to find it unnerving.

"It's been a long time," I confessed before I realized I'd said it. I didn't say *what* had been a long time.

"I doubt that."

"Whether you believe it doesn't matter." I slithered down on the bed beside him and slid one palm up the leg of his trousers. *Yes, nice and hard.* I smiled to myself. "I've got a little too much restless energy and not enough ways to tame it."

His breathing ratcheted up a notch. "You should cover up. We could have visitors at any moment. You'd be at a disadvantage." The words caught in his throat. He forced them out, his breaths coming faster as I slid my other hand under his sweater and found the buckle of his belt.

"True," I conceded. "Then again, maybe my nudity would disarm them." I kissed his hard belly just above the belt and continued to work the buckle. "But you've made your point. We should hurry. We might not have much time tonight." *And I'll never have as long as I'd want with this man.*

He shook his head. "The storm... We should stay on alert."

"I'm very alert, I promise you." I cupped my hand over his erection and fidgeted with the unrelenting buckle. "So are you."

"Aubrey...Simon's men..." He was resisting me, fighting me without moving. "This isn't a good time."

I dipped to kiss the deep-cut muscle that ran parallel to his pelvic bone as I tugged downward on the belt. Why was he being so stubborn? "There may not be another time. There may not be a tomorrow."

He caught my hands in his. "I have a little more faith than you do."

He pulled me up to him, dodged my lips and buried his mouth in the hollow under my chin. I squeezed my eyes shut and let the sensations claim me. He rolled over on top of me, one hand trapped under my back while the other yanked the buckle open. He kissed my neck and then licked at my nipple. I heard his zipper give way, and he pushed his trousers off with one hand.

God, I couldn't wait! This could very well be the last time a man ever touched me in passion, the last time I'd ever let my own fervor play out. I let my want tear through me and push every other worry aside so that there was nothing but this moment in time. I plunged my hand low on his back and grabbed his ass, pulling him to me.

"I want you inside me," I whispered raggedly into his ear. I opened my eyes long enough to see he was watching me, then shut them tightly again.

"Aubrey…"

He went stock-still. By the time I opened my eyes, he was sitting on the side of the bed, shaking his head and looking at me as if I'd just broken his heart.

"Eric?" I extended a hand to his thigh, but he pushed away from my touch.

"It doesn't matter how naked you are, Aubrey. All I see is armor."

"Wh…?" I gripped his shoulder, but he shook me off.

"It doesn't matter how wide you'd spread your legs for me. I'd never get inside you. You're the most emotionally isolated person I've ever met, and that includes stone-cold killers."

"What?" I sat up. He was rejecting me? But I needed him, needed his fire, needed to feel alive again. "You think I'm closed off?"

"I'm saying your armor is too thick for any man to get through. And you like it that way." He stared straight ahead as I cursed him.

"You used to be so alive, Aubrey."

"How would you know what I used to be? Oh, that's right. You work for the Adrianos. You know everything."

"I also work for Myrddin." He turned just his face to me. "I know everything about you that he knows and I know how you once were, how alive you used to be, what kind of destiny you had before you. But you've spent it all on the past. You might as well be dead already. You're already a ghost. You haven't let yourself feel anything in years."

Was that what was happening to me now? The tiles, the ringing ears? I was starting to *feel?* After all these years? Was that this strange electricity in my skin—the letting go of long-lost lovers and the acceptance that my future was something that would never work out as planned? I shook it away and snapped back to Eric instead.

"What would you know about feeling anything? You don't even have a life, Eric Cabordes. You say Benny's your life. Well, he's cute, but he's not yours. Why don't you go get yourself a real wife and kid?"

He flinched as if I'd slapped him, then rose and stalked to the bathroom. He slammed the door behind him, and a few seconds later I heard the shower running.

I sat there, seething. I glanced from the door of his room to the window. I should leave, I decided. Then and there. Not even wait for his return. Except that it was still storming outside, my clothes were in the bathroom with Eric, my key was inside my clothes in the bathroom with Eric and the artifacts were hidden under Benny's bed in the next room—and I absolutely would not sneak naked into a little boy's room.

Damn. What have I done? I ached all over, and in ways I didn't understand.

Twenty minutes later, the shower quieted and the door to the bathroom opened. Eric stepped out, damp and naked. He quickly wrapped a thin towel around his waist to cover up. Resolute and angry, I was still lying naked on his bed. He seemed genuinely surprised to see me there.

"I…I thought you might have gone."

"I considered it." I didn't move except to deepen my glare.

"Aubrey…" He crossed the small room to the bed and sat on the edge, shoulders hunched as he stared at the floor. "I've read every report that's ever been written about you. At least ten years' worth. I know everything there is to know. What you were like as a girl. As a young woman. Later, when Max lured you back to Europe and you gradually turned into one of them. But I like you."

"Yeah. I can tell."

"No." He frowned up at me. A droplet of water traced a path down his temple and fell to the mattress. "I mean it. I like you. I just don't like what you've become."

I flung myself upright and started to slip off the bed and leave him for certain this time, but his next words stopped me cold.

"I had a wife and child."

I settled back onto the bed. *Had. Had a wife and child.* Meaning *no more.*

"A wife and children, actually. One little girl and another on the way."

Girls. Eric had girls. He would understand the specialness of a daughter.

"What happened?" I finally asked.

"You're not the only one who lost everything in your life that was important to you." His breathing slowed. I could see the heaviness on his shoulders. "My wife… she was so full of life. Literally. She was pregnant with our second child. Eight months." His eyes misted over. "I had the most fantastic little girl. She would have been two years older than her sister."

"Eric—" I started to touch his shoulder, but he held up his hand to stop me.

"You think you have all these plans, Aubrey. My wife had plans, too. She had plans and she lived every moment. We both had plans. Plans for our daughters. Plans for growing old together. But life is what happens when you're making plans. And sometimes…sometimes the best things in life are the things you don't plan." He swallowed. "Like when I fell in love with my wife. And our daughters. Neither one of them was planned. Birth control failed every time. We used to say they were fated. Meant to be. But I guess they weren't meant to grow up."

"Eric." This time I managed to touch his shoulder before he shook me off. I felt the resistance in his muscles, but then he relaxed and permitted my fingers on his skin.

"It happened several years ago, right after I started working for Adriano Security. Josh had been my roommate in college, and we'd run into each other and he'd offered me a better job than the one I had heading up corporate surveillance for an American company in Paris. Overnight, we were best friends all over again. And then it happened."

I listened to every word. I had the feeling he didn't divulge his inner world very often.

"I was working a security detail for Josh. He and Pauline had had a big argument and she told him not to come home. He spent the night at my house to cool off. The Adrianos are routinely targets for kidnapping and assassinations. An assassin—he's dead now—went after Josh and thought my home...my family's home...was one of Josh's getaways. Caleb's usually the one with getaways, but that didn't matter. What mattered was that my home—and everyone in it—was blown to nothingness in an explosion. Josh and I weren't even there."

"Oh, Eric." I tried to hug him, but he pushed me aside. "Eric, I'm sorry."

"Sorry won't bring them back. Nothing will. For a long time, I didn't care if I lived or died. I had nothing left. Myrddin was the one who got through to me. That's when I started working for him. And my life started to mean something again. I can't change the way Simon is. Or Caleb. Josh, I don't know. Maybe there's hope for him. But maybe with the next generation. I decided I couldn't change the past but I could change the future. I could have a positive impact on that child. I'm hoping for something better with Benny, that maybe I can have an influence on him."

My throat ached. I could watch my daughter from afar. Eric couldn't. I'd spent all my years mourning a life that had been promised to me but never happened. My lover was gone. My daughter was lost to me. But at least she was still alive. As long as she was alive…as long as I was alive…

"As long as I'm alive, there's hope," I murmured.

"Aubrey? I don't want you just to be alive. I want you to live."

Chapter 12

I woke with a start, and it took a few seconds for me to realize where I was. I lifted my cheek from Eric's bare chest. The hair on my temple was damp from the heat. I blinked up at him. He was still asleep.

Somehow I must have fallen asleep, too. That in itself was unusual. The last time I'd awakened in the arms of a lover, I'd been eighteen and that man had been Matthew.

But Eric wasn't my lover.

No, waking with Matthew was not the last time I'd awakened in the arms of a lover but the last time I'd awakened in the arms of a man. Any man. I'd never let anyone get that close to me again.

Until now. Since Matthew, I'd never allowed a physical surrender to become an emotional one. My bond with Eric had never made it over the threshold of the sexual. This was different. Somewhere in the night, I'd been lulled into an emotional surrender. Or maybe I was so weary that I didn't care anymore. I'd been battling for much too long, not just the Adrianos and the rest of the world but my own heart, as well.

Eric slept. His face was peaceful, and I found myself jealous. He'd dealt with his losses far better than I had, turned them into something positive and honorable, into a reason to live. He'd found a way to transcend the Adriano madness, both by helping the women they were trying to destroy and by protecting and nurturing their future leader. One day, Benedict Adriano might become the good man the rest of the planet thought the Adrianos were.

Nothing could have shocked Eric Cabordes out of his complacency or changed the path of his life except for a drastic plunge into tragedy. Had his wife and daughters lived, he would never have gotten so close to the throne of the Adrianos. Myrddin most likely would have died in the vault. Benny would have fallen to his death from the towers in a dangerous game of hide-and-seek with his uncle Caleb. The Adrianos would have tracked me and recaptured me already. Simon would have had the incunable, a ready-made directory to the families of others of "my kind" who had for centuries been his sworn enemies.

Yet, in spite of Eric's resignation to destiny and all he'd done to change the world, I was certain that, given a choice between his heroics and a normal, ordinary life as a husband and father, he would not have embraced this future but would instead have embraced those he loved. How could anyone human willingly give up everything they loved for this kind of life?

I gently lifted off Eric. My skin was still damp in the valley between my breasts and down between my legs where our heat had merged, if not our bodies. I was careful not to wake him. The storm still raged outside.

I retraced my steps to the bathroom, freshened myself, then tugged on yesterday's clothes with the exception of the boots. Then I checked on Benny. He was still asleep. He hadn't moved. The kitten, however, had shifted from under his chin to the nape of his neck.

Next to Benny's bed, I lowered myself to the floor, taking great care to keep my right leg as straight as possible. After all the activity and pressure on my knee the day before, it was sorer than usual and disproportionately swollen. I cringed at the crackling sound it made every time I bent it. I rubbed a slow circle around it with my palm. Whether it was the warmth of my skin or the pressure of my touch that made it feel better, I wasn't sure.

The tiles under Benny's bed rang louder than before in my ears. I could barely hear anything for the sound of them, even the wind and rain outside. I shook my head, but nothing stopped it. The ringing was overpowering. I felt a little sick to my stomach.

What exactly were those stones made of? Kryptonite?

Their presence was overwhelming. They felt the way I imagined an anxiety attack might feel. Heart palpitations. Edginess. Nervousness. An overwhelming sense of doom. The strong sense that I was about to jump out of my skin. I couldn't stand being so close. The only time I'd ever felt this way before was the last week of that six-week workshop that had ended in me being smack-dab in the middle of a museum heist without meaning to be.

I retrieved the briefcase containing the manuscript from next to the tiles and then ambled back to Eric's room so I wouldn't have to listen to the constant drone. I situated myself on the floor in the corner of the room by a table lamp, my back against the wall so I could see all the entrances around me. I opened the stereolithographic case exactly as Simon had shown me.

With trembling fingers, I extracted the incunable. No doubt, it had touched many lives since the 1430s, mine among them. I turned the pages gingerly and began to translate the tiny script, vaguely aware of the passing hours.

Jeanne has worn a ring, according to the manuscript. A special ring. One passed down to her from her mother. One of two rings, each resembling a blue eye on a pink face. Isabelle, the twin, had put hers away and had never worn it because she'd become ill on every occasion she'd held the ring.

Jeanne had worn hers, though. Throughout her trial and tribulations, she'd worn her ring, up until near the end of her life. While away in battle, she'd looked at it often because it reminded her of her parents, particularly of her mother, with whom she must have been close. An Adriano who had been part of her inquisition had take the ring from her, leaving her with a bloody knuckle. After that, the voices and visions—the ones she'd heard and seen since she'd first worn the ring on her twelfth birthday, those voices and visions of the Archangel Micha-El—had vanished, and she'd thought she'd been forsaken.

Two eyes, I thought. *Two blue eyes.*

Leaving the manuscript wrapped and carefully set aside, I scrambled back into Benny's room. My knee clicked as I crouched on the floor by his bed and pulled back the tapestry. I fumbled through the tiles, hands trembling, until I located two of the tiniest tiles, each one a small blue eye against a background of pink rock. They were square and no bigger than my thumbnail. The perfect fit for a ring.

I pulled out several other tiles, ones I remembered from my own childhood…the baby's face…and pressed the tiny blue eyes into a perfect fit. My breath came out in ragged gasps. The missing bits of my heritage were falling together now, faster than I could absorb them.

Joan of Arc and her sister had been two of my kind. The sister must've been my ancestor. My grandmother had said we were descended from the womb of Joan of Arc, but now I understood. Not the womb inside Jeanne but the womb that had held her and her twin sister.

Isabelle had never worn her ring because it had made her ill, just as these tiles made me ill. And if old Max Adriano had read this manuscript and known that, then he would have known how to pick me out of a crowd of other Joan of Arc scholars. All he had to do was narrow down the number of potential candidates for Aubergine de Lune through our interests and expertise in medieval literature and then lure us to Europe. From there, all he had to do was get close enough to each candidate—or have someone else do his dirty work—with the tiles in his pocket and watch for a reaction.

I'd had the same reaction to the blue-eyed tiles as Isabelle had. They'd affected Jeanne differently. Not just visions, but visions and sound that she'd interpreted as St. Catherine, St. Margaret and Archangel Micha-El telling her to go forth and crown a king and save her people. They'd hidden the remainder of the tiles, the child's face and body, burying them at the church along with a sword that Jeanne would later carry into battle.

According to the incunable, generations of priestesses of the Great Mother had preceded the twins. Jeanne had interpreted the Great Mother as Mother Mary when she'd been told of her legacy on her twelfth birthday. She must have found the stories of warrior priestesses inspiring. Perhaps that's why she was so quick to go into battle for God when such a mission was usually reserved for grown men, not feisty teen girls.

Such priestesses and warrior women had existed from the very beginning of oral history, according to Isabelle's scribbling. Many had come from other races, other cultures, with even one mention of the priestess Dageniam and the Nolalaln priestesses of a country beyond the wide sea, a land Plato had referenced in his writings, a place Isabelle knew only as Atlantis. There had always been—and maybe there always would be—women dedicated to mothering the entire human race.

I placed the two small tiles in my left palm and stared at them. My ears rang fiercely, and my eyes, so close to the created stone ones, twitched and blurred. My stomach flip-flopped. I closed my palm over the tiles, but it did nothing to lessen the effect. My skin seemed to crawl with electricity, energy, some of which felt sexual but only in that life-force sort of way that perpetuates our species. Whatever this radiological electromagnetic energy was all about, the way it affected me and apparently some of my ancestors was through the auditory nerve and, to some degree, visually. Not to the extent of seeing archangels, fortunately.

The blue of the stone seemed both ice-cold and burning in my hand, yet I could not put it down. I pressed it hard against my chest and held it there. It didn't hurt exactly. It wasn't pain. It wasn't pleasure, either. But it was intense…so intense…I could barely breathe!

I held it over my heart. I couldn't move my hand. I knew a lot about stones, about their reputed physical and metaphysical properties. Characteristics of stones in the breastplates of ancient priestesses were recorded in many languages. Fascinating lore, but I was more of the scientific sort myself. What New Agers like Scarlet felt as "vibes" were really more likely to be geological frequencies or geopathic stress, similar to the upsetting pitch of elemental energies Eric had told me about earlier in the day when he had explained radiological electromagnetic energy fields. Even the woo-woo factor could be explained by science, just as refracted sunlight on atmospheric particles made the moon appear to have turned to blood in ancient times.

The blue stone with its waves of light and dark blue, almost like swells of the ocean or waves of clouds, was larimar, what some called the Dolphin Stone or the Atlantean Stone. Geologists and jewelers who aren't familiar with the legends refer to it as blue pectolite. Some texts say it comes from Atlantis, but the one place it's been found naturally in modern times is the Dominican Republic, where it's formed by an unusual combination of hot gases, crystallized minerals, volcanic heat and the sea. All four elements merged in one stone. Was that why it was supposedly so powerful? It was revered as a healing stone, one that, when touched, would sear like ice. And upon feeling that strange sensation, the recipient would know that the stone was actually healing rather than harming.

The pinkish-colored stone around it with tiny flecks of gray was most likely kunzite. The stone had been discovered in the early 1900s in California, but it had been found more recently in Afghanistan, Madagascar and Brazil. This stone was a bit pinker than the violet-hued kunzite I'd seen in museums and private collections. It, too, was said to be a healing stone, one that was particularly good for creating an active mind and yet releasing any worry. It was said to give its wearer a sense of serenity and peace of mind in the midst of trouble. Certainly that would have been handy for Joan of Arc on the battlefield.

The icy burning in my hand and chest faded. I pulled back my hand and opened my palm to look at the tiles. My ears still rang, but not as badly. It's said that the sensation of burning stops when the healing is done, but I had never believed it. I didn't feel any different, except that the ringing in my ears had all but stopped.

I could hear again. Benny's soft breathing. The kitten's purring. I could hear—I could *hear!*

The storm. The storm had stopped.

Chapter 13

My senses lit up and magnified exponentially. Everything around me was alive. The wooden chest with a lamp on top, the Madonna trivet beside it, the wall, the air itself. Everything was alive and connected. And I felt it all!

I pulled back the curtain in the corner of Benny's window. Nothing outside but darkness. No lights anywhere, but this room faced away from the monastery's entrance, so the lack of lights outside meant nothing.

Pocketing the room key, I tiptoed out into the corridor. When I was certain I was alone, I closed the door behind me. Holding my breath, letting it escape just a little at a time, I crept the length of the corridor and back to the reception area. The monastery was so quiet now that I could almost hear it holding its breath, too. The only sound was the slight thud of my bare feet on the stone.

Nothing moved. Nothing. Nothing but me.

The reception area was dark, but I knew something was wrong. I'm not psychic, but I've been in the business long enough to have a sixth sense about these things, and something about all that electromagnetic energy sizzling on my skin amplified every sense. My eyes adjusted to the light in the room. I could see the austere sofas in the sitting room and the desk where the innkeeper's son had urged me to enjoy my "husband" rather than keep *him* awake any longer with my nervous pacing. He'd left the emergency halogen lantern there. I made a mental note of it.

I glanced above the fireplace at the wall of weapons. None of them would hold up against a gun. Their presence reiterated how each successive era of military technology had rendered the previous generation's state-of-the-art weapons useless. The broadsword would be too heavy, I decided quickly. Almost as heavy as Benny. Even though I could wield the blade in a pinch, I still had the disadvantage of an opponent who might be twice my size. I really didn't know what was out there. Or who. Or how many.

I skulked back to the window and peered out as discreetly as possible. Everything outside was still, uncannily still. Security lights outside blinked off, one by one by one.

They were here. My senses screamed it. They'd found us. Could I make it back to the room in time to alert Eric? Or was it better to dispatch them myself and buy Eric some time to hide the artifacts and escape with Benny?

A light in the corridor blinked off, and I was left in total darkness. Night-vision goggles. That's what they were using. They were trying to put me at the disadvantage of being in the dark while they could see me in a sickly, shimmering green. I'd initially experimented with NVGs when I'd first become affiliated with the Adrianos, back when I was still being trained to be the drone of one of their acquisition specialists, before I even knew who the Adrianos were.

Yeah. Back when I'd thought they were so nice to give me work and a new life. What a gullible fool I'd been!

The memory came back like a bolt of lightning. The electromagnetic energy from the tiles had a way of magnifying not just my senses but my memory, as well. Without wanting to be, I was suddenly back there again, ten years ago, the third turning point in my life.

I'd been set up, caught red-handed with a museum artifact in my hand that I didn't know was an artifact. I'd been so naive, so willing to help a stranger who'd asked me to hold his backpack while he chased down his runaway toddler outside a museum. Then I'd been in trouble, deep trouble, and the police officials who'd tried to arrest me hadn't believed me. They'd told me I'd rot in jail for the rest of my life. They'd found drugs in the backpack, too. They'd asked too many questions about whether I had any children or a husband, and their insistence had raised my fears, all the way back to Matthew telling me I wasn't safe and that the police could be bought. I'd refused to give them my name or my passport. One of the men struck me across the cheek.

I'd known then that the situation would not get better and I'd decided then to run.

I shook off the memory and pressed my back against the wall of the reception area as I listened for footfalls. I needed to concentrate, but so much had happened so quickly! I wasn't sure who was the enemy and who wasn't. Maybe I never had been, not even in the beginning of my life of crime.

Had the police officials really been police at all or just part of the setup to make me believe I had no choice but to go with Ricardo, the man who'd rescued me, the same one who'd handed me the backpack, the one who'd later become my trainer in the world of art theft, the one who'd turned me into a thief for real?

He'd given me my new name, too. He'd said Max Adriano had seen me from a distance, admiring the moon as if I were wishing to be that far away, and he'd called me Dr. Ginny Moon. I'd never met Max or I might have been nervous about how similar the name was to my birth name, Aubergine de Lune.

I remembered the night I'd wept under that full moon for the daughter I'd left behind. My emotions had been closely tied to that moon and the notion that somewhere my Lilah might be looking up at the same moon and wishing for me to come home in spite of the news she'd just received that her mother had been killed in a train accident somewhere in Europe.

I heard the snap of something outside. A twig? A leaf? I was here with antique weapons good for little more than decoration, and they were waiting for me out there with access to the most advanced modern weapons available to the Adrianos and most small governments.

Back when I'd first learned about stealth technology, the NVGs had been huge, experimental, so heavy that I'd needed both hands to lift them to my face. Technology had changed a lot even in that short time. Now NVGs were easily strapped onto the forehead with such little weight that the wearer barely nodded under their influence. They didn't create light where there was none but if there was the slightest bit of illumination, even star shine, they amplified the light into an eerie view out of what seemed to be utter darkness. And if there was too much light…

I pulled down an eighteenth-century French épée from the wall, its long double-edged blade still sheathed in a steel guard attached to an ornate corded belt. I gripped the copper-wrapped hilt in one fist and extended the weapon to test its range. It almost tripled my reach.

Tucking the épée under one arm, I felt my way along the wall until my hands tingled all over. Energy. Old energy. Lifetimes ago, but still strong, like a memory left behind on the weapons. I found the crossbow and pulled it down, along with one tiny iron arrow. I pricked my finger while loading it and was thankful I'd had a tetanus shot after a job in the States last spring. No telling where that arrow had been, though I doubted it had been used for hunting stags.

Careful not to drop my makeshift arsenal, I plucked the very modern halogen lantern from the reception desk. A slight sound caught my attention, like a cat landing on the roof. I recognized it. I'd heard my own feet land on many a rooftop in the same way, but my hearing was better than ever tonight and buzzing with sensation. It was the kind of sound that most people would never notice or, if they did, would think was a creak in the roof or perhaps a bird. But I was good at landing quietly on my feet. So was whoever the Adrianos had sent after me.

Feeling my way along the corridor walls, I found a side exit and squeezed through the door. The outside air was damp and unseasonably chilled. Immediately my bare toes sank into mud from the constant pounding of rain for the past twelve hours. Its coolness sent a dull ache up my legs and into my knee. The sky was clear, though. Not a cloud in it or the moon, but there were enough stars to make a night-vision-goggle aficionado bubbly with joy.

I studied the darkness against the stars and waited, separating myself enough from the building so that I might see any shadows on the roof. There!

I flung the halogen lantern around, flicking it on as I did, aiming it directly for the silhouette on the roof. The powerful beam caught one shadow by surprise—a man in all black: black boots, black trousers, black sweater, black mask. A halogen beam in the eyes is bad enough, but with NVGs on?

"Amplify that," I muttered under my breath.

I saw the weapon in his hand, but his reflexes got the better of him. He threw one arm over his face and jerked the headpiece off, blinking into the halogen beam as if he'd just seen his maker. *Not yet, anyway.*

The shadow of another man moved behind him, but I could get only one. I raised the crossbow and took aim. This time he fell to the roof with a heavier thud.

The shadow beside him jerked sideways. Another man in solid black. In the beam of my lantern, he whipped off his NVG headpiece and took aim at me. I dropped the lantern and skidded sideways. I didn't hear the report of his weapon, but I heard his bullet whiz past me, right above the lantern. I left the lamp in the grass, its beam skittering across the stone pathway as I somersaulted to the stone column close to the entrance. Surrounded by stone, I knew the second man could not afford the ricochet.

What was I doing? It was all about instinct. I'd never used weapons like this before, yet there was an energy around them that I could feel, like memories attached to them, and I simply obeyed where they led.

I pulled the épée from its sheath and touched one edge of the double blade, careful not to cut myself. I flattened my body against the column and waited for the second man to come down. Under other circumstances, I might have vaulted onto the roof and fought him there, but my knee hated inclines. Level ground would at least not put me at a disadvantage.

Since I'd held the larimar eyes to my chest, my senses had stayed alive and magnified, more so than they did from my usual adrenaline rush during a heist. I felt it coming before I could react.

Something hard and muscled caught my shoulder. Before I could spin around, his other arm bore hard against my throat, pulling me back, choking me. I swatted at him with the épée, but the blade was too long. I couldn't get a good angle! I choked and sputtered and fought the glimmer of gray in my vision. He brought back memories of Caleb's hands on my throat. This man wasn't Caleb. He was shorter, leaner, younger, but just as ruthless.

The gray in my vision grew denser. I'd pass out soon. I might never wake. Or, if I did, I might find myself tied to Caleb's bed.

I grabbed the hilt of the épée, its decorative pummel hard against my wrist. I aimed the blade directly in front of me. With every ounce of strength I could muster, I slammed the blade against the stone column. As any good swordsman knows—and certainly any good art thief—épée blades don't last forever, especially one this old and this pitted. The blade shattered halfway down its length. I flipped the hilt in my hand, bringing the blade parallel to my forearm, and jabbed it back hard behind me. I felt the resistance when it found its target. I urged the blade deeper, heard a grunt of surprise, and then the arm released. I fell forward onto the grass, sucking in oxygen, heaving, and then struggling back to my feet.

I frowned down at the man on the ground. A pair of sightless eyes stared back at me from underneath the black ski mask.

I heard the motion above me, and before I could move, the first assassin tumbled from the roof onto the ground and fell at the edge of the darkness. Dead. My crossbow's arrow was still lodged in his chest.

I had not killed often. Only a few times. The first time had been seconds after a rival thief had murdered an English professor friend of mine, Drusilla St. Augustine, over a manuscript in Madrid, then turned his knife toward me. In my fury, I'd gained the upper hand and stabbed him through the heart and then I'd fled the burning building with the artifact.

That first time had been the worst, but every time had been in self-defense. Certain old manuscripts, particularly those related to the occult, talk of claiming the power of your enemies as their souls rush out of their bodies at the moment of death. Maybe it was the adrenaline rush of having survived. It was always just enough to get me through the moment so I wouldn't think too much about what I'd done.

I'd think about it later, though. Later, when I was safe and everything was quiet. Then, when I was all alone, my knees pulled up to my chin and my arms wrapped around my knees, I would rock and keen and cry for what I'd done. Later. Not now.

In the darkness, I heard nothing else. Not even the sound of night birds. Everything was quiet. Too quiet. That meant something else was on the prowl besides me.

I retrieved the lantern, but before I turned it off, I noticed the sliver of light across the grounds to the gray BMW parked haphazardly behind some shrubbery. The three men who'd been tailing us, two of whom had been dispatched at my feet. The third?

Eric had hidden the rented Mercedes to throw them off, yet if there'd been another tracker on the automobile, it should have led them in the opposite direction. They would never have come here. That meant that there was a tracker either on me or on Eric…or on Benny!

I bolted back into the building the way I'd come, hauling the bright lantern with me and running on bare wet tiptoes down the corridor. Benny. God, that sweet little boy! Not just the hope for the future of the Adrianos but for anyone dealing with the Adrianos. My knee screamed. I couldn't get to him quickly enough! That little boy had a destiny, the kind that would affect thousands of lives. A true Indigo Child, as the New Agers called them. A future king.

When I rounded the corner, I heard the hum of the tiles. Or maybe I just felt them. The ringing in my ears meant I was close. Almost like a silent alarm. As I reached the rooms, I saw that the corridor doors to both Eric's room and mine were still closed. I caught my breath and leaned against the wall.

The metal key felt warm in my hand as I fished it from my pocket. I glanced up and down the corridor again as I put the metal in the lock and twisted. I cracked the door just enough to see Benny snuggled up with his kitten and facing the wall. His chest rose and fell in tender dreams. He was asleep. Our little prince was still okay.

I pushed through the door, closing and locking it behind me, then turned around. I gasped. A man in black—the last of the trio of assassins—stood between Benny and me.

With his little finger, he caught the hem of his ski mask under his chin and yanked off his camouflage. It landed on the floor at my bare feet. I didn't know him. It was a calculated move to let me know he had no fear of my seeing his face. He grinned at me…then Benny… then me…then Benny. He had a gun in the holster under his left arm and a knife in his right hand.

"Put down the blade," I whispered. I couldn't call to Eric without startling the boy. I didn't want to wake Benny. I didn't want him to see anything violent. Children shouldn't have to witness such things, not even little Adriano boys. "Let's take this outside," I whispered.

Where the hell is Eric? Then my heart skipped a beat. What if the assassin had already found Eric, asleep in the next room? He could have killed the boy's bodyguard first with a plan to dispose of the child afterward. But the assassin wasn't just between Benny and me. He was also between Eric and me. I wanted Benny to stay asleep. If he woke, a panicked child would be a volatile variable I didn't want to deal with.

"Why would I want to take this outside?" The man took a step closer to Benny. He kept his voice as low as mine.

In the periphery of my vision, in the outer circle of the lantern's light, the kitchen knife above the doorway gleamed like a beacon. Purposely I didn't look directly at it. I knew better than to do anything to call attention to the weapon before I leaped for it. Other than that, the quickest weapon was the lantern in my grip. If it didn't kill him, it still would make a dent in his skull.

I had to get this assassin away from Benny. Any way I could.

"You want a piece of me?" I offered. "Come on. We'll take it outside."

He twisted his jaw to one side. "I'll get a piece of you when you're dead." He took another step toward Benny.

"Get away from him!" I ordered. Another damned necrophiliac thug!

The assassin shook his head. "I have orders to kill you both. Him first. Then you."

"That's not going to happen." I took a step toward him, another step closer to both the blade in his hand and the one I'd left in the wall just above his head.

"It's too bad you eluded us for so long. Caleb said the Duke was willing to make you a trade. Now you're too late."

He fingered a cell phone at his belt. An Adriano cell phone, no doubt. Probably sending every word of our conversation direct to the palazzo's security center. To Caleb. Yes, to Caleb! Simon would never have sent an assassin to kill the Adriano heir. But Caleb would have. These men worked for Caleb, not for Simon.

"What would Simon have to trade? I have the tiles, I have the manuscript and I have his grandson. Looks like I'm the one with the leverage."

The man turned on his heels, grinning in the halogen light. I saw the flash of steel toward Benny's bed. The whoosh of a bullet disguised by a silencer split the air. The man froze, then crumpled to the ground. The knife fell from his hand.

Eric appeared in the doorway exactly as I'd left him—without a stitch on. He held out a gun in his extended hand. He slanted a quick glance in my direction. "Are you all right?" he whispered.

I blinked at his nakedness. The hardness of his chest, over his abs, all the way down to a muscle that dipped low on his groin. Weapon in his hand. And not looking the least bit fazed. It was a picture I intended to hold in my mind for the rest of my life.

"Never better," I murmured so softly that not even an Adriano could hear it.

Eric stalked over to the assassin on the floor and rolled him over onto his back. The man wasn't dead. He pressed his left fist hard against the growing dampness on his black shirt. A trickle of blood escaped with a cough.

Eric put his finger to his lips and nodded at the cell phone. He kicked at it and it fell off the man's waist. Eric stepped on it with one bare foot, bearing down his full weight on it and twisting his heel until the phone crunched. As he stepped off it, he kicked it across the room. Bits of electronics scattered on the wooden floor.

Eric shrugged. "They don't make cell phones like they used to."

The assassin squinted up at Eric. "Cabordes… I should have known. When they find out you're helping her, the Duke will have your heart cut out!"

"Sorry. Already had my heart cut out on behalf of the Adriano family."

"Eric?" I motioned to get his attention. "Your cover's been blown."

He shook his head. "No. Not yet, anyway. This man's certainly not going to tell anyone."

Benny mumbled something in his sleep, a waking sound as if he'd incorporated any sounds he'd heard into a bad dream. I left the lantern on the floor and tiptoed closer to him. I sat on the corner of his bed and brushed my fingers over his hair the way I used to do Lilah's. He waved away my touch as if he either wasn't used to the gesture or had been trained to find it uncomfortable.

"Shhh, sweetie. It's okay. You go back to sleep."

His sleepy eyes blinked open just enough to see my fingers over his face as I traced his delicate eyebrows with a featherlight touch. "You're bleeding," he said softly. He pointed to my finger where I'd cut myself on the iron crossbow arrow.

"Yes, honey. That's what happens when you play with sharp things." I kissed his cheek. "Now you go back to sleep and don't wake your kitten."

He nodded, hugged a tolerant kitten momentarily harder, then relaxed back into sleep. For that, I was grateful.

The assassin coughed again. He made a funny sound like a cross between a gurgle and a laugh. "You can't get away from the Adrianos, bitch. As long as you're alive, they will hunt you. Sooner or later, they will find you."

He was right. I glanced up at Eric. "There's another tracker on us. It's not in the car. It's on one of us."

The assassin's right hand moved. He grasped the gun in his holster and swung the weapon toward Benny. Without thinking, I threw myself over the child.

The bullet sliced through the air. I waited a split second that seemed forever. Lilah would never know, never know me, never know what I'd done, either the good or the bad.

No. Not a bullet. I hadn't been hit. Tentatively I looked up.

Eric stood over the man, his arm still extended, still in play. The handle of the kitchen knife wobbled in the man's chest next to his heart.

I expelled a ragged breath and pulled myself off Benny, who merely flung an annoyed hand at me for disturbing his sleep. I sat up, stiff with tension.

The assassin steadied his gaze on me. It took all his effort to focus on my face. Words tumbled out of his mouth. Raw, venomous. Stabbing to my core. Then the light went out in his eyes, long after his words hung in the air.

"The Duke…has…your daughter."

Chapter 14

Eric, completely naked, strolled around me and picked up a blanket off the pallet I'd made earlier for Benny. He covered the body on the floor, careful to hide anything that might frighten the child when he woke.

Me? I sat on the corner of Benny's bed and stared at the floor. Eric was talking, something about going outside to take care of the other two assassins who'd sure be right behind this one.

"Been there, done that," I whispered. Not even an armed and naked Eric could raise my spirits.

Eric raised an eyebrow, then nodded approvingly. "My research had indicated you might be able to take care of yourself without my help." He thumbed his hand at the lump under the blanket. "Hope you still don't have trouble accepting help from others, me included."

He meant it as comic relief, but I simply shook my head. "I don't mind." I didn't look at him. I felt myself sinking into an abyss. That sense of doom. And it wasn't from the high vibrations of the tiles under the bed.

"Come," Eric said. "Caleb will know where his men are. We can't stay here. We need to get moving. Now." He stalked back into the bathroom and dressed.

When he returned, I hadn't bothered to get Benny dressed or make any preparations of my own. I sat in the same position as when he'd left.

"Aubrey." I vaguely heard him but didn't respond. "Aubrey," he said urgently. "We have to get out of here."

I shook my head. It was no use. I had lost.

"My cover's still safe. When we find that second tracker, you'll be free to go to France to your friend Catrina. Take the tiles and the manuscript. Myrddin and the others will contact her soon enough. I'll spend the day on the coast with Benny and I'll take him back when I know for certain that his father is at the palazzo and the boy will be safe from his uncle. Benny will—" He thought I wasn't listening. "Aubrey? Aubrey, what's wrong?"

I didn't move. Nothing but my eyes. "That man." I made an abrupt gesture at the lumpy blanket on the floor. "He said Simon has my daughter."

"So?" Eric shrugged. "You don't have a daughter."

"Yeah…I *do*."

"What?" Eric froze. "No. You don't."

"Eric…Eric, it's true."

"That's not what Myrddin told me. He had Max's records on you. I've seen them myself. There was nothing in there about a daughter. Nothing, I'm telling you!" He clenched his jaws as if he'd been lied to and didn't care for it.

"Myrddin didn't know. Neither did Max."

"Myrddin told me that you and Matthew Burns, uh…" He stumbled for the right words. "That Burns impregnated you. But you miscarried before you left Britain. You lost your baby."

"No. Not then. I didn't lose my baby until eleven years later when I came back to France."

Realization shone in his eyes. He nodded. "The setup. And you couldn't go back. How…how old is she now?"

"She's in college."

My eyes burned. I'd never talked about Lilah, not since I'd left the States, not since I'd left her behind. I'd never talked about her. Not to anyone. Not to Catrina. Not to Therese. Not to any of the female friends who'd disappeared. Not to my colleagues in the underworld of art. Not to a lover. Not to anyone. Not even to the private investigator who sent me photographs of her every month and a short report on her activities. I'd taken great care to contact the P.I. through a third party so there'd be no chance of interception.

I'd always wanted to talk about her. I wanted to tell someone how special she was and how much I loved her. I wanted to be like any other proud mother of a beautiful, smart, savvy, sassy, sweet, wonderful daughter who'd grown into the kind of woman I'd always hoped she'd be. I'd wanted to tell the world about the flesh-and-blood legacy of hope and love I'd created with my mysterious Matthew. But I'd had to stay silent all these years. I'd never even spoken her name aloud.

"Lilah." Tears ran down my cheeks. I didn't wipe them away. "Lilah," I said louder, but it came out as a sob. The syllables stuck in my throat and fell off my lips like a prayer to an ancient goddess. *"Lilah."*

Eric opened his mouth to say something, but nothing came out. For all the weapons in his arsenal, he didn't seem to have anything effective against tears. Finally he asked, "How did you keep her a secret for all these years?"

"When I was pregnant, Matthew smuggled me into the Highlands. He said he had to get me out of the country and we had to hide the baby or they'd kill us. He never said who 'they' were. But it didn't matter to me. I was young and I believed him. Matthew, he was young, too, but he was a good man. Barely older than Lilah is now."

Eric nodded. "He was working for Max, but he was working for others like you, too. That's what Myrddin told me. Matthew knew who you were before he ever met you. They sent him to kill you, but he saved you. It wasn't just because he fell in love with you. He was probably in love with you before he ever laid eyes on you. Maybe that's why he volunteered to work so closely with the Adrianos. Others like you were trying to reconnect and build a force against Max. Some of them had sons who infiltrated Max's organization."

"You?" I asked.

"No. Not me. But Myrddin's trying now to rally women like you. Warriors at heart. It's been tried many times over the past fifteen hundred years."

"And Matthew tried, too." I backhanded my tears and then sniffed them away.

"Yes. Myrddin once told me that Matthew Burns knew Max was onto him. That's why he went back. To buy you time. So you could safely get out of Europe. He thought he'd be able to join you. At least, it appears that he did."

I sighed. "I was young then. Just a hopeless romantic. I'd thought he'd come to the States after me. He never showed up at our rendezvous point. He never contacted me. Just vanished from the face of the earth. I waited for a few months until I ran out of money." I twisted my hands in my lap. "I found a relative in the States, though. Not a blood relative. She was married one time to my mother's cousin. She took me in and I started a new life under the name of Lauren Hartford, a name I'd found on a tombstone in a little town in North Carolina. My mother's cousin knew some people…shady people…who were able to forge some papers under my new name. I was eighteen and about six months pregnant."

"And afraid," Eric added.

"My daughter was born, and I kept looking for Matthew, but I never heard from him. We were together for such a short period of time. I'm not sure how much of it was a lie or a cover story. I'm not sure I even knew the real Matthew, but I always imagined the kind of husband he would have made for me. And what a great father he would have been. He used to tell me about how he'd told his baby sister, Nonny, bedtime stories when he'd been a teen. Stories about warrior women. That's what he used to tell her. I didn't know he was talking about my ancestors…or his. I just thought they were stories."

"They're not stories. They're real."

"As real as Jeanne…Joan of Arc. I read the rest of Isabelle's manuscript while you were sleeping."

"You mean Joan of Arc's manuscript."

"No. It wasn't written by Jeanne. The incunable was written by her sister. It's an indictment against the Adrianos, about how they manipulated the pope, countries, kingdoms. Myrddin was right—my daughter is from the double bloodline, and my half of that bloodline dates back to Joan of Arc's mother and before."

Eric sighed. "That makes her all that much more valuable to Simon."

"But, Eric, I don't understand how they would know about Lilah. I was so careful. Her birth certificate has my guardian's name on it as her mother. There is nothing to do with Lilah that has my name on it. There's nothing that has my claim on her. I raised her as my daughter, yes, but there's nothing in writing anywhere that says I have a daughter."

Eric sat down on the bed beside me. He took my hand and squeezed it. Words between us weren't important. The gesture let me know he cared. He lost himself deep in thought, then jerked his head up. "Therese!" He nodded to himself and then to me.

"That's how Simon found out who you were before. About your identity between the time you were Aubrey de Lune and the time you became Dr. Moon. The patriarch—Max—he was the one who set you up. He kept you on a leash all these years but never told Simon." He lowered his voice in an aside. "Adriano men don't always trust their sons. More than once, a son has turned against his father or brother if it meant taking control of the family dynasty."

I folded my hand over Eric's. I let him soothe the skin on the back of my hand with his thumb. I let myself take comfort in his touch.

"Max never told Simon who you really were. Simon found out only a few months ago, right before you went to San Francisco for the manuscript."

"Therese?" I remembered Max's secretary. I'd met her a couple of times in Paris and once in Athens when she'd made personal deliveries to me, usually instructions on a job Simon wanted me to do. Always something that was too problematic to be delivered electronically, even with Pretty Good Privacy—or PGP—protocols to safeguard the information. In spite of advances in technology, some things still didn't lend themselves well to encryption.

Therese had been young and pretty, in her mid-twenties. She was more of a courier, really, than a secretary, and I had no doubt that she could use her looks to slip through the tightest of security. Therese and I had become friendly, if not friends, and had shared lunch on several occasions. After Max was hospitalized—Therese had told me he'd actually died and Eric had confirmed it—Therese had been moved to a different position within the organization. I hadn't seen her since.

"A few months ago, Therese asked Simon what to do with Max's files on Aubrey de Lune as well as some other women. He'd left some files with Therese instead of in his office. Therese didn't know Max hadn't intended for the files to go to Simon. Max had been shot. He'd retired from the family business, so it made sense that all his personal files would go to Simon. Myrddin saw those files years ago and recreated some of them from memory. He tried to keep those files out of Simon's hands, but he failed."

"That's how Myrddin knew who I really was?"

"Yes. That's how Myrddin knew all about you. And how I knew all about you. And eventually how Simon knew all about you. But, Aubrey, there was nothing in those files about a child born to you. Nothing at all to indicate you and Matthew ever had a daughter. So if you took great care in hiding her as you say you did, I don't know how Simon would have found her. He didn't find her through those files. I know that. I've seen copies of them myself." He slipped an arm around my shoulder. "They can't possibly have your daughter."

"I can't take that chance."

"It's probably a bluff."

"Maybe. But I still can't take that chance. We have to go back."

"What about the tiles? The manuscript? You're just going to march back to the palazzo and hand those over?"

"No." I shook my head. "Never. But I'll hand myself over if I can set my daughter free."

"Aubrey! Think about it!" He grabbed my shoulders and bent into my face. "You don't want to go back there."

"No, I don't *want* to go back. But I don't have a choice."

"You always have a choice, Aubrey. Always. Life is always about the choices you make." He let go of my shoulders. He sounded as if he was channeling Myrddin. "Sometimes they're good, sometimes they're bad. But you do have choices."

"Eric, if Simon has my daughter and I don't do something about it, then I could not live with that choice. I want nothing more than to get as far away from life with the Adrianos as I can get, but my top priority is and always will be my daughter's safety."

He clamped his mouth shut and thought for a second. Then he nodded. "I know. I do, Aubrey. I know. If I were in your position, I'd do the same thing. I…I never had the choice. The choice was made for me. But, Aubrey, if Simon gets that manuscript and those tiles, do you realize how many people might die?"

I wanted to say I didn't care, that I cared only about Lilah. But I couldn't. Not honestly.

"You know," I said, "Joan of Arc had a secret weapon. And I don't mean the tile ring she wore. She had a sister. A twin. An identical twin."

"You told me about the sister." He shrugged. "I don't remember reading about her."

"You wouldn't have. That's because when she was captured, part of her punishment was that no one would ever speak her name or write it. Years after Jeanne was burned at the stake and Isabelle escaped, Isabelle lived in seclusion, courtesy of some priests who hid her from the Adrianos. Her punishment from the Church was that 'her name be obliterated from the annals of man.' The pope that the Adrianos installed decreed that no one would ever utter her name. Not a scribe, not a husband, not a child. The only one who could was her. So she learned to write. And she, not Joan of Arc, is the one who wrote this manuscript."

"An identical twin?" Eric raised an eyebrow. "Useful, I suppose."

"Very. She's the one who, when Jeanne was wounded on the battlefield, stood in Jeanne's place, inspiring the troops so that they thought Jeanne was invincible. She was taken, too, tortured like Jeanne, but she escaped when she jumped from a three-story window. Jeanne wasn't so lucky. The inquisitors took their rings, the ones with bits of the tiles in them. Isabelle had given her ring to Jeanne to wear, so both rings were confiscated." I motioned to the mosaic under the bed, then flipped my hand in a grand gesture at the tiny tiles on the chest by Benny's bed. "The eyes of the child."

Eric picked up one of the eye-shaped tiles and held it up to the halogen light to get a better look.

"This incunable," I continued, "this manuscript isn't so much about Joan of Arc but an indictment against Simon's ancestors. Could you imagine if the press got a copy of it? It tells how the Adrianos manipulated popes and fought against a line of strong women that Isabelle and Jeanne were descended from." I frowned. "That I'm descended from. That

Lilah is descended from. That's why they had to keep it hidden. This manuscript was written in an attempt to get the word out to others of their kind. To pull them together so others would know what the Adrianos of their time had done. To get others to unite with them against the Adriano front and bring them down. Isabelle put the family crests in the margins, but instead of being used to bring together these women, the incunable was used to hunt them down and destroy them.

"It's said," I added, "that Joan of Arc was discovered, alive and well, several years after she was burned at the stake. That a woman came back claiming to be her. Her brothers recognized her as their sister. Everyone who'd fought beside her recognized her as Jeanne. The king denied it. The pope denied. Officially she was declared an impostor. Even fairy tales said that the only remains of Jeanne's body was the still beating heart they discovered in the ashes. All kinds of legends sprang up. But the best legend of all-and the truth of it all—no one ever knew. It was all buried right here." I kicked my foot in the direction of the briefcase. "Right here in this manuscript. All of it. That's why this book is so important to the Adrianos. They don't want this news to get out."

"That and the possibility of using it to track down their enemies."

"The woman they'd claimed was an impostor was the real thing, Eric. Well, half of the real thing. The woman who was on the battlefield when Jeanne was injured was the impostor. No one was the wiser and the stunt kept the battle going. Maybe we should take a lesson from her. From Jeanne…and Isabelle."

Eric fidgeted with one of the child's-eye tiles. If his ears rang or he felt sick, he didn't show it. He walked over to the bits of cell phone on the floor and knelt over the pieces. He ran the tile over the bits. He shook his head and looked up. "I don't understand. What does Joan of Arc's twin have to do with you going back to the palazzo and getting yourself killed?"

"I'm going to make a trade with Simon. My daughter for me. Me and the tiles. And the book. The manuscript will be easy enough to hide, at least for as long as it takes to get my daughter to safety. I won't hand over the real thing. I'll hand over impostors."

I watched as Eric held the tile a hand's width from his arm, almost as if he were scanning his whole body with it. He did the same over his chest, his waist, his hips, over the bulge in his trousers. Down each leg. Around his boots.

"Continue," he urged. "I'm listening."

"The manuscript will be easy enough to provide an impostor for. Newspaper wrapped in a cloth, then placed inside the stereolithographic case and snapped shut. Then put inside the briefcase. They'd have to get through several layers before they'd know if it is or isn't the manuscript."

Eric held the tile over my head and scanned back and forth around my face. I shooed him away.

"What are you doing?"

"Checking for bugs. There's a tracker on one of us. I'm betting it's you."

I stood up and held my arms out to either side so he could hold the tile close to my skin, along the lines of my body. He tested me as thoroughly as an airport security guard with a metal-detecting wand.

"We won't be able to duplicate the tiles," he reminded me. "Not like your mother did. We'd need plaster and gemstones. Several days of time you don't have."

"I don't intend to duplicate them. I want only to provide an impostor that will slow Simon down and buy me some time."

He followed the lines of my velvet dress, then bent to his knees and skimmed the child's-eye tile over my bare legs and muddy feet. Something about him kneeling in front of me and tilting his chin upward to me gripped my throat. I liked this man. I really liked him.

I didn't know much about him—not his favorite color or his shoe size or his mother's name—but I knew the really important things. Like why he wanted to live when he'd lost everything to live for. Like how he planned to leave his mark on the world. Like how his palm curved against the back of my head when he stroked my hair when he thought I was asleep. I wanted more of those moments. More of him.

"You're clear," he said, rising to his feet.

I picked up one of the trivets from the night table beside Benny's bed and held it up to the light. The red Mother Mary glimmered in the halogen beam. "See? Tiles."

Eric eyed me doubtfully. "Simon will know the difference."

"As long as he doesn't know the difference immediately. I need the weight and the appearance. Rocks and tile. That will suffice."

Eric smiled, but it didn't quite reach his eyes. "You always have a plan, don't you, Aubrey de Lune?"

"You don't approve." A statement of fact, not an expectation.

"I have a plan of my own," he said, "but let's hope I don't need it."

He bent over Benny's bed and skimmed the boy's shoulder and chest. He moved up closer to the child's head, and the tiny tile in Eric's fingertips shimmered.

I blinked. Had I seen it correctly? "What was that?" The tile had just changed from pink and blue to gray and black, then back to its original color.

Eric sighed. "I think we just found the other tracking device." He skimmed Benny's jawline, and the tile changed hue again. "It's in his tooth. The tracker must be in one of his fillings." Eric cursed under his breath. "Josh never told me. I guess it was a safeguard against even me."

"The tile…the way it changed."

"Radiological electromagnetic energy field. It can detect frequencies. More important, it can amplify communication signals. As long as Benny was in your rental car, the tiles amplified his tracking signal's location."

"But we lost the three men in the BMW yesterday. For a while, at least."

"The storm. That was meant to slow us down. We made it here and Benny got separated from the tiles. The signal was too weak then."

Yes. Benny had spent the afternoon far from the tiles,

playing with the innkeeper's grandson and the kittens elsewhere in the cluster of old monastic buildings.

"And then," I continued for Eric, "Benny went to sleep literally atop the tiles and boosted the transmission of his signal. So they knew exactly where to look for us."

Eric and I stared at each other. We both knew what that meant. We needed to find a safe place for the tiles—one as far away from Benny as possible—so we could reach the palazzo before the Adrianos' men found us again.

Chapter 15

Twelve hours later, we were on our way back to the palazzo. Eric drove while I wrung my hands. We'd had a busy morning and afternoon, and even with all the exhaustion, my nerves were raw and inflamed.

"Pull over." I felt sick, so sick.

"We're almost there," Eric said.

"I know. Pull over. I need air and I need it now."

He obeyed, steering the Volkswagen sedan we'd borrowed from the innkeeper after the old man had seen the bodies of the three assassins and had understood how important it was to get Benny safely to his father. Benny, headphones glued to his ears, sat quietly in the backseat, legs swinging as he stared out the window, oblivious to the tremors I felt in my stomach.

Eric had barely stopped the car before I opened the door and tumbled out, gasping for breath. He ran around to the passenger side and knelt in front of me as he helped me to my feet.

"You don't have to do this, Aubrey," he said. "You don't."

"Yes, I do."

"What if they don't have your daughter? It may just be a bluff."

"I can't risk it."

"I can take Benny back. My cover isn't blown. I'll say you escaped and I had a choice between you and Benny. Josh will believe me." He chuckled halfheartedly. "He'll probably raise my salary. It'll buy you time to get away and it'll buy time for me to find out if they really do have your daughter."

I shook my head. They'd come after me again. I'd never stop running. Plus, they might really have Lilah, and how could I run away from that? "We're too close to turn back."

"I'll hide the car. There's a spot about fifty meters from here. We can walk to the gate from there." Eric patted the disposable phone in his pocket, one we'd bought several hours before. "Josh is at the palazzo. He's waiting for me. He'll protect Benny. Pauline won't dismiss me again. When I tell Josh what Caleb tried to do to Benny, do you know what's going to hit the fan?"

"You're going to tell Josh you hid Benny in my car?"

"Of course not. I'll let Josh think Caleb did that, too. I know where the cameras are on the grounds. They won't see that I was the one. And Benny will confirm how much unnecessary medication his uncle gave him before carrying him to the tower. Caleb is already in enough trouble with his father. It won't take anything for Josh to believe me over his brother. Between Caleb and me, I'm the one with the better track record."

I braced my hands against my knees and bent forward, sucking in air. I was glad now that we'd changed clothes in Naples and I'd traded my velvet dress for skintight leggings and a bulky red sweater that hid a utility belt underneath. I'd also exchanged my boots for athletic shoes, which were easier on my achy knee. I wished for some tiles to give me supersensitive strength, but they were well hidden, far away. Still, the aftereffects of their energy buzzed in my skin.

"I have a plan." Maybe I was just reassuring myself. I did have a plan, but the probability of escaping with Lilah was slim to none. "The thing is to get Lilah out of there and then I'll do what I can to get myself out."

"And if you can't?"

"Then…then…" I couldn't even say it. For the past hour I'd been able to think of nothing but Caleb's hands on my throat, almost as if I could feel them there already. "You've explained to Josh? The plan's all set?"

Eric tapped the disposable cell phone on his hip. "I didn't tell him about Caleb. Not yet. Josh's phone is probably bugged. But I told him enough. I'm bringing you back for a trade with Simon. You're willingly bringing Benny back and you'll trade the artifacts for your daughter."

I hesitated to ask. "Did he know what daughter you were talking about?"

Eric looked away. "He never said anything about a daughter. He was interested only in Benny's safety. But he agreed to whatever swap you want as long as Benny's unharmed. The exchange will take place on the towers, out in the open, like you wanted."

In the open. Good. I'd be able to see everything, without the likelihood of a sniper hiding in the trees below or on top of a building. No one would be able to get a clear shot at me once I entered the eastern tower. The four watchtowers were situated with crosswalks between them and an X in the center, with stone handrails missing in some places. I was comfortable in midair, more so than anyone else would be. As long as I was up there, I'd be safe. They wouldn't try anything underhanded up there. They wouldn't want me to drop anything important.

I glanced down the narrow road. The shadows were growing longer, but the sun was still bright. "They'll be watching for us. Too likely a sniper will pick me off when we get out of the car."

"That's why you're going to carry Benny and I'll carry the fake artifacts. Josh won't dare let anyone get a shot at you. No matter how good they are. He won't take the chance. Not with his son. And not with Caleb calling the shots or the shooters."

"Hide the automobile then. We should walk from here. Any closer and they'll be watching for us."

"The walk will be worse on your knee."

I shrugged. "Doesn't matter. I just have to get through the day. After today, there'll be no more hanging from threads." I attempted a smile. "One way or the other."

He glanced at Benny in the backseat. The boy didn't know where he was yet. No sign of excitement at being so close to his home or seeing his mother.

"Eric? I think we should say goodbye now."

Eric frowned and I looked away, focusing my attention on a spot in the grass.

"Once they see us," I continued without looking at him, "we won't want to show any evidence of camaraderie. If Lilah and I are able to get away..." I swallowed. "If I should survive...if I should...survive..." What was I saying? That if I lived, I might actually have a relationship with this man? Even if I survived the next twenty-four hours, how could I have *anything* with Eric Cabordes?

He planted one hand on my shoulder and with the other lifted my chin. "If you survive, I will meet you in six weeks. A friend of mine has a vacation home in London. You know him...professionally. His name is Robert Fraser."

I jerked my head up at the name of the notorious thief. I hadn't seen Robert in months, not since he'd appeared out of the blue with Analise Reisner in tow. The night Simon had ordered me to track Analise and retrieve a Madonna statue from her. Before that, I hadn't seen him in years. I'd heard he was strictly legit now. "You know Robert?"

"And he knows you. All your identities, too. He and

I have been working together for a while now. I'll have business with the Adriano London office in six weeks. I'll meet you at Robert's flat."

Something wistful flashed in his eyes. He moved to kiss me. I opened my mouth, but instead he kissed the side of my neck. His tenderness sent shivers through me. I wanted so badly to go back to that monastery bed and lie on his chest again and have him hold me. Wish for all of this to go away. No more worries about Lilah disappearing.

"That's your plan?" I whispered. I sniffed. The last thing I needed was a teary goodbye, but my eyes burned and my throat lumped up. How unfair to have this promise of the kind of life I wanted, the kind of man I wanted, like a beautiful mirage calling to me, and to be faced with Simon…Caleb…the likelihood that in a few days I'd be too brain-damaged to care or to recognize Lilah's name.

"No." He kissed the other side of my neck. "That's not my plan." He brushed his lips across mine but didn't stop for a kiss. Instead he pressed his lips against my forehead and held them there. He pulled my body in close to his chest, hard against him as he whispered in my ear.

"Don't worry, Aubrey de Lune. I won't let you suffer. If Caleb gets his hands on you—" his voice caught "—the only way I'll be able to save you will be to put a bullet in your brain as quickly as possible. I'm an excellent shot."

He stroked my hair and kissed the skin of my neck passionately. "Don't worry," he moaned. "I'll make it quick."

So this is what it's like to walk before a firing squad,

I thought an hour later as we approached the palazzo gates and the security guards opened them for us without a word.

I didn't need a red silk scarf, either for a blindfold or to tuck into my neckline over my heart for a better mark. I wore a bright red sweater they couldn't possibly miss, but it was part of my escape plan. They'd be looking for me in red. If I couldn't escape—and I had serious doubts—then I'd need to buy time for Lilah to find the boat and get away. Better to call attention to myself than her, and I would gladly sacrifice myself for my daughter, just as I had for years sacrificed my desire to see her again because I'd wanted to keep her safe.

On the other hand, a firing squad would have been preferable over being given to Caleb for disposal if I failed. No doubt I'd spend my last hours bound or drugged and violated in every way imaginable. Caleb was a gifted enough lover to use my body against me. I couldn't imagine a worse death than being brought to orgasm by a man I hated while he choked the air out of me again and again. He'd wake me every time and remind me how I'd eventually suffer brain damage and how he'd keep my body alive for a few days after my mind was gone.

I understood now why some informants carried cyanide pills or shot themselves through the temple. There are things worse than death.

I thought I'd wanted to have sex with Eric. Just sex. Exuberant, crazy, wild, passionate, hot, make-me-feel-alive-one-last-time sex. A coupling with no strings and with no thoughts of anything permanent.

I hadn't gotten what I'd wanted.

Instead Eric had given me something I barely remembered experiencing with any man. He'd given me exactly what I really needed and hadn't even realized I wanted.

Tenderness.

I clutched Benny to me as I limped up the hill to the palazzo and the towers. The buildings gleamed in the sunshine. Scaffolding crawled up the side of the eastern watchtower, the place I'd named as mine in the upcoming exchange.

Benny laid his head on my shoulder. I kissed his cheek and told him everything would be okay. I wasn't so sure. Maybe he'd at least remember me when he was all grown up and the newest Duke of the Adriano family.

Eric walked behind, pointing his revolver at my lower back and hauling a tapestry filled with ceramic trivets—small tiles, some broken, that were imprinted with a red-inked Mother Mary. The sale had made a street vendor very, very happy. The real artifacts, including the manuscript, were safely hidden in a bathroom in the train station at Pompeii. Either I would retrieve them later or Eric would. The most important thing right now was for Eric to retain his cover. And that meant the gun at my back and the occasional shove forward.

My knee throbbed with every step. I knew we were being watched. If there's one thing the Adriano Security team excelled at, it was watching. The sun was still high enough in the sky to light the deeper shades of the manicured gardens leading up to the main house.

My limp grew more pronounced with each footfall

as I retraced my steps along the driveway to the main house, the same path I'd clomped along less than forty-eight hours ago with a package in hand that was indeed the most important artifact of the last millennium.

In the periphery of my vision I saw the movement of men as they stepped out from behind trees, columns, walls, gates, everywhere. Within a few slow, steady minutes, men in black and camouflage lined the way ahead. Every man had a weapon drawn. Every man was silent.

I held my breath as I pressed forward. Benny snuggled closer against me. "Keep your eyes closed, sweetheart. I don't want you to see anything ugly." He nodded, and I felt the muscles around his eyes scrunch up as he turned his face into my neck. Trusting, sweet. Eric was probably to blame for that.

Men kept coming out of the gardens ahead of me, lining the drive for as far as I could see, all the way to the main house and to the path beyond to the eastern tower of the four. Still, I had clear passage as long as I held their little prince. Clear passage *to* the tower. I'd known twenty paces ago that there'd be even less of a chance of escape for me than I'd ever dreamed. I was safe only until the "artifacts" I carried could be authenticated—or not. Simon wouldn't kill me and risk losing the whereabouts of the real artifacts.

My knee was killing me. I grimaced with every step.

A man up ahead, a hulking blonde, stepped out in front of me, legs spread, his weapon aimed directly at Benny and me. I stopped.

"Algernon!" I heard Eric's sharp command from

behind me. "Stop being a hero and move aside! She's been promised a clear path to get the child to his father. No one's to touch her until the authenticity of those artifacts has been validated."

Algernon's smile quirked to one side. "Caleb says otherwise."

I knew what he meant. It didn't matter if he killed me. He needed to shoot through Benny to get to me. As the old saying goes, two birds with one stone.

I pressed Benny closer to me, holding his head tight against my cheek and his little legs wrapped furtively around my waist. He held on to my neck in a crushing squeeze.

"Algernon!" a voice above bellowed.

Benny shuddered. "Is my father angry?" he whispered. "Was my mother bad again?" I shushed him and he buried his face in my neck.

I glanced up into the sun to see a shadow leaning out over the stone battlements of the northern tower. Another figure joined him, much thinner and smaller. Pauline. Josh and Pauline, already in position and waiting for me. As long as they stood toward the center, they couldn't be seen from below, but if they moved to the edge, a sniper could pick them off from this distance. I was glad now that Caleb had once courted me with a candlelit dinner on the western tower, so I knew the layout of the semirefurbished ruins. But step close to the edge? The men on the driveway could easily take aim at me. I'd have to remember that when I took my place on the eastern tower.

"Algernon!" Josh bellowed again.

That startled me. I'd never heard Josh raise his voice. I'd hadn't known he was capable of it.

"Algernon! Put that weapon down! Dr. Moon has been granted safe passage to bring my son to me. If one hair on his head is harmed, I'll come down there and kill you myself."

I smiled to myself. I'd known Josh for a long time, but I'd never seen him so passionate about anything. Tension vibrated in the timbre of his voice. For as cold as Pauline seemed as a parent, Josh was her polar opposite. At the moment, though, Josh believed I was a kidnapper, and so our previous friendly relationship was now in doubt.

Algernon cursed in a language I'd never heard and stepped to the edge of the drive. He didn't put down his gun, but he lowered it in deference to his employer.

In the two minute exchange, my knee had stiffened, and it creaked as I took a step forward. I winced again, took another step, and kept limping. So much for not showing my weaknesses to my enemies. They all knew I was wounded. If I hadn't been, I might have pretended to be wounded, the way a mother bird feigns a broken wing to lure a predator from her young. But this was real, and I was in real trouble.

I limped past the main house, up the hill, a little farther. The incline would be slight but it was still an incline and I felt it multiplied in my tendons. Descending the hill would be even worse, but my plan was to escape in a different direction. Then again, most of my plans had not worked out so well recently.

By the time I reached the gaping doorway of the eastern tower, I was almost dragging my right leg behind me. Benny hadn't seemed too heavy when I'd first extracted him from the backseat of the Volkswagen, but now he seemed to be the weight of the world. Obviously Eric had noticed. He'd ceased giving me the obligatory shove forward.

"Keep going!" he barked loudly from behind me. Then under his breath he whispered, "Keep going, Aubrey."

I glanced over my shoulder at the henchmen on the driveway. They'd closed ranks behind us and stood at the base of the eastern tower. Not one of them came near the door or the tower walls.

I frowned upward at sunlight seeping through the stairwell openings of the stone floors above me. Stairs. Stone stairs. God, why stairs? I'd known about the stairs when I'd formulated my plan, but my weight had been off my knee at that moment and my mind had not registered how much climbing stairs would hurt. I whimpered before I realized it.

Eric moved in behind me. He must have heard me, because he scooped an arm around my waist, gathering me up and helping to pull me along the stairs beside him. No one was watching. He had to bear my weight, Benny's and the fake artifacts in the tapestry over his shoulder.

Three stories up, I emerged in sunlight and fell to the stone floor of the upper deck of the tower. Benny tumbled down unharmed beside me, and the two of us scooted to the center of the tower floor, where we wouldn't be seen by snipers below when we stood.

Eric didn't bother to crouch. He stood to his full height and looked around, pointing his gun to one side but making it appear that he had the gun on me. "The players are all here," he said without moving his lips.

"My daughter? Do you see my daughter?"

He squinted into the western sun, raised a hand to shade his eyes. Then he looked at the southern tower back to the western tower, and then to the north. "There's a girl here," he said. "I don't know her. Never seen her before."

God. Oh, God! It was true.

"Where is Dr. Moon?" I heard Simon's voice coming from the south. Player number one on the southern tower. Josh and Pauline on the northern tower.

"It's okay, Duke," Eric yelled back. "She's right here. So is Benedict. And the artifacts. It's all here."

"Then tell Dr. Moon to get to her feet. She's tried my patience long enough."

Eric didn't move. "Aubrey," he whispered, "are you ready?"

I shook my head. "No. But it doesn't matter. I have to do this. Just..." I remembered the touch of his hand and the stroke of his palm against my hair. "Just remember what you said. That you won't let Caleb take me."

He nodded. "I swear by the Mother."

"No snipers up there?" I asked.

"None. Just stay to the center of the tower. No one's going to take aim at you as long as you're carrying either Benny or the artifacts. They won't risk anything being dropped."

"She's keeping the artifacts here for the exchange," Eric called out. "I'm taking Benny back to his parents."

I heard Pauline's waiflike voice thanking God and all the saints in Italian. Most likely she was terrified that her little insurance policy might get hurt in the exchange and she'd lose her prize position as the wife and mother of an Adriano.

Benny opened his eyes and realized where he was. The tower. A tall tower. The poor little boy was afraid of heights, terrified of them. He grabbed Eric's thigh and clung to him.

"Come, Benny. I'm going to carry you back to your mother and father now, but I want you to wrap your arms around my neck and keep your eyes closed and hold on tight. And I will take you there. Okay?"

The child nodded emphatically.

Eric glanced back one last time before he started across the narrow bridge to the northern tower. We locked gazes for a brief second. He seemed to will me to see the promise in his eyes. *I swear.*

Chapter 16

I rose to my feet, the tapestry loaded with fake artifacts drawn close to my chest, and watched as Eric made his way gingerly across the stone bridge to the tower were Josh and Pauline waited. It seemed to take forever for Eric and the boy to reach the other side. When they did, Josh grabbed Benny and hugged him while Pauline made a fuss over her baby boy's mussed hair. My eyes stung, even though the reunion wasn't mine.

"Take my grandson below!" Simon ordered from the southern tower.

As Pauline, Josh and Benny disappeared from sight, I scanned the other two towers. Simon stood at the edge of the southern tower, two figures behind him at the other edge but too distant for me to recognize. Caleb stood at the western tower, the sun behind him and in my eyes. I could see his silhouette but not his features, though I knew his physique all too well. A woman stood beside him, also in silhouette. She appeared to be taller than me, although next to Caleb she looked short.

I fully expected Caleb to spew some profanity at me. His stance was defiant, and with the sun in my eyes I could tell no more than that, but it was enough.

"Cabordes!" Simon shouted. "Get below! See to my grandson!"

Eric shot me a helpless look. He paused for a split second, just long enough for Simon to frown. His Adam's apple bobbed with a swallow. I knew I was on my own. And so did he.

"Cabordes!"

Eric raised his weapon skyward, nonthreateningly but so Simon could see it.

"Do you have a problem, Cabordes?" Simon's tone was one that I had heard much more often from Caleb, but Caleb remained silent, subdued, and leaned close to the woman at his side.

"I would prefer to remain here, Duke." Eric answered him strongly, confidently. I had been close enough to the man for the past twenty-four hours to feel the fear rise off him. "In case we need an extra weapon. Should she…try to escape."

Simon's head jerked in a nod. "Very well. You may stay. But she's not going anywhere." Simon pivoted and called to me. "Dr. Moon? Aubrey! Aubergine de Lune!"

Then he grinned. "My, you're looking worse for the wear, aren't you? Did you bring my tiles back?"

I held up the tapestry bundle of clinking ceramics but said nothing.

"I can't hear you, Dr. Moon. Did you bring my tiles back?"

"I have the tiles," I yelled back in a hoarse voice. "I'm willing to exchange them for my daughter. To let her go free."

I heard a female voice protest and glanced back at Caleb and the woman at his side. She was questioning something, but I couldn't hear her words on the wind. I saw her silhouette against the sun. I should know that profile anywhere. I'd seen it often enough in the photographs my private investigator had taken of Lilah and I remembered it, very tenderly from so many years ago…from Matthew when he'd been a young man, when he'd been alive and when he'd been mine.

"And the book? Jeanne la Pucelle's heresy?"

"Actually, it was Isabelle's heresy," I mumbled under my breath, "and it wasn't heresy at all.

"Yes," I lied. "I have your book." I cringed at my own words. I'd spent so many years lying—lying to cover up, lying to be something I wasn't. Maybe to some degree I'd always have to live a lie, but I didn't have to like it. Not anymore. I didn't want that kind of life. I wanted one where I could speak the truth and be proud of it, where I could be myself, where I could just *be.*

"Quiet," Simon said to someone behind him. I could barely see the figure of a woman and a man behind him, though I could tell that the man was one of the younger henchmen. Then Simon turned to the western tower across from me. "Caleb. Send her over to get the tiles." He gestured at the woman at Caleb's side.

I squinted to see her. Lilah? It had to be. Again I saw the profile—beautiful. Shoulder-length hair pulled back into a ponytail that sprayed out around the back of her head. She was probably scared. She said something to Caleb, but I still couldn't hear her words. I could tell that Caleb was talking to her softly. He didn't seem threatening toward her as she shook her head, hard enough to shake her ponytail from side to side. Young, vibrant, full of life. I hadn't seen her since she'd been ten years old. My arms ached to hold her again. But there'd be no time, no time at all. *I have to get her out of here.*

"Caleb!" Simon thundered, and it surprised me to see Caleb startle at his father's voice. "Did you not hear me? Get her out there—now!"

Caleb scowled back at his father. I couldn't actually see the scowl, but I could feel it in his posture. I held my palm above my eyes against the sun and squinted harder. I'd chosen the eastern tower as my own because of the scaffolding, because of my escape plan. I had probably waited a little too late in the day, because the sun sinking in the western sky put me at a definite disadvantage.

"She says heights make her dizzy," Caleb called back.

Simon threw up his hands. "I don't care if she's—" I knew very little Italian, but I knew profanity when I heard it. "She's expendable."

My heart caught in my throat. Expendable? Lilah?

"Not if you want these artifacts!" I screeched back at him. "You let her stay where she is."

Simon ignored me. "Caleb, I told you not to bring her up here. You're the one who made her a part of this."

"Father—"

"I will not have you turned into a weakling by a woman. Do you understand me, Caleb? She might as well be of some use, and you're too heavy for that walk or I'd have you out there on the crosswalk." He gestured at the stone bridge between the towers. "Get her out there."

"My daughter!" I screeched loud enough that my throat ached, raw. "I'll give you the artifacts. Just let my daughter go!"

Caleb made an openhanded gesture. "Please, Father—"

I'd heard Caleb desperate before but desperate in different ways. But I'd never seen Caleb Adriano like this. He conferred with the woman again. This time I saw her silhouette perch one hand on his chest. Briefly, calming. Then she nodded and turned toward me. It made my skin crawl to see her touching Caleb like that, and I prayed that he had not charmed her into his bed as he had with me.

With cupped hands around his mouth, Caleb yelled back to me, "She's coming over. You bring the tiles. She'll meet you halfway."

I pulled the tapestry bundle close to me and stepped to the edge of the eastern tower's wall. Despite the earthquake activity over the past few years, the crosswalks were still in place. Most of them, anyway. Between my tower and the one where Simon and the two other figures stood, a span twice the length of my body was missing. The crosswalk that Eric had traversed to the northern tower was still intact and even had stone guard-rails. The crosswalk formed a square, with each angle being one of the towers, but it also formed an X between the towers, and X marked the spot of the exchange exactly as I'd directed. I would meet my daughter in the center and wait there with the tiles until she had crossed safely to the eastern tower and I would scramble back to join her, hook my utility belt over the scaffolding and swing her over the fence of the Adriano compound to safety. From there, while Simon figured out how to get to the tiles in the X, we'd scramble down to the opening of the tunnel Myrddin had shown me and hide there until we could make our way back to where Eric and I had hidden the car, even if it meant waiting for days.

If I couldn't get away with Lilah, I'd do everything in my power to slow down the Adriano henchmen so she could escape. I smiled to myself, realizing suddenly that I knew there was no way Simon would live up to his end of the agreement when it came to exchanging artifacts for my daughter. Then again, these weren't the real artifacts.

I stepped out onto the narrow crosswalk without bothering to put any pressure on the there-sometimes-and-sometimes-not handrails. I caught my breath at last. I felt safer here, up high, than on the ground. This was my turf, the air. I'd spent so many nights clinging to ropes and the sides of walls. I had no fear of heights, no fear of falling and—at the moment—no fear of the sudden stop at the end of a long fall. I limped forward, the bundle in my arms. Within seconds, I was at the center, waiting for my daughter.

Lilah was much more timid. I'd spent the last decade hanging from threads and wasn't afraid of heights, but this girl was. As terrified of them as Benny. She'd seemed so confident moments ago, yet now uncertainty took over and the light around her faded. She stepped tentatively onto the crosswalk, right foot first, and then sidestepped in my direction.

Something about her profile reminded me of Matthew. Of one time in particular. We'd been at the Tor in Glastonbury, the mound where Druid priestesses had once gathered to learn and to heal, and we'd lain there in the grass and talked of the child I carried and how nothing else in the world mattered but being together. I'd reclined in his arms, full of joy, his child growing inside me, and I'd admired his profile against the misty sky.

Lilah inched closer to me, one side step after another. A breeze stirred and caught her ponytail. It fluttered all the way to the clip close to her head. She bent her knees and rocked unexpectedly.

"Don't look down," I called to her.

The breeze slapped at her wide-legged pants, gathered at the ankle as if fresh from a fairy tale of harem girls and belly dancers. I couldn't tell the color of the cloth with the sun behind her, but it glinted off the gold flat shoes she wore. I strained to see her face in the shadow. Would I see Matthew in her eyes as I once had? She looked down at her feet, her chin close to the leather vest she wore zipped to the neck. Sunbeams caught the gold of a hoop at one ear.

I ached to see her face, to look into her eyes again. Would she recognize me? Would she hate me for having left her? Would she be happy that I wasn't dead after all?

She kept her arms at her sides for balance, since the path back to Caleb was missing its railing. Long, dark fingernails and rings of both gold and silver. The light shifted around her head as she came closer.

I laid the bundle of fake artifacts in the middle of the X of the crosswalk but kept the bundle closed. I reached for her. She let me. I grabbed her outstretched hand and pulled her toward me. She let out a moan of relief as I steadied her. She grabbed the rail closest to me.

"Dr. Moon!" she gasped.

"Scarlet?" I stared. The last time I'd seen her, she'd worn her hair in a bob. The long hair…the ponytail… A trendy cascade of fake hair. Dying her hair or bobbing it was nothing new, but I hadn't expected Scarlet. My God, I'd thought she was Lilah. I'd *expected* her to be Lilah. It was obvious up close, though not from a distance and not with the sun in my eyes. Their eyes were different. And the mouth. But the profile…the profile was a perfect match. It had been a ruse. All of it. This was Scarlet, not Lilah.

"Quit dawdling." From the southern tower, Simon leaned forward over the edge. "Look in the bag. What do you see? Are there tiles?"

Scarlet hesitated, watching me intently through veiled lashes. White knuckles on the rail, she slowly lowered herself to the bundle of tiles and allowed one tentative hand to pull back the edge of the tapestry. "Yes," she called back without looking up. "They're tiles. With pictures of the Madonna on them."

Simon's laughter caught in the wind. "Excellent! And the book? Is there a briefcase with a book in it?"

Scarlet touched the briefcase. "I…I guess that's what it is."

"Good. Good. Then gather them up and carry them back to Caleb. Without dropping them."

I caught Scarlet's hand and held it. "I can get you out of here."

She looked as if she might laugh. "I don't want to get out of here. And I don't want to hear any more of your lies about Caleb."

"They're not lies. And Scarlet?" I glanced up at Simon. He'd already made it quite clear that he found her a threat to his control over Caleb. "Scarlet, you're in danger here."

Her face twisted in disgust. "You're the one who's dangerous. Caleb's never done a thing to hurt me. I've never met anyone as special as he is."

I gripped her wrist and shook it. "Didn't you hear Simon? You're expendable."

"So his dad's an ass. I've dealt with worse."

"No. No, you haven't. The Adrianos—and that includes Simon and Caleb—are killers. They'll do anything for power. Don't you understand?"

"You know what?" She yanked her wrist out of my grip. "I don't know what this—" she waved at the exchange going on around her "—is all about, but I do know one thing. To steal from your employer like you did and then kidnap that little boy to save your own ass and *then* try to tell me that Caleb and his family are the bad guys? Dr. Moon—or whatever your name really is—you make me *sick!*"

I watched her go. I stood in the middle of the X, in the crosshairs of the Adrianos, and watched Scarlet Rubashka go. She was indeed in danger if Simon discovered who she really was. She was one of "my kind." One of my lineage. Or rather, Matthew's lineage. I knew it in her profile. Matthew's little sister, the little girl Matthew's mother had adopted from a relative, the child they'd called Nonny, my daughter's only other living relative. And she hated me.

I let her go. I let her take the only leverage I had left—the fake artifacts—and go. They didn't have my daughter. They had an unwitting accomplice who was Matthew's sister. *But they didn't have my daughter.* I felt the glorious release inside my throat and wanted to cry out in victory in spite of my situation. They didn't have Lilah. My daughter was safe.

Scarlet inched along the crosswalk a little faster as she neared Caleb. He stepped out onto the edge of the stone bridge and drew her in by the waist. He lifted her onto the tower beside him, setting the bundle on the deck at their feet. He hugged her close, and she pressed her cheek into his chest.

"Good," Simon called back. "Now get rid of her."

Caleb glowered. The sun had dropped another degree on the horizon, and I could barely see his face now. The look was one of pure hatred. I knew it personally.

For a moment I thought Simon's order had been directed at me, not Scarlet. Caleb drew Scarlet into a deep embrace and turned his back on his father, protecting Scarlet, hiding the naive little fool from the man who'd just pronounced her expendable.

"Dr. Moon?" Simon's voice wasn't nearly so loud since I'd closed half the distance between us.

I rose to my feet in the center of the X but didn't look down. I knew better. There was nowhere to look except directly at him.

"Dr. Moon? Aren't you forgetting something?"

A security guard, the man behind him, stepped to one side. He pulled a second figure with him, a woman, and shoved her to the tower's edge next to Simon's right. A slight woman. Judging by the lack of ripeness in her figure, I guessed she was no more than twenty. White T-shirt, jeans. Her arms pulled behind her back. A thick blue scarf covering her forehead and eyes.

Lilah?

Sunlight washed cross the blue swath on her face. She was close enough that I could see her chin quiver. Dread twisted in my stomach. I'd expected to see Lilah in Caleb's hands. I'd been so worried about Caleb getting his hands on my precious daughter that I'd forgotten what a bastard his father could be. No, this was much more Simon's forte. Torture the ones you love, then torture you.

Oh, God.

"Dr. Moon, did you think you could outsmart my family? We made you. We turned you into what you are today."

"And for that," I whispered, "I hate you." I breathed through gritted teeth. "Let her go!"

"Why would I do that?"

I was vaguely aware of Scarlet asking what was going on and Caleb trying to talk her into going back downstairs. "You have me," I told Simon.

"Don't be silly. Of course I have you. I've always had you. Did you think you'd ever be able to leave us? I'll own you until the day you die…whichever day I decide that to be." He grabbed Lilah's jaw and twisted her to look at me, even though she couldn't see me through the blindfold. "Don't you have something to say to your mother?"

"M-mom?" she croaked out. That voice. So frail, so fragile. My baby?

"Let her go!" My voice cracked on the last syllable. If there was any doubt that I'd shown my weaknesses to everyone watching—Simon, Caleb, Eric, Scarlet, even Lilah—all doubt was now gone. Lilah was my weakness. She always had been. From the moment she was conceived. But she was also my strength. The one thing that had kept me going through the all the dark times. Knowing that she was safe. Knowing that she was living the life I could never have and that she was free to live and love as she wanted.

"No," was all he said.

"Simon…Duke? Please? Let her go!"

He seemed to think for a moment. Hope surged through me. We'd had a good working relationship for so long. He owed me, I'd thought. He cared, I'd thought. Didn't all those years count for anything? He seemed to reconsider. He still didn't know the tiles were fake or that the manuscript in the tapestry was a fake. He still thought those were real. Maybe he'd keep his end of the bargain, at least long enough to let her go.

"Please," I said, lowering my voice. I would never beg for myself. But for Lilah, I would die. "Please let her go."

He shrugged. "Okay."

I saw the blur of white shirt and blue blindfold, the whirl of motion. She took flight. She tumbled forward, over. I was vaguely aware of a scream from Scarlet's direction.

Chapter 17

"Caleb, what happened? What happened?" I barely heard Scarlet's voice.

My baby.

I stared openmouthed at Simon. We locked gazes. I couldn't miss the amusement in his eyes.

"Oops." He grinned back.

My eyes searched the courtyard below, the grounds, out into the gardens. She'd fallen beyond the security fence on the compound's perimeter. I caught a flash of white T-shirt as she tumbled down the hill and out of sight.

A three-story fall. Could she be okay? Could she be alive? Could— I let out a yelp as reality set in.

I felt Eric's eyes on me. I sensed his pain at seeing my own, but I had no time for it.

Lilah. Lilah, my life.

I bounded across the crosswalk toward the eastern tower, snatching the utility belt from under my sweater. I flung it into the sky as I ran, bringing it down into the scaffolding in a fast loop around the upper bar as I launched myself into thin air. The utility hook grabbed the bar and held. I heard the chaos behind me. Simon yelling. Scarlet crying. Caleb yelling. None of it mattered. The only thing that mattered was getting to my baby. The cord unraveled behind me as I swung out wide beyond the southern tower and over the security fence. I let go and tumbled to the grass. My knee gave way under me, but I pulled myself up and kept going. I had to keep going. I had to.

I plunged toward Lilah where she'd plummeted down the hill. She was sprawled like a broken doll. Arms still tied behind her at the wrists but in an awkward angle that didn't seem human. One leg askew, obviously broken. She didn't move.

I hit the ground and tumbled toward her. It was faster than limping. I knew before I touched her that she was dead.

"Ah, baby." I crawled to her, touched her hair, soothed the dirty wisps that escaped from the edges of the blindfold. A scarf. Robin's-egg blue. A beautiful blue. With gold threads through it. Probably Scarlet's. It matched her outfit of the day. They'd used Scarlet's scarf to blindfold my daughter. I wonder if she even knew.

"My baby," I whispered. Full-grown. I never got to meet her full-grown. In my mind, despite the private investigator's photographs, she was still ten years old. "I'm so sorry, baby." I kissed her forehead. "If I could rewrite my life, I swear, Lilah, this would all be different."

Gently I lifted the blindfold and peeled it back to look into her beautiful eyes one last time.

What the hell?

I blinked. I didn't know these eyes.

Then I realized that I did. Green eyes. Nose ring. *Nicole.* The runaway. The girl in San Francisco. The girl who'd posed as my daughter to escape her stepfather. My contact in L.A.—George, who created new identities for various Adriano assignments—had betrayed me. Betrayed her. Had given her to Simon thinking she was my child. Mine and Matthew's.

Damn you! I sobbed, sinking a clenched fist into her shoulder and then pounding her shoulder again. *Damn you, damn you, damn you, you naive little girl!* I let my fist rest on her shoulder and then pressed my forehead to hers. It wasn't her fault. It wasn't Nicole I wanted to strike but the man who'd done this to her. I'd sworn to keep her safe and to kill anyone who hurt her, but all I had to pour my shame into was a broken body. I pulled her to me and kissed her forehead. "I'm sorry. So sorry."

I shook off a deep need to stay and mourn this girl. There'd be time for that later. Because if Nicole was the only child Simon had attached to me, then Simon didn't know about Lilah. This girl had been sacrificed in my daughter's place. And that meant—

Lilah's still alive! Safe!

I pushed up off my feet and quickly checked the direction of the sun. I made my way to the trees and brush, the rocks, heading as fast as I could go toward the entrance of the tunnel Myrddin had shown me. I needed a place to hide, at least until things calmed down. Then, after dark, I'd head toward the place we'd hidden the car. I could hear shouting from within the Adriano compound. They'd be here within moments. I couldn't look back. I would never look back again. Only forward.

"Leaving empty-handed?" A voice spun me around and I came face-to-face with Interpol agent Analise Reisner. With a gun. She couldn't have picked a worse time.

"Look," I said, palms in the air, angling to get around her, "I don't want to fight you."

She smiled grimly. "You don't look like you have any fight left in you."

Reisner was right about the way I looked. Bedraggled and exhausted. Not calm, athletic, robust like Reisner, but still with plenty of fight in me, especially if it meant Lilah was alive.

"Dropping off another artifact you acquired for your benefactor?"

"Simon's not my benefactor. Not anymore. And I can't stay here or they'll kill me. And no, I didn't make my delivery."

"But I saw—"

"They had my…something very important to me. I mean, I thought they did. Look, you don't owe me anything, but—"

"I'm here to help you." The air seemed to crackle between us. My skin tingled.

I eyed her suspiciously. Help? She'd been chasing me for months. I'd saved her life in France and in return she'd let me get away, but I'd always known I'd have to face her again. No doubt, she could tell I didn't believe her.

"Myrddin."

"Myrddin?" I repeated. She knew Myrddin?

"I was sent to make sure you didn't come back from San Francisco with a present for the Duke. I failed. Yesterday morning, Myrddin told Cat you were on your way to Paris with some important artifacts that had to stay out of Adriano hands. I was to tag you." She holstered her weapon. "When I lost you, I retraced my path to here."

"You were going to…help me?" I glanced over my shoulder at the sounds of chaos behind me. I couldn't linger much longer. "Why would you help me?"

"I understand we have some ancestors in common."

I froze and stared at her. No, not a descendant of Isabelle. An ancestry that went farther back than that. To a time when our foremothers had been sisters in their mission, priestesses of the Mother. She was one of my kind, too. How many of us were there?

"I have to get out of here. Now."

"I have a boat." She dug a set of keys out of her pocket and pitched them to me. "It's down at the water access. Only one there. Will I see you at Cat's?"

I nodded. "And you? What about you?"

She shrugged. "I'll see what I can do to stir up some trouble here with the guards. Give you a delay. And don't worry. I've called the local police for backup. They'll make sure I get away in one piece."

I caught my bottom lip between my teeth and frowned in the direction of Nicole's rag-doll body. "The girl…"

We locked gazes, both of us silently acknowledging the casualties of this war with the Adrianos.

"Innocent bystander," I whispered, swallowing the lump in my throat. The words were lost between us, but she read my lips and nodded.

"I'll see that the police take care of that, too." She gestured toward the bay. "Now, go. I'll be safe. See? My backup's already at the main gate."

I twisted my jaw to one side. "One more thing. I'm not going to be able to retrieve those artifacts for a while, and they can't stay where I left them."

Reisner nodded. "I'd be more than happy to pick them up for you."

"I thought so. But don't go hauling them all back to Interpol. Some of those artifacts belong to me personally." I frowned. "Some may belong to you personally, too." I had no idea if she'd inherited tiles, as well. "Go to Naples. Get on the *Circumvesuviana* train line. Get off at the Pompeii Scavi. I left a navy-blue blanket hidden in the ceiling above the toilets. You'll know it when you see the Adriano logo on the blanket."

I heard her wish me luck as I ran toward the water access. I had to slide down between the rocks, digging my heels into the ground to keep from plunging down to the water. Once the Adrianos found out I hadn't delivered the real tiles, they'd never stop hunting me. I'd have to die to escape them.

I have to die.

I wished I could tell Eric. I wished I could say goodbye to him. As long as he was a man of his word, there would be nothing for either of us to worry about.

"Ha!" Algernon shot up in front of me, grabbing my arm, spinning me around. I punched him hard in the nose, not once but twice. His face contorted and he raised a fist…then sank at my feet.

Reisner stood behind him, a big rock in her grip. "Go!" she urged. "Now!"

I pounced into the boat and started the motor before my feet were firmly on the floor. Within seconds I was out in open water, looking back at the palazzo on the hill and the four towers. I circled the boat back around, not so close as to be hit if they decided to shoot but close enough that they would know who it was.

As soon as I saw more men appear on the towers, I tugged off the red sweater and tied the arms to the steering wheel, letting the bright red flap in the wind beside me. Then I turned the boat toward the rocks, going faster and faster and faster—

At the last possible moment, I slipped over the edge and let the water cover me. Plumes of fire exploded above me, and I knew I had a long swim ahead to my rebirth.

Chapter 18

Six weeks later
London, England

I was late. Train service from Paris had been disrupted, and the London Underground had been closed down for nearly a day due to a gas leak of some sort. But Robert's flat looked inviting as I strolled toward the stoop.

Had I not stayed too long in Paris with Cat and Analise Reisner—who I now knew as Ana—I might have made it to Robert's flat two days ago. Both women had helped me locate a safe house and make some real plans for the future, plans that included both Europe and North America. In the six weeks since I'd confiscated the tiles, not a single rainstorm had threatened the Italian countryside. The three of us had celebrated a victory over the Adrianos. If they were responsible for the scientifically induced bad weather, we now had the tiles and their energy far from the ley lines at the palazzo. We weren't sure whether they had used the energy to create storms, but since the weather had improved, we assumed they didn't have the needed energy stored for another attempt. The only thing we were sure of was that the storm had stopped.

I held my breath and knocked at the side door Robert had suggested I use. I waited. Maybe I was too late. Maybe Eric hadn't been able to meet me after all. Maybe I'd seen the last of him.

The curtain above the door moved very, very slightly, then fluttered. The door opened with a flourish and strong, masculine hands pulled me inside. The door slammed behind me.

"You look damned good for a dead woman." Eric grinned down at me. His lips found my cheek and then kissed my hairline all the way to my neck. "I thought I'd lost you."

"I thought I'd lost me, too." I pushed away and peered into his pale blue eyes. Ah, yes. The same fire I'd seen in them on the steps of the main house at the palazzo. "Not anymore, though," I added. "I know exactly where I'm going now."

He kissed me then, full on the lips, his mouth sinking into mine with a hunger I'd thought was mine alone. I thumbed open the buttons on his black shirt as he carried me into what I was vaguely aware was a bedroom. I fumbled with his jeans and tugged them down. He barely had my dress off before I'd pressed him down on the bed on his back and eased my body down onto his. I heard him cry out.

Or maybe it was me who cried out.

A little later, I sat facing him, both of us naked with our legs wrapped around one another, with him deep inside me and with his mouth hungry for mine. I felt the warmth of his body and my own tenderness for him, felt his flesh inside me, felt myself in his arms.

Then the sensation of the tile energy wafted over me. Something inside me had been activated, and my senses had been on overload for weeks. I felt the essence of my soul shift in a half circle until it seemed that I was no longer in my body but in his. I felt the strength of his body from the inside. I felt the woman in his arms, the woman wrapped around his flesh. And then—

I gasped. I felt his emotions, all those just-below-the-surface and oh-so-intense feelings he had for me, felt him trying to pull my body and soul closer to him as if he couldn't get enough, felt the stirrings of a deep affection that made me shift back into my own body, break the seal of his mouth and cry out in surprise.

"Shhh," he whispered. "Did I hurt you?"

I shook my head. I could never explain the thing that had just happened, but whatever healing the tiles had given me, this gift of seeing Eric's feelings for me was a marvelous treasure.

Sometime after that, I rolled over in bed and stretched like a cat. The linens in Robert's unoccupied flat were crisp, white and felt oh-so-good against my skin. Then again, so did Eric.

I snuggled against him. He was still hot, breathing heavily. I sighed a little too loudly.

"Damn!" Eric grinned. "You sound like a contented woman!"

I laughed. Laughing felt good, sounded good in my own ears. I couldn't remember a laugh that felt so real.

Propping on one elbow, I stared into his face. He closed his eyes as a genuine smile lifted his cheeks all the way into his eyes. I smoothed the damp curls on his forehead, then traced his nose to its tip. At his mouth, I pressed one finger against his lips. He kissed it. We'd been reunited for a whole two hours and had yet to come up for air.

"Eventually," I said, "we're going to have to stop touching each other and actually talk."

"No, we're not." He gave his head a little shake. "Talking's overrated, but touching's good." He opened his eyes and pulled me toward him.

I brushed my lips over his and pulled back. "No, you don't," I whispered. "Luring me in again like that. I'm serious. At some point, we do need to talk."

"Oh, all right. I suppose I could use a rest." He grinned at me.

Eric Cabordes had been well worth my wait. This time I'd met him with open arms and an open heart. He'd said I looked different, happier, lighter somehow, as if the weight of the world had been lifted from my shoulders.

I fell back into the bed beside him and pulled the sheet around me.

"No, no, no. Don't cover up."

"I have to. Or you won't hear a word I say!"

He pretended to be exasperated. "Oh, all right. Fine. I'm listening."

I closed my eyes and inhaled his scent. *God, I could get used to this.* "I don't know if we can keep this up."

"As long as you let me rest every now and then…"

"No. I mean meeting like this."

I hadn't been to London in almost a year. The last time, I'd lifted a classified document from inside the Ministry of Defence at Whitehall. Those days were gone now. I didn't do that anymore. I didn't have to. To the rest of the world, Dr. Ginny Moon was dead, the result of a fiery boating accident. So was Dr. Lauren Hartford. So was Aubrey de Lune. As far as the Adrianos were concerned, I was dead. And that meant I was free.

"We shouldn't meet again here," I advised. "It was nice of Robert to let us meet at his flat, but it's too dangerous for us to come here again."

"Then we'll meet someplace different. Josh has me couriering information and items for him several times a month when he's with Benny. I could arrange to meet you for a day or two every few weeks. Different cities around Europe. Occasionally in the States."

I nodded. "I'm willing. I'd like to see you again." I glanced down at his groin dip. *And again…and again…* "I will meet you wherever I need to, Eric Cabordes, but I am concerned that the Adrianos will find out and you'll be in danger."

"No danger. Josh trusts me. Completely. In fact, he

even told me about Benny's dental chip. Volunteered the information."

"Why now? Because you brought Benny home?"

"More than that. He knows I saved his son from Caleb. He knows what Caleb tried to do. So does Simon."

I couldn't help but smile. "I take it Caleb's not too happy now."

"Not in a lot of ways. It doesn't help that he and Scarlet had a big fight. She was gone before you left the premises, but he's trying desperately to sweet-talk her back into his arms."

"Really?" I lowered my voice, anxious to hear the gossip. "I tried to warn her about him. Not just at the towers. Earlier this year, too."

"Nothing you could have said would have made any difference, and Caleb will probably talk her around. Scarlet didn't see exactly what happened. And no one would give her straight answers. Not even Josh knows for sure it wasn't an accident, which is the official family position in the police investigation. She's not sure what she witnessed, but she knew enough to be scared when she left."

"About time."

"Simon disapproves of Scarlet, thinks she makes Caleb weak. He's been after Caleb to get rid of her. And I'm not talking about breaking her heart over a candlelit dinner for two."

"And they don't know about Lilah?"

He shook his head. "They never knew you gave birth. When one of their men in California tipped them off that you had a daughter, it was a complete surprise. So now they think you had a daughter and she's dead at their hands."

I winced, remembering poor Nicole. I would always feel responsible.

"What about me? Are they absolutely convinced I'm dead?"

"Yes. Thoroughly. They saw your red sweater before the boat crashed. I saw…I…" He stopped. "I thought you were dead, too. When you showed up here at Robert's…" He kissed the top of my head and then fell back into his pillow. "They think you're dead and that the artifacts were either on the boat when it blew up or that you'd hidden them away somewhere. They're not sure which. Everyone at the palazzo is walking on eggshells right now. The tensions are high. Simon plans to step up his efforts to find others of your kind, but he's not sure where to start. But yes, as far as you're concerned, they think you're dead."

Dead. Dead! I was dead! I was *free.*

"Aubrey? Why are you smiling? And it had better be because of me." He kissed the underside of my chin and worked his way up to my mouth.

"Among other things."

"What things?" he asked between kisses, but I answered with a giggle. "Do you have a plan, Aubrey de Lune?"

"Don't I always?"

"Yes. How long have you been concocting this one?"

"Hmm." I deepened his kisses and pressed my body into his.

"You do have a plan, don't you?"

"I do, but it's one that life presented me. An opportunity came up, and I'm taking it, seeing where it leads me."

He pressed against my leg and then prodded his way between my thighs. No more than that. Not yet. But the promise was there.

"I'll be in Madrid in two weeks. Meet me there."

"Can't."

He pushed away enough to frown into my face.

Before he could say anything, I pressed a finger to his lips. "There's something I have to do before I see you again. Someone I have to see."

Eric kissed my fingertip. "Your daughter."

My life was in that big cardboard box. My heart and my soul. The only earthly possessions I cared anything about.

Other women at my stage in life would've moved into a new house with plenty of baggage: clothes that hadn't been worn in ten years, dishes from their first marriage, mementos of their travels. Not me—and that's saying a lot, considering how much I've traveled in my lifetime.

I'd dipped into my bank accounts in South America and withdrawn enough money to buy a small cottage in a sleepy little college town in central Florida. The house I'd selected had big oak trees on either side, and it was white with a red door. The house hadn't been for sale. With the help of a local attorney, I'd offered three times the real-estate value to the old woman who'd lived here. I'd had to have this house and only this house. No other would do. I never met the previous owner, but my attorney said she had been happy. I'd paid an extra hundred thousand for her to move out and turn over the keys to him by last night so that I could move in today.

I hadn't had time to buy any furniture. The floors were bare but clean, beautiful hardwood. The kind a real family might have. The walls were white, but they wouldn't stay that way for long. I wanted color and lots of it. The steps outside were brick, just two, with a handrail, so I wouldn't have much trouble getting in and out of the house before my knee healed. Most of all, I liked the fireplace and the broad mantel over it. It was the perfect place for pictures of friends—or of Eric, next time I saw him. And a picture of Cat, too. And a picture of…of other friends I'd make in the future. Friends who wouldn't disappear overnight.

I held my breath as I ripped open the box. Since there were no chairs yet in the entire house, I eased down to the floor and sat while I lifted out my treasures. My father's journals. I sighed at the touch of them. A man I had never really known, yet he'd left journals about my mother and her mother before her. These I would dedicate to the local university library, to their special-collections department.

I'd made a deal with the university. They would allow me to donate several million dollars to a special, secret trust. The books would not be advertised, particularly not the next one in the box…the incunable that had changed my life more than once. The manuscript would stay in a special vault inside the special-collections department. I had already paid to have the fireproof, burglarproof, Adriano-proof vault built. The books would be protected and safe, and as I could, I would add more "dangerous books" like these to their collection.

In exchange, I was to be a guest lecturer at the university. They'd created a Chair of Medieval Antiquities for me. Funny how that happens when you make million-dollar donations! I would be allowed to lecture as I pleased, come and go as I pleased. I would spend much of my time in Europe, visiting with Eric when we could meet discreetly every couple of weeks, at least until the Adriano reign was brought to an end. The long-distance relationship wouldn't be long-distance forever, but for now he had work to do and I had a new life to build. I could wait for him to join me. I'd waited longer for far less.

All of this I'd done under another name. Another identity I'd created for myself. One I'd borrowed from the literature professor acquaintance I'd seen die during an art theft years ago in Europe. I had a new, legitimate life as Dr. Drusilla St. Augustine.

I took a sip of my pomegranate juice, then reached deeper into the box and pulled out a shoebox of mementos. Pictures, clippings, things my private investigator had sent to me over the years. Photographs of Lilah in junior high, in high school, in college.

I was making a life for myself, finally. The life I wanted. Reclaiming my life and reshaping my future into something I wanted.

The first time I heard the knock on the door, I ignored

it. No one knew I lived here. Not yet. There'd been no moving van or announcements of a new resident. I'd never even allowed a for sale sign or a sold sign to be placed in the front yard.

Leaving the glass of pom juice on the floor, I tiptoed to the front door and pulled back the sheer curtain. Old habits die hard, I decided. Already I found myself reaching for a weapon, nervous. That would take time, I admitted. Time to settle into this new life of peace, love, friendship, of everything I'd wanted. All the things I had missed.

I opened the door to a young woman on the steps, a big plate of brownies in her arms. She smiled at me through the screen door. A big, wide smile with a little bit of a quirk at the corner of her mouth. I blinked at her.

The girl frowned for a second, as if she recognized me, then shook it off. "Hi," she said through the screen. "I heard Miss Ida Mae had sold her house. I wanted to come meet my new neighbor. I hope you like brownies." When I didn't say anything, she added, "I live right across the street." She jerked her thumb in the direction of the duplex apartment behind her.

She was pretty. Beautiful green eyes that I would know anywhere. A little taller than I'd expected. Slim and athletic with dark hair that just skimmed her shoulders. Very different from the way she'd looked at ten—but then, I'd changed a lot, too.

She didn't need to tell me where she lived. I already knew. That's why I'd picked this house, why I'd picked this town, this college, everything. To be close to her.

"Oh! I'm sorry," she said as I opened the screen door to her. "Where are my manners?" She balanced the brownies and extended one hand. "My name's Lilah."

* * * * *

Don't miss the next riveting story in
THE MADONNA KEY *series!*
SHADOW LINES
by Carol Stephenson
will be on sale in October 2006
wherever Silhouette Books are sold.
Only from Silhouette Bombshell!

Set in darkness beyond the ordinary world.
Passionate tales of life and death.
With characters' lives ruled by laws the everyday world can't begin to imagine.

Introducing NOCTURNE, *a spine-tingling new line from Silhouette Books.*

The thrills and chills begin with UNFORGIVEN by Lindsay McKenna

Plucked from the depths of hell, former military sharpshooter Reno Manchahi was hired by the government to kill a thief, but he had a mission of his own. Descended from a family of shape-shifters, Reno vowed to get the revenge he'd thirsted for all these years. But his mission went awry when his target turned out to be a powerful seductress, Magdalena Calen Hernandez, who risked everything to battle a potent evil. Suddenly, Reno had to transform himself into a true hero and fight the enemy that threatened them all. He had to become a Warrior for the Light….

* * * * *

Turn the page for a sneak preview of UNFORGIVEN by Lindsay McKenna.
On sale September 26 wherever books are sold.

Chapter 1

One shot...one kill.

The sixteen-pound sledgehammer came down with such fierce power that the granite boulder shattered instantly. A spray of glittering mica exploded into the air and sparkled momentarily around the man who wielded the tool as if it were a weapon. Sweat ran in rivulets down Reno Manchahi's drawn, intense face. Naked from the waist up, the hot July sun beating down on his back, he hefted the sledgehammer skyward once more. Muscles in his thick forearms leaped and biceps bulged. Even his breath was focused on the boulder. In his mind's eye, he pictured Army General Robert Hampton's fleshy, arrogant fifty-year-old features on the rock's surface. Air exploded from between his lips as he brought the avenging hammer down. The boulder pulverized beneath his funneled hatred.

One shot...one kill...

Nostrils flaring, he inhaled the dank, humid heat and drew it deep into his massive lungs. Revenge allowed Reno to endure his imprisonment at a U.S. Navy brig near San Diego, California. Drops of sweat were flung in all directions as the crack of his sledgehammer claimed a third stone victim. Mouth taut, Reno moved to the next boulder.

The other prisoners in the stone yard gave him a wide berth. They always did. They instinctively felt his simmering hatred, the palpable revenge in his cinnamon-colored eyes, was more than skin-deep.

And they whispered he was different.

Reno enjoyed being a loner for good reason. He came from a medicine family of shape-shifters. But even this secret power had not protected him—or his family. His wife, Ilona, and his three-year-old daughter, Sarah, were dead. Murdered by Army General Hampton in their former home on USMC base in Camp Pendleton, California. Bitterness thrummed through Reno as he savagely pushed the toe of his scarred leather boot against several smaller pieces of gray granite that were in his way.

The sun beat down upon Manchahi's naked shoulders, grown dark red over time, shouting his half-Apache heritage. With his straight black hair grazing his thick shoulders, copper skin and broad face with high cheekbones, everyone knew he was Indian. When he'd first arrived at the brig, some of the prisoners taunted him and called him Geronimo. Something strange happened to Reno during his fight with the name-calling prisoners. Leaning down after he'd won the scuffle, he'd snarled into each of their bloodied faces that if they were going to call him anything, they would call him *gan,* which was the Apache word for *devil.*

His attackers had been shocked by the wounds on their faces, the deep claw marks. Reno recalled doubling his fist as they'd attacked him en masse. In that split second, he'd gone into an altered state of consciousness. In times of danger, he transformed into a jaguar. A deep, growling sound had emitted from his throat as he defended himself in the three-against-one fracas. It all happened so fast that he thought he had imagined it. He'd seen his hands morph into a forearm and paw, claws extended. The slashes left on the three men's faces after the fight told him he'd begun to shape-shift. A fist made bruises and swelling; not four perfect, deep claw marks. Stunned and anxious, he hid the knowledge of what else he was from these prisoners. Reno's only defense was to make all the prisoners so damned scared of him and remain a loner.

Alone. Yeah, he was alone, all right. The steel hammer swept downward with hellish ferocity. As the granite groaned in protest, Reno shut his eyes for just a moment. Sweat dripped off his nose and square chin.

Straightening, he wiped his furrowed, wet brow and looked into the pale blue sky. What got his attention was the startling cry of a red-tailed hawk as it flew over the brig yard. Squinting, he watched the bird. Reno could make out the rust-colored tail on the hawk. As a kid growing up on the Apache reservation in Arizona, Reno knew that all animals that appeared before him were messengers.

Brother, what message do you bring me? Reno knew one had to ask in order to receive. Allowing the sledgehammer to drop to his side, he concentrated on the hawk who wheeled in tightening circles above him.

Freedom! the hawk cried in return.

Reno shook his head, his black hair moving against his broad, thickset shoulders. *Freedom? No way, Brother. No way.* Figuring that he was making up the hawk's shrill message, Reno turned away. Back to his rocks. Back to picturing Hampton's smug face.

Freedom!

* * * * *

COMING NEXT MONTH

#109 DRESSED TO SLAY by Harper Allen
Darkheart & Crosse
On the eve of her wedding, trendy society-girl and triplet Megan Crosse found out about her mother's legacy as a vampire slayer the hard way—when her fiancé turned on her and her sisters, fangs bared! Now it was up to Megan to trade in her bridal bouquet for a sharp stake and hunt down her mother's undead killer....

#110 SHADOW LINES by Carol Stephenson
The Madonna Key
Epidemiologist Eve St. Giles had never seen anything like it—an influenza outbreak that *targeted* women. But this was no natural disaster—someone was manipulating the earth's ley lines to wreak havoc. Could the renowned Flu Hunter harness the ancient healing rites of her Marian foremothers in time to avert a modern medical apocalypse?

#111 CAPTIVE DOVE by Judith Leon
When ten U.S. tourists were kidnapped in Brazil, the hostages' family connections to high political office suggested a sinister plot to bring American democracy to its knees. Only CIA operative Nova Blair—code name, Dove—could pull off a rescue. But would having her former flame for a partner clip this free agent's wings?

#112 BAITED by Crystal Green
Pearl diver Katsu Espinoza was never one to turn down an invitation to cruise on multimillionaire Duke Harrington's yacht. But when her dying mentor announced he was disinheriting his assembled family and making Katsu his heir, the voyage turned deadly. Stranded on an island in a raging storm, with members of the party being murdered one by one, Katsu had to wonder if she was next—or if she was the bait in a demented killer's trap....

SBCNM0906